CRITICAL ACCLAIM FOR

Colin Dexter

The Remorseful Day

'Morse's last case is a virtuoso piece of plotting . . .
by quitting the game on the top of his form [Dexter]
has set his fellow crime-writers an example they will
find hard to emulate' *Sunday Times*

Death Is Now My Neighbour

'Dexter has created a giant among fictional
detectives and has never short-changed his readers'
The Times

The Daughters of Cain

'This is Colin Dexter at his most excitingly devious'
Daily Telegraph

The Way Through the Woods

'Morse and his faithful Watson, Sergeant Lewis,
in supreme form . . . Hallelujah' *Observer*

The Jewel that Was Ours

'Traditional crime writing at its best; the kind
of book without which no armchair is complete'
Sunday Times

The Wench Is Dead

'Dextrously ingenious'
Guardian

The Secret of Annexe 3
'A plot of classic cunning and intricacy'
Times Literary Supplement

The Riddle of the Third Mile
'Runs the gamut of brain-racking unputdownability'
Observer

The Dead of Jericho
'The writing is highly intelligent, the atmosphere
melancholy, the effect haunting'
Daily Telegraph

Service of All the Dead
'A brilliantly plotted detective story'
Evening Standard

The Silent World of Nicholas Quinn
'Morse's superman status is reinforced by an
ending which no ordinary mortal could have
possibly unravelled'
Financial Times

Last Seen Wearing
'Brilliant characterization in original whodunnit'
Sunday Telegraph

Last Bus to Woodstock
'Let those who lament the decline of the English
detective story reach for Colin Dexter'
Guardian

SERVICE OF
ALL THE DEAD

Colin Dexter graduated from Cambridge University in 1953 and has lived in Oxford since 1966. His first novel, *Last Bus to Woodstock*, was published in 1975. There are now thirteen novels in the series, of which *The Remorseful Day* is, sadly, the last.

Colin Dexter has won many awards for his novels, including the CWA Silver Dagger twice, and the CWA Gold Dagger for *The Wench Is Dead* and *The Way Through the Woods*. In 1997 he was presented with the CWA Diamond Dagger for outstanding services to crime literature, and in 2000 was awarded the OBE in the Queen's Birthday Honours List.

The Inspector Morse novels have been adapted for the small screen with huge success by Carlton/Central Television, starring John Thaw and Kevin Whately.

THE INSPECTOR MORSE NOVELS

Last Bus to Woodstock
Last Seen Wearing
The Silent World of Nicholas Quinn
Service of All the Dead
The Dead of Jericho
The Riddle of the Third Mile
The Secret of Annexe 3
The Wench Is Dead
The Jewel that Was Ours
The Way Through the Woods
The Daughters of Cain
Death Is Now My Neighbour
The Remorseful Day

Also available in Pan Books

Morse's Greatest Mystery and Other Stories
The First Inspector Morse Omnibus
The Second Inspector Morse Omnibus
The Third Inspector Morse Omnibus
The Fourth Inspector Morse Omnibus

COLIN DEXTER

SERVICE OF ALL THE DEAD

PAN BOOKS

First published 1979 by Macmillan

First published in paperback 1980 by Pan Books

This edition published 2007 by Pan Books
an imprint of Pan Macmillan, a division of Macmillan Publishers Limited
Pan Macmillan, 20 New Wharf Road, London N1 9RR
Basingstoke and Oxford
Associated companies throughout the world
www.panmacmillan.com

ISBN 978-0-330-45121-5

5 7 9 8 6

A CIP catalogue record for this book is available from
the British Library.

Printed and bound by
CPI Group (UK) Ltd, Croydon, CR0 4YY

Visit **www.panmacmillan.com** to read more about all our books
and to buy them. You will also find features, author interviews and
news of any author events, and you can sign up for e-newsletters
so that you're always first to hear about our new releases.

For John Poole

I had rather be a doorkeeper in the house of
my God: than to dwell in the tents of ungodliness

(Psalm 84:10)

The First Book of Chronicles

CHAPTER ONE

LIMPLY THE REVEREND Lionel Lawson shook the last smoothly gloved hand, the slim hand of Mrs Emily Walsh-Atkins, and he knew that the pews in the old church behind him were now empty. It was always the same: whilst the other well-laundered ladies were turning their heads to chat of fêtes and summer hats, whilst the organist played his exit voluntary, and whilst the now discassocked choirboys tucked their T-shirts into flare-line jeans, Mrs Walsh-Atkins invariably spent a few further minutes on her knees in what had sometimes seemed to Lawson a slightly exaggerated obeisance to the Almighty. Yet, as Lawson knew full well, she had plenty to be thankful for. She was eighty-one years old, but managed still to retain an enviable agility in both mind and body; only her eyesight was at last beginning to fail. She lived in north Oxford, in a home for elderly gentlewomen, screened off from the public gaze by a high fence and a belt of fir-trees. Here, from the front window of her living-room, redolent of faded lavender and silver-polish, she could look out on to the well-tended paths and lawns where each morning the resident caretaker unobtrusively collected up the Coca Cola tins, the odd milk bottle and the crisp packets thrown over by those strange, unfathomably depraved young people who, in Mrs Walsh-Atkins' view, had little right to walk the streets at all – let alone the streets of her own beloved north Oxford. The home was wildly expensive; but Mrs W.-A. was a wealthy woman, and each Sunday morning her neatly sealed brown envelope, lightly laid on the collection-plate, contained a folded five-pound note.

'Thank you for the message, Vicar.'

'God bless you!'

This brief dialogue, which had never varied by a single word in the ten years since Lawson had been appointed to the parish of St Frideswide's, was the ultimate stage in non-communication between a priest and his parishioner. In the early days of his ministry, Lawson had felt vaguely uneasy about 'the message' since he was conscious that no passage from his sermons had ever been declaimed with particularly evangelistic fervour; and in any case the rôle of some divinely appointed telegram boy was quite inappropriate – indeed, quite distasteful – to a man of Lawson's moderately high-church leanings. Yet Mrs Walsh-Atkins appeared to hear the humming of the heavenly wires whatever his text might be; and each Sunday morning she reiterated her gratitude to the unsuspecting harbinger of goodly tidings. It was purely by chance that after his very first service Lawson had hit upon those three simple monosyllables – magical words which, again this Sunday morning, Mrs Walsh-Atkins happily clutched to her bosom, along with her Book of Common Prayer, as she walked off with her usual sprightly gait towards St Giles, where her regular taxi-driver would be waiting in the shallow lay-by beside the Martyrs' Memorial.

The vicar of St Frideswide's looked up and down the hot street. There was nothing to detain him longer, but he appeared curiously reluctant to re-enter the shady church. A dozen or so Japanese tourists made their way along the pavement opposite, their small, bespectacled cicerone reciting in a whining, staccato voice the city's ancient charms, his sing-song syllables still audible as the little group sauntered up the street past the cinema, where the management proudly presented to its patrons the opportunity of witnessing the intimacies of Continental-style wife-swapping. But for Lawson there were no stirrings of sensuality: his mind was on other things. Carefully he lifted from his shoulders the white silk-lined hood (M.A. Cantab.) and turned his gaze towards Carfax, where already the lounge-bar door of the Ox stood open. But public houses had never held much appeal for him. He sipped, it is true, the occasional glass of sweet sherry at some of the diocesan functions; but if Lawson's soul should have anything to answer for when the archangel bugled the final trumpet it would certainly not be the charge of drunkenness. Without disturbing his carefully parted hair, he drew the long white surplice over his head and turned slowly into the church.

Apart from the organist, Mr Paul Morris, who had now reached the last few bars of what Lawson recognized as some Mozart, Mrs Brenda Josephs was the only person left in the main body of the building. Dressed in a sleeveless, green summer frock, she sat at the back of the church, a soberly attractive woman in her mid- or late thirties, one bare browned arm resting along the back of the pew, her finger-tips caressing its smooth surface. She smiled dutifully as Lawson walked past; and Lawson, in his turn, inclined his sleek head in a casual benediction. Formal greetings had been exchanged before the service, and neither party now seemed anxious to resume that earlier perfunctory conversation. On his way to the vestry Lawson stopped briefly in order to hook a loose hassock into place at the foot of a pew, and as he did so he heard the door at the side of the organ bang shut. A little too noisily, perhaps? A little too hurriedly?

The curtains parted as he reached the vestry and a gingery-headed, freckle-faced youth almost launched himself into Lawson's arms.

'Steady, boy. Steady! What's all the rush?'

'Sorry, sir. I just forgot ...' His breathless voice trailed off, his right hand, clutching a half-consumed tube of fruit gums, drawn furtively behind his back.

'I hope you weren't eating those during the sermon?'

'No, sir.'

'Not that I ought to blame you if you were. I can get a bit boring sometimes, don't you think?' The peda-gogic tone of Lawson's earlier words had softened now, and he laid his hand on the boy's head and ruffled his hair lightly.

Peter Morris, the organist's only son, looked up at Lawson with a quietly cautious grin. Any subtlety of tone was completely lost upon him; yet he realized that everything was all right, and he darted away along the back of the pews.

'Peter!' The boy stopped in his tracks and looked round. 'How many times must I tell you? You're not to run in church!'

'Yes, sir. Er – I mean, no, sir.'

'And don't forget the choir outing next Saturday.'

''Course not, sir.'

Lawson had not failed to notice Peter's father and Brenda Josephs talking together in animated whispers in the north porch; but Paul Morris had now slipped quietly out of the door after his son, and Brenda, it seemed, had turned her solemn attention to the font: dating from 1345, it was, according to the laconic guide-book, number one of the 'Things to Note'. Lawson turned on his heel and entered the vestry.

Harry Josephs, the vicar's warden, had almost finished now. After each service he entered, against the appropriate date, two sets of figures in the church register: first, the number of persons in the congregation, rounded up or down to the nearest five; second, the sum taken in the offertory, meticulously calculated to the last half-penny. By most reckonings, the church of St Frideswide's was a fairly thriving establishment. Its clientèle was chiefly drawn from the more affluent sectors of the community, and even during the University vacations the church was often half-full. It was to be expected, therefore, that the monies to be totalled by the vicar's warden, then checked by the vicar himself, and thereafter transferred to the church's number-one account with Barclays Bank in the High, were not inconsiderable. This morning's takings, sorted by denominations, lay on Lawson's desk in the vestry: one five-pound note; about fifteen one-pound notes; a score or so of fifty-pence pieces and further sundry piles of smaller coinage, neatly stacked in readily identifiable amounts.

'Another goodly congregation, Harry.' 'Goodly' was a favourite word in Lawson's vocabulary. Although it had always been a matter of some contention in theological circles whether the Almighty took any great interest in the counting of mere heads, it was encouraging, on a secular assessment, to minister to a flock that was at least numerically fairly strong; and the word 'goodly' seemed a happily neutral word to blur the distinction between the 'good', by purely arithmetical reckoning, and the 'godly', as assessed on a more spiritual computation.

Harry nodded and made his entries. 'Just check the money quickly if you will, sir. I made it a hundred and thirty-five in the congregation, and I make it fifty-seven pounds twelve pence in the collection.'

'No ha'pennies today, Harry? I think some of the choirboys must have taken my little talk to heart.' With the dexterity of a practised bank clerk he riffled through the pound notes, and then passed his fingers over the piles of coins, like a bishop blessing heads at a confirmation service. The addition of monies was correct.

'One of these days, Harry, you're going to surprise me and make a mistake.'

Josephs' eyes darted sharply to Lawson's face, but

the expression there, as the minister put his signature to the right-hand column of the church register, was one of bland benignity.

Together vicar and warden placed the money in an ancient Huntley & Palmer biscuit tin. It looked an unlikely repository for any great store of wealth; but when at one of its recent meetings the church council had discussed the problem of security no one had come up with any brighter suggestion, except for the possibility that a slightly later vintage of a similar tin might perhaps more firmly corroborate the notion that the receptacle open to view on the back seat of Josephs' Allegro contained nothing more precious than a few ginger-snaps and arrowroots left over from a recent social.

'I'll be off, then, Vicar. The wife'll be waiting.'

Lawson nodded and watched his warden go. Yes, Brenda Josephs would be waiting; she had to be. Six months previously Harry had been found guilty on a charge of drunken driving, and it was largely through Lawson's plea for mitigation that the magistrate's sentence of a fifty-pound fine and one year's suspension had seemed so comparatively lenient. The Josephs' home was in the village of Wolvercote, some three miles north of the city centre, and buses on Sundays were a rarer sight than five-pound notes on a collection-plate.

The small vestry window looked out on the south side of the church, and Lawson sat down at the desk and stared blankly into the graveyard where the grey, weathered tombstones tilted at their varied angles from the vertical, their crumbling legends long since overgrown with moss or smoothed away by centuries of wind and rain. He both looked and felt a worried man, for the simple truth was that there should have been *two* five-pound notes in the collection that morning. Was there just a possibility, though, that Mrs Walsh-Atkins had at last exhausted her store of five-pound notes and put five separate one-pound notes into the collection? If she had, though, it would have been the first time for – oh, years and years. No. There was a much more probable explanation, an explanation that disturbed Lawson greatly. Yet there was still the slimmest chance that he was mistaken. 'Judge not that ye be not judged.' Judge not – at least until the evidence is unequivocal. He took out his wallet and from it drew a piece of paper on which earlier that same morning he had written down the serial number of the five-pound note which he himself had sealed in a small brown envelope and placed in the morning collection. And only two or three minutes ago he had checked the last three numbers of the five-pound note which Harry Josephs had placed in the biscuit tin: they were not the numbers he had written down.

Something of this sort Lawson had suspected for several weeks, and now he had proof of it. He should, he knew, have asked Josephs to turn out his pockets on the spot: that was his duty, both as a priest and as a friend (friend?), for somewhere on Josephs' person would have been found the five-pound note he had just stolen from the offertory. At last Lawson looked down at the piece of paper he had been holding and read the serial number printed on it: AN 50 405546. Slowly

he lifted his eyes and stared across the churchyard once
more. The sky had grown suddenly overcast, and when
half an hour later he walked down to the vicarage in St
Ebbe's the air was heavy with the threat of rain. It was
as if someone had switched off the sun.

CHAPTER TWO

ALTHOUGH HE PRETENDED still to be asleep, Harry Josephs had heard his wife get up just before seven, and he was able to guess her movements exactly. She had put on her dressing-gown over her nightdress, walked down to the kitchen, filled the nettle, and then sat at the table smoking her first cigarette. It was only during the past two or three months that Brenda had started smoking again, and he was far from happy about it. Her breath smelt stale, and the sight of an ash-tray full of stubs he found quite nauseating. People smoked a lot when they were worried and tense, didn't they? It was just a drug really, like a slug of aspirin, or a bottle of booze, or a flutter on the horses . . . He turned his head into the pillow, and his own anxieties once more flooded through his mind.

'Tea.' She nudged his shoulder gently and put the mug down on the small table that separated their twin beds.

Josephs nodded, grunted, and turned on to his back, watching his wife as she stood in front of the dressing-table and slipped the nightdress over her head. She was thickening a little round the hips now, but she was still leggily elegant and her breasts were full and firm. Yet

12

Josephs did not look at her directly as she stood momentarily naked before the mirror. Over the past few months he had felt increasingly embarrassed about gazing at her body, as if somehow he were intruding into a privacy he was no longer openly invited to share.

He sat up and sipped his tea as she drew up the zip at the side of her nigger-brown skirt. 'Paper come?'

'I'd have brought it up.' She bent forward from the waist and applied a series of cosmetic preparations to her face. Josephs himself had never followed the sequence with any real interest.

'Lot of rain in the night.'

'Still raining,' she said.

'Do the garden good.'

'Mm.'

'Had any breakfast?'

She shook her head. 'There's plenty of bacon, though, if you – ' (she applied a thin film of light pink to her pouting lips) ' – and there's a few mushrooms left.'

Josephs finished his tea and lay back on the bed. It was twenty-five past seven and Brenda would be off in five minutes. She worked mornings only at the Radcliffe Infirmary, at the bottom of the Woodstock Road, where two years ago she had taken up her nursing career once again. Two years ago! That was just after . . .

She came across to his bedside, lightly touched her lips to his forehead, picked up his mug, and walked out of the room. But almost immediately she was back again. 'Oh, Harry. I nearly forgot. I shan't be back for lunch today. Can you get yourself something all right?

I really must go and do some shopping in town. Not that I'll be late – three-ish at the latest, I should think. I'll try to get something nice for tea.'

Josephs nodded and said nothing, but she was lingering by the door. 'Anything you want – from town, I mean?'

'No.' For a few minutes he lay quite still listening to her movements below.

'By-ee!'

'Goodbye.' The front door clicked to behind her. 'Goodbye, Brenda.'

He turned the bedclothes diagonally back, got up, and peered round the side of the curtained window. The Allegro was being backed out carefully into the quiet, wet street and then, with a sudden puff of blue exhaust smoke, was gone. To the Radcliffe was exactly 2.8 miles: Josephs knew that. For three years he had made the identical journey himself, to the block of offices just below the Radcliffe where he had worked as a civil servant after his twenty years' service in the forces. But two years ago the staff had been axed following the latest public-expenditure cuts, and three of the seven of them had been declared redundant, including himself. And how it still rankled! He wasn't the oldest and he wasn't the least experienced. But he was the least experienced of the older men and the oldest of the less experienced. A little silver handshake, a little farewell party, and just a little hope of finding another job. No, that was wrong: almost no hope of finding another job. He had been forty-eight then. Young enough, perhaps, by some standards. But the sad truth had slowly seeped into his soul: no one really wanted him any longer. After more than a year of dispiriting idleness, he had, in fact, worked in a chemist's shop in Summertown, but the branch had recently closed down and he had almost welcomed the inevitable termination of his contract. He – a man who had risen to the rank of captain in the Royal Marine Commandos, a man who had seen active service against the terrorists in the Malayan jungles – standing politely behind the counter handing over prescriptions to some skinny, pale-faced youth or other who wouldn't have lasted five seconds on one of the commando assault-courses! And, as the manager had insisted, saying 'Thank you, sir,' into the bargain!

He shut the thought away, and drew the curtains open.

Just up the road a line of people queued at the bus-stop, their umbrellas raised against the steady rain which filtered down on the straw-coloured fields and lawns. Lines he had learned at school drifted back into his mind, serving his mood and seeming to fit the dismal prospect before him:

> And ghastly thro' the drizzling rain
> On the bald street breaks the blank day.

He caught the 10.30 a.m. bus into Summertown, where he walked into the licensed betting-office and studied the card at Lingfield Park. He noticed that by some strange coincidence The Organist was running in the two-thirty, and Poor Old Harry in the four o'clock. He wasn't usually over-influenced by names, but when he recalled his lack of success through undue reliance on the form-book he suspected that it might have been more profitable if he had been. In the ante-post betting odds, The Organist was one of the co-favourites, and Poor Old Harry wasn't even quoted. Josephs walked along the series of daily newspapers affixed to the walls of the office: The Organist was napped in a couple of them; Poor Old Harry seemed to have no support whatsoever. Josephs allowed himself a rueful grin: probably neither of them was destined to be first past the post, but ... why not? Take a chance, Harry boy! He filled in a square white betting-slip and pushed it over the counter with his money:

Lingfield Park: 4 p.m.
£2 win: Poor Old Harry.

A year or so previously, after purchasing two tins of baked beans from a supermarket, he had been given change for one pound instead of for the five-pound note he knew he had handed over. His protestations on that occasion had necessitated a full till-check and a nervy half-hour wait before the final justification of his claim; and since that time he had been more careful, always memorizing the last three numbers of any five-pound note he tendered. He did so now, and repeated them to himself as he waited for his change: 546 ... 546 ... 546 ...

The drizzle had virtually stopped when at 11.20 a.m. he walked unhurriedly down the Woodstock Road.

Twenty-five minutes later he was standing in one of the private car parks at the Radcliffe where he spotted the car almost immediately. Threading his way through the closely parked vehicles, he soon stood beside it and looked through the offside window. The milometer read 25,622. That tallied: it had read 619 before she left. And if she now followed the normal routine of any sensible person she would walk down into Oxford from here, and when she got home the milometer would read 625 – 626 at the most. Finding a suitable vantage-point behind a moribund elm tree he looked at his watch. And waited.

At two minutes past twelve the celluloid doors leading to E.N.T. Outpatients flapped open and Brenda Josephs appeared and walked briskly to the car. He could see her very clearly. She unlocked the door and sat for a few seconds leaning forward and viewing herself in the driving-mirror, before taking a small scent-bottle from her handbag and applying it to her neck, first to one side, then to the other. Her safety-belt remained unfastened as she backed none too expertly out of the narrow space; then the right blinker on as she drove out of the car park and up to the Woodstock Road; then the orange blinker flashing left (left!) as she edged into the traffic departing north and away from the city centre.

He knew her next moves. Up to the Northern Ring Road roundabout, there cutting through Five Mile Drive, and then out on to the Kidlington Road. He knew his own move, too.

The telephone kiosk was free and, although the local

directory had long since been stolen, he knew the number and dialled it.

'Hello?' (A woman's voice.) 'Roger Bacon School, Kidlington. Can I help you?'

'I was wondering if I could speak to Mr Morris, Mr Paul Morris, please. I believe he's one of your music teachers.'

'Yes, he is. Just a minute. I'll just have a look at the timetable to see if . . . just a minute . . . No. He's got a free period. I'll just see if he's in the staff-room. Who shall I say?'

'Er, Mr Jones.'

She was back on the line within half a minute. 'No, I'm afraid he doesn't seem to be on the school premises, Mr Jones. Can I take a message?'

'No, it doesn't really matter. Can you tell me whether he's likely to be at school during the lunch-hour?'

'Just a minute.' (Josephs heard the rustling of some papers. She needn't have bothered, though, he knew that.) 'No. He's not on the list for lunches today. He usually stays but—'

'Don't worry. Sorry to have been a nuisance.'

He felt his heart pounding as he rang another number – another Kidlington number. He'd give the bloody pair a fright! If only he could drive a car! The phone rang and rang and he was just beginning to wonder . . . when it was answered.

'Hello?' (Just that. No more. Was the voice a little strained?)

'Mr Morris?' (It was no difficulty for him to lapse into the broad Yorkshire dialect of his youth.)

'Ye-es?'

'Electricity Board 'ere, sir. Is it cónvénient for us to come along, sir? We've—'

'Today, you mean?'

'Aye. This lunch-taime, sir.'

'Er – er – no, I'm afraid not. I've just called in home for a second to get a – er – book. It's lucky you caught me, really. But I'm due back at school – er – straight away. What's the trouble, anyway?'

Josephs slowly cradled the phone. That would give the sod something to think about!

When Brenda arrived home at ten minutes to three, he was clipping the privet hedge with dedicated precision.

'Hello, love. Have a good day?'

'Oh. Usual, you know. I've bought something nice for tea, though.'

'That's good news.'

'Have any lunch?'

'Mouthful of bread and cheese.'

She knew he was telling a lie, for there was no cheese in the house. Unless, of course, he'd been out again . . .? She felt a sudden surge of panic as she hurried inside with her shopping bags.

Josephs continued his meticulous clippings along the tall hedge that separated them from next door. He was in no hurry, and only when he was immediately alongside the offside front door of the car did he casually glance at the fascia dials. The milometer read 25,633.

As he always did, he washed up after their evening meal by himself, but he postponed one small piece of investigation until later, for he knew that as surely as night follows day his wife would make some excuse for retiring early to bed. Yet, strange as it seemed, he felt almost glad: it was he who was now in control of things. (Or, at least, that is what he thought.)

She was on cue, all right – just after the news headlines on BBC 1: 'I think I'll have a bath and an early night, Harry. I – I feel a bit tired.'

He nodded understandingly. 'Like me to bring you a cup of Ovaltine?'

'No, thanks. I shall be asleep as soon as I hit the pillow. But thanks anyway.' She put her hand on his shoulder and gave it the slightest squeeze, and for a few seconds her face was haunted by the twin spectres of self-recrimination and regret.

When the water had finished running in the bathroom, Josephs went back into the kitchen and looked in the waste bin. There, screwed up into small balls and pushed right to the bottom of the débris, he found four white paper bags. Careless, Brenda! Careless! He had checked the bin himself that same morning, and now there were four newcomers, four white paper bags, all of them carrying the name of the Quality supermarket at Kidlington.

After Brenda had left the next morning, he made himself some coffee and toast, and sat down with the *Daily Express*. Heavy overnight rain at Lingfield Park had upset a good many of the favourites, and there were no congratulatory columns to the wildly inaccurate prognostications of the racing tipsters. With malicious glee he noticed that The Organist had come seventh out of eight runners; and Poor Old Harry – had won! At sixteen to one! Whew! It hadn't been such a blank day after all.

CHAPTER THREE

THE LAST LESSON of the week could hardly have provided a more satisfactory envoi. There were only five of them in the O Level music group, all reasonably anxious to work hard and to succeed, all girls; and as they sat forward awkwardly and earnestly, their musical scores of Piano Sonata Opus 90 on their knees, Paul Morris vaguely reminded himself how exquisitely Gilels could play Beethoven. But his aesthetic sense was only minimally engaged, and not for the first time during the past few weeks he found himself wondering whether he was really cut out for teaching. Doubtless, these particular pupils would all get decent O Level grades, for he had sedulously drilled the set works into them – their themes, their developments and recapitulations. But there was, he knew, little real radiance either in his own exposition of the works or in his pupil's appreciation of them; and the sad truth was that what until so recently had been an all-consuming passion was now becoming little more than pleasurable background listening. From Music to Muzak – in three short months.

Morris had moved from his previous post (it was almost three years ago now) primarily to try to forget that terrible day when the young police constable had come to tell him that his wife had been killed in a car accident; when he had gone along to the primary school to collect Peter and watched the silent, tragic tears that sprang from the boy's eyes; and when he had wrestled with that helpless, baffled anger against the perversity and cruelty of the Fates which had taken his young wife from him – an anger which over those next few dazed and despairing weeks had finally settled into a firm resolve at all costs to protect his only child whenever and wherever he could. The boy was something – the only thing – that he could cling to. Gradually, too, Morris had become convinced that he had to get away, and his determination to move – to move anywhere – had grown into an obsession as weekly the Posts Vacant columns in *The Times Educational Supplement* reminded him of new streets, new colleagues, a new school – perhaps even a new life. And so finally he had moved to the Roger Bacon Comprehensive School on the outskirts of Oxford, where his breezy interview had lasted but fifteen minutes, where he'd immediately found a quiet little semi-detached to rent, where everyone was very kind to him – but where his life proved very much the same as before. At least, until he met Brenda Josephs.

It was through Peter that he had established contact with St Frideswide's. One of Peter's friends was a keen member of the choir, and before long Peter had joined, too. And when the aged choirmaster had finally retired it was common knowledge that Peter's father was an organist, and the invitation asking him to take over was accepted without hesitation.

Gilels was lingering *pianissimo* over the last few bars when the bell sounded the end of the week's schooling. One of the class, a leggy, large-boned, dark-haired girl, remained behind to ask if she could borrow the record for the weekend. She was slightly taller than Morris, and as he looked into her black-pencilled, languidly amorous eyes he once more sensed a power within himself which until a few months previously he could never have suspected. Carefully he lifted the record from the turntable and slipped it smoothly into its sleeve.

'Thank you,' she said softly.

'Have a nice weekend, Carole.'

'You, too, sir.'

He watched her as she walked down the steps from the stage and clattered her way across the main hall in her high wedge-heeled shoes. How would the melancholy Carol be spending her weekend? he wondered. He wondered, too, about his own.

Brenda had happened just three months ago. He had seen her on many occasions before, of course, for she always stayed behind after the Sunday morning service to take her husband home. But that particular morning had not been just another occasion. She had seated herself, not as usual in one of the pews at the back of the church, but directly behind him in the choir-stalls; and as he played he'd watched her with interest in the organ-mirror, her head slightly to one side, her face set in a wistful, half-contented smile. As the deep notes died away around the empty church, he had turned towards her.

'Did you like it?'

She had nodded quietly and lifted her eyes towards him.

'Would you like me to play it again?'

'Have you got time?'

'For you I have.' Their eyes had held then, and for that moment they were the only two beings alive in the world.

'Thank you,' she whispered.

Remembrance of that first brief time together was even now a source of radiant light that shone in Morris's heart. Standing by his side she had turned over the sheet-music for him, and more than once her arm had lightly brushed his own . . .

That was how it had begun, and how, he told himself, it had to end. But that couldn't be. Her face haunted his dreams that Sunday night, and again through the following nights she would give his sleeping thoughts no rest. On the Friday of the same week he had rung her at the hospital. A bold, irrevocable move. Quite simply he had asked her if he could see her some time – that was all; and just as simply she had answered 'Yes, of course you can' – words that re-echoed round his brain like the joyous refrain of the Seraphim.

In the weeks that followed, the frightening truth had gradually dawned on him: he would do almost anything to have this woman for his own. It was not that he bore any malice against Harry Josephs. How could he? Just a burning, irrational jealousy, which no words from Brenda, none of her pathetic pleas of reassurance could assuage. He wished Josephs out of the way – of course he did! But only recently had his conscious mind accepted the stark reality of his position. Not only did he wish Josephs out of the way: he would be positively happy to see him dead.

'You stayin' much longer, sir?'

It was the caretaker, and Morris knew better than to argue. It was a quarter past four, and Peter would be home.

The regular Friday evening fish and chips, liberally vinegared and blotched with tomato sauce, were finished, and they stood together at the kitchen sink, father washing, son drying. Although Morris had thought long and hard about what he would say, it was not going to be easy. He had never before had occasion to speak to his son about matters connected with sex; but one thing was quite certain: he had to do so now. He remembered with devastating clarity (he had only been eight at the time) when the two boys next door had been visited by the police, and when one of the local ministers had been taken to court, and there convicted and sentenced to prison. And he remembered the new words he had then learned, words that his school-fellows had learned, too, and laughed about in lavatory corners: slimy words that surfaced ever after in his young mind as if from some loathsome, reptilian pool.

'I think we may be able to get you that racing bike in a couple of months.'

'*Really*, Dad?'

'You have to promise me to be jolly careful . . .'

But Peter was hardly listening. His mind was racing as fast as the bike was going to race, his face shining with joy . . .

'Pardon, Dad?'

'I said, are you looking forward to the outing tomorrow?'

Peter nodded, honestly if comparatively unenthusiastically. "Spect I'll get a bit fed up on the way back. Like last year.'

'I want you to promise me something.'

Another promise? The boy frowned uncertainly at the serious tone in his father's voice, and rubbed the tea-towel quite unnecessarily round and round the next plate, anticipating some adult information, confidential, and perhaps unwelcome.

'You're still a young lad, you know. You may think you're getting a bit grown-up, but you've still got a lot to learn. You see, some people you'll meet in life are very nice, and some aren't. They may seem nice, but – but they're not nice at all. It sounded pathetically inadequate.

'Crooks, you mean?'

'In a way they're crooks, yes, but I'm talking about people who are bad inside. They want – strange sorts of things to satisfy them. They're not normal – not like most people.' He took a deep breath. 'When I was about your age, younger in fact . . .'

Peter listened to the little story with apparent unconcern. 'You mean, he was a queer, Dad?'

'He was a homosexual. Do you know what that means?'

27

"Course I do.'

'Listen, Peter, if any man ever tries anything like that – anything! – you have nothing at all to do with it. Is that clear? And, what's more, you'll tell me. All right?'

Peter tried so very hard to understand, but the warning seemed remote, dissociated as yet from his own small experience of life.

'You see, Peter, it's not just a question of a man – touching' (the very word was shudderingly repulsive) 'or that sort of thing. It's what people start talking about or – or photographs that kind of—'

Peter's mouth dropped open and the blood froze in his freckled cheeks. So *that* was what his father was talking about! The last time had been two weeks ago when three of them from the youth club had gone along to the vicarage and sat together on that long, black, shiny settee. It was all a bit strange and exciting, and there had been those photographs – big, black and white, glossy prints that seemed almost clearer than real life. But they weren't just pictures of *men*, and Mr Lawson had talked about them so – so naturally, somehow. Anyway, he'd often seen pictures like that on the racks in the newsagent's. He felt a growing sense of bewilderment as he stood there by the sink, his hands still clutching the drying-cloth. Then he heard his father's voice, raucous and ugly, in his ears, and felt his father's hand upon his shoulder, shaking him angrily.

'Do you hear me? Tell me about it!'

But the boy didn't tell his father. He just couldn't. What was there to tell anyway?

CHAPTER FOUR

THE COACH, A wide luxury hulk of a thing, was due to leave Cornmarket at 7.30 a.m., and Morris joined the group of fussy parents counterchecking on lunch bags, swimming gear and pocket money. Peter was already ensconced between a pair of healthily excited pals on the back seat, and Lawson once more counted heads to satisfy himself that the expedition was fully manned and could at last proceed. As the driver heaved round and round at the huge horizontal steering-wheel, slowly manœuvring the giant vehicle into Beaumont Street, Morris had his last view of Harry and Brenda Josephs sitting silently together on one of the front seats, of Lawson folding his plastic raincoat and packing it into the overhead rack, and of Peter chatting happily away and like most of the other boys disdaining, or forgetting, to wave farewell. All *en route* for Bournemouth.

It was 7.45 a.m. by the clock on the south face of St Frideswide's as Morris walked up to Carfax and then through Queen Street and down to the bottom of St Ebbe's, where he stopped in front of a rangy three-storeyed stuccoed building set back from the street behind bright yellow railings. Nailed on to the high wooden gate which guarded the narrow path to the front door was a flaking notice-board announcing in faded capitals ST FRIDESWIDE'S CHURCH AND OXFORD PASTORATE. The gate itself was half-open; and as Morris stood self-consciously and indecisively in the deserted street a whistling paper boy rode up on his bicycle and inserted a copy of *The Times* through the front door. No inside hand withdrew the newspaper, and Morris walked slowly away from the house and just as slowly back. On the top floor a pale yellow strip of neon lighting suggested the presence of someone on the premises, and he walked cautiously up to the front door where he rapped gently on the ugly black knocker. With no sound of movement from within, he tried again, a little louder. There must be someone, surely, in the rambling old vicarage. Students up on the top floor, probably? A housekeeper, perhaps? But again as he held his ear close to the door he could hear no movement; and conscious that his heart was beating fast against his ribs he tried the door. It was locked.

The back of the house was enclosed by a wall some eight or nine feet high; but a pair of gates, with NO PARKING amateurishly painted in white across them, promised access to somewhere, and turning the metal ring Morris found the gate unlocked. He stepped inside. A path led alongside the high stone wall beside an ill-tended stretch of patchy lawn, and quietly closing the gates behind him Morris walked up to the back door, and knocked with a quiet cowardice. No answer. No sound. He turned the door-knob. The door was unlocked. He opened it and went inside. For several seconds he stood stock-still in the wide hallway, his eyes

unmoving as an alligator's. Across the hall *The Times*
protruded downwards through the front-door letter-
box like the tongue of some leering gargoyle, the whole
house as still as death. He forced himself to breathe
more naturally and looked around him. A door on his
left was standing ajar, and he tiptoed across to look
inside. 'Anyone there?' The words were spoken very
softly, but they gave him an odd surge of confidence as
though, should anyone be there, he was obviously trying
to be noticed. And someone was there; or had been,
until very recently. On a formica-topped table lay a
knife, stickily smeared with butter and marmalade, a
solitary plate strewn with toast crumbs, and a large mug
containing the dregs of cold tea. The remains, no
doubt, of Lawson's breakfast. But a sudden shudder of
fear climbed up Morris's spine as he noticed that the
grill on the electric cooker was turned on full, its bars
burning a fierce orange-red. Yet there was the same
eerie stillness as before, with only the mechanical tick-
tock of the kitchen clock to underline the pervasive
silence.

Back in the hallway, he walked quietly across to the
broad staircase, and as lightly as he could climbed up
to the landing. Only one of the doors was open; but
one was enough. A black-leather settee was ranged
along one side of the room, and the floor was fully
carpeted. He walked noiselessly across to the roll-top
desk beside the window. It was locked, but the key lay
on the top. Inside, two neatly written sheets of paper –
on which he read the text and notes for some forth-
coming sermon – lay beneath a paper-knife, curiously

fashioned in the shape of a crucifix, the slitting-edge, as it seemed to Morris, wickedly (and quite needlessly?) sharp. He tried first the drawers on the left – all of them gliding smoothly open and all of them apparently fulfilling some innocent function; and the same with the top three drawers on the right. But the bottom one was locked, and the key to it was nowhere to be seen.

As a prospective burglar Morris had anticipated the stubbornness of locks and bolts only to the extent of a small chisel which he now took from his pocket. It took him more than ten minutes, and when finally the bottom drawer lay open the surrounding oblong frame was irreparably chipped and bruised. Inside lay an old chocolate-box, and Morris was slipping off the criss-cross of elastic bands when a slight sound caused him to whip round, his eyes wide with terror.

Standing in the doorway was a man with a lathered face, his right hand holding a shaving-brush, his left clutching a dirty pink towel about his neck. For a second Morris felt a shock that partly paralysed his terror, for his immediate impression was that the man was Lawson himself. Yet he knew he must be mistaken, and the logic that for a moment had threatened to disintegrate was swiftly reasserting itself. The man was about the same height and build as Lawson, yes. But the face was thinner and the hair was greyer; nor was the man's voice, when finally he spoke, in any way like Lawson's own, but a voice and a mode of expression that seemed to mask a curious combination of the cultured and the coarse:

'May I ask what the 'ell you're doing 'ere, mate?'

Morris recognized him then. He was one of the drop-outs who sometimes congregated in Bonn Square or Brasenose Lane. Indeed, Lawson had brought him to church a few times, and there was a whisper of rumour that the two men were related. Some had even suspected that the man was Lawson's brother.

At Bournemouth the sun shone brightly out of a clear sky, but the wind was chill and blustery, and Brenda Josephs, seated in an open deck-chair, envied the other holiday-makers who sat so snugly, it seemed, behind their striped wind-breaks. She felt cold and bored – and more than a little disturbed by that little remark of Harry's on the coach: 'Pity Morris couldn't make it.' That was all. That was all . . .

The boys had thrown themselves around with phenomenal energy: playing beach football (Harry had organized that), running into the sea, clambering up and down the rocks, guzzling Coke, guttling sandwiches, crunching crisps, then back into the sea. But for her – what an empty, fruitless day! She was officially the 'nurse' of the party, for invariably someone would feel sick or cut his knee. But she could have been with Paul all day. All day! No risk, either. Oh God! She couldn't bear to think of it . . .

The farther stretches of the sea twinkled invitingly in the sun, but along the shore-line the crashing breakers somersaulted into heavy spray. It was no day for tentative paddlers, but huge fun for the boys who were still leaping tirelessly against the waves, Lawson with them, white-skinned as a fish's underbelly, laughing, splashing, happy. It all seemed innocent enough to Brenda, and she couldn't really believe all that petty church gossip. Not that she liked Lawson much; but she didn't dislike him, either. In fact she'd thought more than once that Lawson must suspect something about herself and Paul; but he'd said nothing . . . so far.

Harry had gone for a walk along the esplanade, and she was glad to be left to herself. She tried to read the newspaper, but the sheets flapped and billowed in the breeze, and she put it back into the carrier bag, alongside the flask of coffee, the salmon sandwiches, and her white bikini. Yes. Pity about the bikini . . . She had become increasingly conscious of her body these past few months, and she would have enjoyed seeing the young lads gawping up at her bulging breasts. What was happening to her . . .?

When Harry returned an hour or so later it was quite clear that he had been drinking, but she made no comment. As a concession to the English summer he had changed into a pair of old shorts – long, baggy service-issue in which (according to Harry) he and his men had flushed the Malaysian jungles of all the terrorists. His legs had grown thinner, especially round the thighs, but they were still muscular and strong. Stronger than Paul's, but . . . She stemmed the gathering flood of thoughts, and unfolded the tin-foil round the sandwiches.

She averted her eyes from her husband as he slowly masticated the tinned salmon. What *was* happening to her? The poor fellow couldn't even eat now without her experiencing a mild disgust. She would have to do something, she knew that. And soon. But what *could* she do?

It was not on that joyless day at Bournemouth (although it was very soon after) that Brenda Josephs recognized the ugly fact that had been standing at the threshold of her mind: she now hated the man she had married.

'Have you heard that somebody might be helping himself from the collection? It's only a rumour but . . .' It was the following morning when Morris heard the first whisperings; but in his mind – as in many others' – the alleged hebdomadal thefts were already firmly substantiated in the higher courts of heaven and now stood only in need of a little terrestrial corroboration. There were – surely – only two obvious opportunities, and two possible suspects: Lawson at the altar and Josephs in the vestry. And during the penultimate verse of the offertory hymn Morris turned the organ-mirror slightly to the right and adjusted the elevation so that he had a good view of the large, gilt crucifix standing on the heavily brocaded altar cloth; and of Lawson holding high the collection-plate, then lowering it and leaning forward in a tilted benediction before handing it back to the vicar's warden. It had been impossible to see Lawson's hands clearly, but nothing had been taken – Morris could have sworn to it. So it must be that contemptible worm Josephs! Much more likely – counting the cash all alone in the vestry. Yes. And yet . . . And yet, if the church funds *were* being pilfered, wasn't there a much likelier culprit than either? The scruffy-looking man from the Church Army hostel, the man who had been there again this morning, sitting next to Josephs at the back of the church, the man Lawson had befriended – and the man whom Morris himself had encountered the previous morning in the vicarage.

A few minutes later he closed the organ-door quietly behind him and managed a cheerful 'Good morning' to Mrs Walsh-Atkins as she finally rose from her knees. But in truth he was far from cheerful; and as he walked slowly up the central aisle his mind for once was not wholly preoccupied with thoughts of Brenda Josephs, whom he could now see waiting for him by the font. Like Lawson at this time a week ago, he felt a very worried man.

CHAPTER FIVE

ON WEDNESDAY OF the same week, no one seemed to mind the woman as she stood by the shop window examining with slow deliberation one bulky sample-book after another. 'Just looking,' she told the assistant. She'd known what would happen, of course: from the bus-stop in Woodstock Road he would walk down South Parade (where Cromwell had once arranged his Roundheads), turn right into Banbury Road, and then go into the licensed betting-office just opposite the carpet-shop. And he had already done so. She knew, too, that he would have to come out sooner rather than later, since he was due home for lunch – lunch with *her* – at about one o'clock; and he had another call to pay before then, had he not?

It was 11.20 a.m. when Harry Josephs at last emerged, and his wife drifted quietly behind a line of vertically stacked linoleum rolls, watching him. Back up to South Parade, where he pushed the button at the pelican crossing and waited to cross the Banbury Road. Just as she'd thought. She left the shop with a guilty 'Thank you', and kept well behind him as he walked with his slightly splay-footed gait up towards north Oxford, his brown suit clearly visible beyond the other pedestrians.

He would turn right very soon now (how much she knew!) into Manning Terrace; and she skipped and waltzed her way in and out of the prams as soon as he disappeared. He was on the right-hand side of the terrace, about seven or eight houses along, and he would be stopping just about there (yes!) and walking up the short path to one of the front doors. She knew not only the number of the house but also the woman who lived there; knew the style and colour of her hair even – long and prematurely grey, like the strand she'd found on Harry's suit one day the previous week. Ruth Rawlinson! That was the name of the woman who lived at number 14, the woman whom her husband had been seeing; and it was all just as Lionel Lawson had told her it was. She hurried back to the Summertown car park. She would just have time to put in a brief appearance at the Radcliffe Infirmary, and to tell the nursing officer that her dental appointment had taken much longer than expected and that she'd make up the time tomorrow.

As she drove down into Oxford her lips were curled in a cruelly contented smile.

At 8 p.m. on the Wednesday of the following week, Ruth Rawlinson took little notice when she heard the click and the creak of the north door opening. People often came in to look around, to admire the font, to light a candle, to pray even; and she silently wiped her wet cloth over the wooden floor of the pew behind one of the pillars in the south aisle. The stranger, whoever he might be, was now standing still, for the echo of his footsteps had died away in the empty, darkening church. This was just about the time when the place could get almost eerie – and time for Ruth to go home. Of indeterminate age, anywhere between mid-thirties and late forties, she wiped her pale forehead with the back of her wrist and brushed back a wisp of straggling hair. She'd done enough. Twice a week, on Mondays and Wednesdays, she spent about two hours in St Frideswide's (usually in the mornings), cleaning the floors, dusting the pews, polishing the candlesticks, turning out the dying flowers; and once every three months washing and ironing all the surplices. For these good works her motives were obscure, not least to Ruth herself: sometimes she suspected they sprang from an almost pathological need to escape for a brief while her demanding, discontented, self-centred invalid of a mother, with whom she shared her house; at other times, especially on Sundays, she felt her motives sprang from a deeper source, for she found herself profoundly moved in spirit by the choral mass, especially by Palestrina, and then she would approach the altar of the Lord to partake the host with an almost mystical sense of wonder and adoration.

The footsteps had started again, and as they moved slowly up the central aisle she peered over the top of the pew. He looked somehow familiar, but he was half turned away from her and for a while she failed to recognize him: his subfusc suit seemed of good quality cloth, though loose-fitting and shabby; and his face (so far as she could see it) was matted with greyish stubble.

He peered vaguely across the pews, first to the left, then to the right, before stopping at the chancel steps. Was he looking for something – or someone? Instinctively Ruth felt it better if he remained unaware of her presence, and very very quietly she wiped the cloth over the winking suds.

The north door clicked and groaned again, and she dipped the soapy cloth more boldly into the dirty water; but almost immediately her body froze over the bucket.

'You came, then?'

'Keep your voice down!'

'There's nobody here.'

The newcomer walked down the central aisle and the two men met half-way. They spoke in hushed voices, but the few snatches of their conversation that carried to Ruth's ears were readily and frighteningly comprehensible.

'. . . given you more than enough already and you're not getting a penny more . . .'

'. . . *told* you, Mister Morris. It's just to tide me over, that's all. And I'm sure you wouldn't want me to tell my brother . . .' The voice seemed a curious combination of the cultured and the coarse.

The ugly word 'blackmail' rose to the surface of Ruth's mind; but before she could learn more the door had opened again to admit a small group of tourists, one of whom in a nasal twang was soon admiring 'that cute lil farnt'.

*

Half of the long school holiday had now passed and the August sun shone gloriously. Brenda and Harry Josephs were in Tenby for a week; Lawson had just come back from a brief holiday in Scotland; Peter Morris was away at scout camp; and his father was decorating the staircase – amongst other things.

It was at 1.30 p.m. that he was sitting in the Old Bull at Deddington and deciding that he oughtn't to drink any more. After all, he had to drive home. And he had the additional responsibility of a passenger.

'I think we ought to go now,' he said.

Carole nodded, and drained her third Babycham. From the start she had felt embarrassment at being with him, and things hadn't been helped much by the way he'd been speaking to her – so naturally! So unendearingly! It wasn't at all what she'd expected. Or hoped. She'd been in a pub before, of course – quite a few times; but only for a giggle round the juke-box with some of the others from school. But this? The whole thing had been a ghastly mistake, somehow; and yet it could have been so very different . . .

The car was parked at the far end of the tarmac behind the pub, and Morris politely unlocked and opened the door for his passenger before getting into the driver's seat and fitting the key into the ignition.

'You won't say anything at all about this, will you?'

''Course I won't.'

'You mustn't tell anyone.'

'I shan't tell a soul,' she said. Her eyes, the lids shaded in a lurid blue, were dull with disappointment.

Morris took a deep breath. 'Put your safety belt on, my girl. Better safe—'

He leaned over to help fix the awkward thing, and was aware of the softness of her breast against his arm. With what seemed almost paternal affection he took her hand in his; and as she turned her head towards him he put his mouth lightly to hers and felt her full lips softly cushioning his own. He had meant no more than that; but he lingered there as the girl's lips gently – yet so perceptibly! – pushed forward against his own. And still he lingered, savouring long the sensual delight. He put his arm along the seat, easing her more closely towards him; and then the tip of her tongue tentatively tried the entrance to his mouth, and the smouldering smoke burst forth in a blazing flame ... Eagerly she pulled down his hand to her naked thigh, and her legs opened slowly and invitingly, like the arms of a saint in a holy benediction.

They broke away from each other guiltily as a car backed into the space beside them, and Morris drove off to Kidlington, dropping her (where he had picked her up) on the north side of the village.

'Would you like to come to see me sometime?' They were the first words that either of them had spoken on the way back.

'When do you mean?'

'I dunno.' His throat was very dry. 'Now?'

'All right.'

'How long will it take you from here?'

'Ten minutes.'

'You'd better come in the back way.'

'All right.'

'I want you, Carole!'

'I want you, sir.' ('Sir'! My God! What was he doing?)

'Be as quick as you can.'

'I will, don't worry.'

In the kitchen he opened a bottle of Beaujolais, fetched two glasses from the living-room, and looked yet again at his watch. Just another five minutes. Come on, Carole! . . . Already in his mind he was unfastening the buttons down the front of her white blouse, and his hands were slipping inside to fondle her breasts . . . He breathed deeply and waited with an almost desperate impatience.

When finally he heard the timid knock, he walked to the back door like a man newly ushered through the gates of Paradise.

'Good afternoon,' said Lawson. 'I hope I've not called at an inconvenient time? I wonder if I can come in and talk to you. It's – er – it's rather important.'

The Second Book
of Chronicles

CHAPTER SIX

BUT FOR HIS dilatoriness and indecisiveness Detective Chief Inspector Morse would have been cruising among the Greek islands. Three months earlier, in January, he had discussed Easter bookings with the Town and Gown travel agency, taken home a Technicolor brochure, rung up his bank manager to discover the going rate for the drachma, bought a slim Modern Greek phrase-book, and even managed to find his passport again. He had never been to Greece; and now, a bachelor still, forty-seven years old, he retained enough romance in his soul to imagine a lazy liaison with some fading film star beside the wine-dark waves of the Aegean. But it was not to be. Instead, on this chilly Monday mid-morning in early April, he stood at a bus-stop in north Oxford, with a fortnight's furlough before him, wondering exactly how other people could organize their lives, make decisions, write a letter even.

Still no bus in sight.

A heavily pregnant mother pushed a rickety, collapsible pram into the shelter, unstrapped the infant within it, and then stuck her head out to admonish her slightly older offspring, already exhibiting, as it seemed to Morse, the lively potential of a fully fledged criminal. 'Stop frowin' dem bricks, Jason!'

Jason! Jason and the Argonauts sailing up to the Hellespont . . . Morse felt he could have done without the reminder – the second reminder, in fact, that morning; for Radio Oxford had just broadcast an interview with the new vicar of St Frideswide's, recently returned from a fortnight in a monastery on the island of Patmos.

Morse stood aside to allow Jason's formidable mother to enter the bus first. She asked for 'St Frideswide's', and as she fiddled one-handedly in her purse the other passengers watched in helpless silence as the hero of the *Argosy* wiped his filthy shoes over the nearest seat-cover.

Morse knew where St Frideswide's was, of course: one of the string of ecclesiastical edifices along Corn-market . . . where there had been some rather curious occurrences the previous Autumn . . . when he him-self had been away on an eight-week secondment in west Africa . . .

'Where to, mate?'

'Er' (it was more than a year since Morse had been on a bus) 'St Frideswide's, please.' It was as good a stop as any for the Ashmolean, and Morse had prom-ised himself an hour or so in the galleries: it would be good to see the Tiepolo again; and the Giorgione.

But he saw neither that morning.

Whilst Mrs Jason was extricating his pram from the luggage-rack, the triumphant young vandal himself was already at large in the street, and very soon the bottom half of a notice affixed to the church railings was torn from its moorings.

''Ow many times 'ave I *told* you, Jason?' This rhetorical question was accompanied by a clumping clout across the youngster's ears, and the bawling brat was finally dragged away.

The notice now read: ST FRIDESWIDE'S EASTER JUMBLE SALE. That was all. Any details of date, time and place had vanished with the passing of Jason.

Morse was a believer neither in the existence of God nor in the fixity of the Fates. About such things he never quite knew what he should think; and, like Hardy's, his philosophy of life amounted to little more than a heap of confused impressions, akin to those of a bewildered young boy at a conjuring show. Yet, as he looked back, it seemed somehow pre-ordained that his steps should take him on only one course that morning; and he took that course now as, in obedience to some strangely compelling impulse, he walked the few steps across the pavement and unlatched the door at the north porch of St Frideswide's.

CHAPTER SEVEN

As a schoolboy, Morse had once paid a few shillings for a book on architecture and had traipsed around a good many churches, earnestly tracing the development of Early English into Gothic. But the enthusiasm, like so many, had been short-lived. And as he stood in the vaulted silence, looking down the central aisle towards the altar, with the heavily curtained vestry to the right behind him, few of the architectural features were familiar any longer; and his mind, whilst not uninformed, remained maddeningly blank – like that of an amnesic ornithologist at a duck-pond. A ring of candles burned around the effigy of some saint or other, and an occasional elongated asterisk of light was reflected in a gleaming flash from an adjacent crucifix. The air was heavy with incense.

As he walked slowly towards the chancel, Morse realized that he'd been wrong about the silence, though. Somewhere he could hear a quiet, rhythmic scratching noise, like that of a church mouse scampering about in the wainscoting. But the noise was too regular for that; and suddenly Morse knew that he was not alone. A grey head rose above the level of the front pew and nodded neutrally as the visitor stopped alongside. She wiped her pale forehead with the back of her wrist and blew a stray hair from her vision before bending over her work once more, the concentric rings of soap on the wooden floor dissolving beneath her wiping-cloth, the bucket rattling as she moved to the next rectangle.

'Good morning.' Morse smiled amiably as he looked down at her. 'You don't seem to have got any of those brochure things – you know, telling people what to look at.'

'No. We ran out last week, but the Vicar's having some more printed.'

'The Vicar? That's Mr Lawson, isn't it?'

'No, it isn't.' Her large brown eyes looked up at him cautiously, and she suddenly seemed a good deal younger than he'd thought. 'It's Mr Meiklejohn. He's been here since last November.'

'I must have been thinking of one of the other churches.'

'No. Mr Lawson *was* here.' She hesitated. 'He – he died last October.'

'Oh dear. I'm sorry about that.'

For a few seconds there was silence between them.

'I think you knew he was dead,' said the woman quietly.

Morse blinked at her happily. 'Did I?'

'You're another one of those reporters, aren't you?'

Morse shook his head and told her. He was a police officer attached to the Thames Valley Police H.Q. in Kidlington – not to the City Police in St Aldates; he'd heard vaguely about the case but had never been on it himself; in fact, he'd been out of the country at the time.

'Were you involved in any way?' he asked.

'As a matter of fact I was, yes.'

'Pardon?' She spoke so very quietly now that Morse took a step nearer to her.

'I was here in the church on the night of the murder.'

'I see. Do you mind telling me something about it?'

She dried her hands along her faded blue jeans, worn almost threadbare at the knees, and stood up. 'Wait a minute.'

There was a natural elegance about her walk, and Morse's eyes followed her with a slightly quickened interest as she disappeared somewhere at the back of the church, and re-emerged a minute later carrying a brown handbag. She had taken the opportunity to arrange her straggling hair, and Morse began to realize that she must once have been an attractive woman.

'Here you are.' She handed him a cheap brown envelope containing several cuttings from the *Oxford Mail*, and Morse sat down in the pew opposite her and carefully unfolded the thin sheets. The first cutting was dated Tuesday, 27 September of the previous year:

CHURCHWARDEN MURDERED DURING SERVICE

WHILST the congregation was singing the last hymn, Mr H. A. Josephs was stabbed to death in the vestry of St Frideswide's Church, Cornmarket.

Chief Inspector Bell of the Oxford City Police, who is in charge of the murder enquiries, told our reporter that Mr Josephs, one of the two churchwardens at St Frideswide's, had just taken the collection and was almost certainly counting it as he was attacked.

When the police arrived there was no sign of the collection-plate itself or of the money. Inspector Bell said that if robbery had been the sole motive the murder was doubly tragic, since only a dozen or so people had attended the evening service, and the offertory could have amounted at most only to about two or three pounds.

Several members of the congregation had heard sounds of some disturbance at the back of the church, but no one suspected that anything was seriously wrong until Mr Josephs had shouted for help. The vicar, the Reverend L. Lawson, immediately suspended the service and summoned the police and the ambulance, but Mr Josephs died before either could arrive.

The knife used by the murderer was of a dull, golden colour, cast in the shape of a crucifix, with the blade honed to a razor sharpness. Police are anxious to hear from anyone who has knowledge of such a knife.

Mr Josephs, aged 50, was married and lived in Port-Meadow Drive, Wolvercote. He came to Oxford after the bar brilliantly pushed over left-foot shot was serving as a regular officer in the Royal Marine Commandos and saw active service in Malaya. Until two years ago he worked for the Inland Revenue Department. There are no children. The inquest is to be held next Monday.

Morse quickly read through the article again, for there were a couple of things, quite apart from the extraordinary typography of the last paragraph, that puzzled him slightly.

'Did you know him very well?'

'Pardon?' The woman stopped her scrubbing and looked across at him.

'I said did you know Josephs well.'

A flicker of unease in those brown eyes? Had she heard him the first time?

'Yes, I knew him quite well. He was a churchwarden here. It says so, doesn't it?'

Morse let it go and turned his attention to the second cutting, dated Tuesday, 4 October:

INQUEST RIDDLE

THE inquest on Mr H. A. Josephs, who was stabbed to death last week at St Frideswide's Church, was adjourned yesterday after a twenty-minute hearing, but not before the court had heard some startling new evidence. The post-mortem report on Mr Josephs showed that a lethal quantity of morphine was present in the stomach, but it seemed clear that it was the stab-wound which had been the immediate cause of death.

Earlier, Mr Paul Morris, of 3 Home Close, Kidlington, had given evidence of formal identification. He had been the organist during the service and was in fact playing the last hymn when Mr Josephs was murdered.

Another witness, Miss Ruth Rawlinson, of 14 Manning Terrace, Summertown, said that she heard noises coming from the vestry during the singing of the last hymn, and had turned to see Mr Josephs call out and slump beside the vestry curtains.

Chief Inspector Bell, of the Oxford City Police, informed the Coroner that he was as yet unable to re-

port on any firm develop-
ments in the case but that
enquiries were proceeding.
The Coroner extended his
deepest sympathy to Mrs
Brenda Josephs, the de-
ceased's wife.

The funeral service will be
held at St Frideswide's on
Thursday at 2.30 p.m.

The narrative was bald, but interesting enough, wasn't it? What was morphine doing in the poor beggar's innards? Somebody must have wanted him out of the way pretty badly, and that somebody had so far got away with it and was still walking around – probably walking around the streets of Oxford – a free man. Or a free woman perhaps, he reminded himself, as he glanced across the aisle.

Morse looked about him with renewed interest. He was actually sitting a few yards from the scene of the crime, and he tried to imagine it all: the organ playing, the few members of the congregation standing, heads bowed over their hymn books – one minute, though! Where was the organ? He got to his feet and walked up the broad, shallow steps of the chancel. Yes. There it was, on the left-hand side behind two rows of choir-stalls, with a blue curtain stretched across in front of it to hide the body of the organist; and a mirror, too, fixed just above the high top manual, so that, however much he was concealed from the view of all others, the organist himself could keep an observant eye on the minister and the choir – and on the congregation as well, if he wanted to. If you swung the mirror round a bit . . . Morse sat himself behind the curtain on the organ-seat and looked into it. He could see the choir-stalls behind him and the main body of the chancel. Mm. Then, like a nervous learner before starting off on a driving test, he began adjusting the mirror, finding that it moved easily and noiselessly: up and down, right and left – wherever he wanted it. First, to the right and slightly down, and he found himself looking straight at the intricately woven gold design on the front of the green altar-cloth; then to the left and down, and he could see the head and shoulders of the cleaning woman, her elbows circling sedulously over the soapy suds; then further still to the left and up slightly, almost as far as the mirror would go – and Morse suddenly stopped, a needle-sharp sensation momentarily flashing across his temples. So very clearly he could now see the front curtains of the vestry, could even see the fold where they would swing back to let the choir on its way; the fold where they had once opened – perhaps only slightly? – to reveal the figure of a man shouting desperately above the swell of the organ notes, a man with a knife stuck firm and deep through his back, a man with only a moment or two to live . . . What if the organist – Morris, wasn't it? – had actually been looking at the vestry curtains during those fateful, fatal seconds? What if he'd seen something? Something like . . .

The rattle of the pail brought his airborne fancies down to earth. What possible reason could Morris have had for turning the mirror to such an improbable angle as he played the last hymn? Forget it! He turned on the smooth bench and looked over the curtain. The cleaner was packing up by the look of things, and he hadn't read the other cuttings yet. But before he got off the bench his mind again took wing and was floating as effortlessly as a kittiwake keeling over the cliffs. It was the organ-curtain . . . He was himself a man of just over medium height, but even someone three or four inches taller would be fairly well concealed behind that curtain. The back of the head would be showing, but little else; and if Morris was a small man he would have been almost completely concealed. Indeed, as far as the choir and congregation were concerned, the organist might . . . might not have been Morris at all!

He walked down the chancel steps. 'Mind if I keep these cuttings? I'll post them back to you, of course.'

The woman shrugged. 'All right.' It seemed a matter of little concern to her.

'I don't know your name, I'm afraid,' began Morse, but a small middle-aged man had entered the church and was walking briskly towards them.

'Morning, Miss Rawlinson.'

Miss Rawlinson! One of the witnesses at the inquest. Well, well! And the man who had just come in was doubtless Morris, the other witness, for he had already seated himself at the organ, where a few switches were clicked on and where a whirr of some hidden power was followed by a series of gruff bass blasts, as if the instrument were breaking wind.

'As I say, I can post 'em,' said Morse, 'or pop 'em through your letter-box. 14 Manning Road, isn't it?'

'Manning *Terrace*.'

'Oh yes.' Morse smiled at her good-naturedly. 'Memory's not what it was, I'm afraid. They tell me we lose about 30,000 brain cells a day once we're past thirty.'

'Just as well we all have plenty to start with, Inspector.' There was perhaps just a hint of mockery in
her steady eyes, but Morse's lightheartedness had
evoked no reciprocal response.

'I'll just have a quick word with Mr Morris before—'

'That's not Mr Morris.'

'Pardon?'

'That's Mr Sharpe. He was deputy organist when Mr
Morris was here.'

'And Mr Morris isn't here any longer?' said Morse
slowly.

She shook her head.

'Do you know where he's gone?'

Did she? Again there seemed some hesitation in the
eyes. 'N-no, I don't. He's left the district. He left last
October.'

'Surely he must have—'

'He left his post at the school and, well, he just went.'

'But he must have—'

She picked up the bucket and prepared to leave.
'Nobody knows where he went.'

But Morse sensed she was lying. 'It's your duty to tell
me, you know, if you've any idea at all where he went.'
He spoke now with a quiet authority, and a flush arose
in the woman's cheeks.

'It's nothing really. Just that he – he left at the same
time as someone else. That's all.'

'And it was fairly easy to put two and two together?'

She nodded. 'Yes. You see, he left Oxford the same
week as Mrs Josephs.'

CHAPTER EIGHT

MORSE LEFT THE church and strolled over to the snack bar.

'One coffee, please,' he said to the girl lounging by the pay-desk.

'If you go an' si' down, one of the girls'll come.'

'Oh.' It all seemed a roundabout business.

He sat and stared abstractedly through the large window, flecked now with drizzle, and watched the people walking to and fro along Cornmarket. Immediately opposite him, fencing in the church and the churchyard, were the sharply pointed, black-painted railings of St Frideswide's, against which a bearded, damp-looking tramp was leaning uncertainly, a bottle of something hanging loosely in his lefthand.

'Order, please?' It was the same waitress.

'You just had it,' snapped Morse.

'I'm sorry, sir, bu'—'

'Forget it, luv.'

He left and walked back across the street.

'How goes it, brother?'

The tramp looked at Morse warily through an incongruous pair of dark sunglasses: unsolicited interest in his well-being was quite clearly no everyday occurrence. 'Could do wiv a cup o' tea, guv.'

Morse pushed a couple of ten-pence pieces into a surprisingly clean hand. 'Do you usually stand here?'

'Nah. Usually be'ind Brasenose College. Makes a change, though, don't it?'

'Some nice kind people come out of the church, do they?'

'Sometimes.'

'You know the minister here?'

'Nah. Tell yer to push off, like as not, this one. Knew the other one, though. Real gent he was, guv. Sometimes 'e'd take yer down to the vicarage an' give yer a real square meal, 'e would.'

'Is he the one who died?'

The tramp looked at Morse with what could have been a glint of suspicion behind the dark lenses, and took a swig on the bottle. 'Christ, you can say that again, mister.' He shuffled along the railings towards Carfax, and was gone.

Morse crossed the road yet again, and walked past the snack bar, past a well-stocked bicycle-shop, past the cinema, and then turned left into the curving sweep of Beaumont Street. Momentarily he debated between the Ashmolean, just opposite on his right, and the Randolph, immediately on his left. It wasn't a fair contest.

The cocktail-bar was already quite full as Morse waited rather impatiently for a group of Americans to sort out their gins and tarnics. The barmaid wore a low-cut dress and Morse watched with what he told himself was a fascinated indifference as she finally leaned forward over the beer pump to pull his order. She was too young, though – no more than twenty-odd – and Morse was beginning to formulate the philosophy that men were attracted to women of roughly their own age – well, give or take ten years or so either way.

He sat down, savoured his beer, and took out cutting number three from his pocket. It was dated Wednesday, 19 October.

TRAGIC FALL FROM CHURCH TOWER

YESTERDAY morning the Reverend Lionel Lawson fell to his death from the tower of St Frideswide's Church in Cornmarket. Only ten minutes earlier he had conducted the regular 7.30 a.m. Communion Service, and two members of the congregation were among the first to discover the tragedy.

The church tower, formerly a favourite viewing-point for tourists, has been closed to the public for the last two years as signs of crumbling have become evident in the stone fabric on the north side. But the tower was not considered unsafe, and only a year ago workmen had been up to check the leads.

Mr Lawson, a bachelor, aged 41, had been vicar of St Frideswide's for almost eleven years. He will be remembered above all, perhaps, for his social work, since in addition to his deep involvement with the church's flourishing youth activities he invariably took a compassionate interest in the plight of the homeless, and there can be few regular down-and-outs in Oxford who have not at some time or another enjoyed his hospitality.

As a churchman he made no apologies for his High Anglican views, and although his strongly voiced hostility towards the ordination of women was not universally popular his large and loyal congregation will mourn the death of a dear friend and pastor. He studied theology at Christ's College, Cambridge, and later at St Stephen's House, Oxford.

Only last month Mr H. A. Josephs, churchwarden of St Frideswide's, was found stabbed to death in the church vestry.

Mm. Morse looked at the last sentence again and wondered why the reporter had deemed it his duty to stick it in. Wasn't there a bit too much of that *post hoc, propter hoc* suspicion about it? Yet a murder followed very shortly afterwards by a suicide was by no means uncommon, and the reporter would hardly have been the only one to suspect some causal connection. For if Lawson had somehow managed to murder Josephs, then it was surely only honourable and proper for a servant of the Lord to be stricken so sorely in conscience as to chuck himself off the nearest or most convenient pinnacle, was it not?

Morse drained his beer, fiddled in his pockets for some more change, and looked vaguely around him. A woman had just walked up to the bar and he studied her back view with growing interest. A good deal nearer his own age than the barmaid, certainly: black-leather, knee-length boots; slim figure; tight-belted, light-fawn raincoat; spotted red headscarf. Nice. On her own, too.

Morse sauntered up beside her and heard her order a dry Martini; and the thought crossed his mind that all he had to do was to pay for her drink, ask her over to his lonely corner, and talk of this and that in a quiet, unassuming, intelligent, fascinating, masterly way. And then – who knows? But a middle-aged customer had risen from his seat and clapped a hand on her shoulder.

'I'll get that Ruth, love. You sit down.'

Miss Rawlinson unfastened her headscarf and smiled. Then, as she appeared to notice Morse for the first time, the smile was gone. She nodded – almost curtly, it seemed – and turned away.

After his third pint, Morse left the cocktail-bar and from the foyer rang through to the City Police Station. But Chief Inspector Bell was on holiday, he was told – in Spain.

It was a long time since Morse had undertaken any extended exercise, and he decided on impulse to walk up to north Oxford. Only half an hour, if he stepped it out. As if to deride his decision, bus after bus passed him: Cutteslowe buses, Kidlington buses, and the eternally empty Park and Ride buses, subsidized at huge cost by the City Fathers in the vain hope of persuading shoppers to leave their cars on the outskirts. But Morse kept walking.

As he came up to the Marston Ferry crossroads he watched, almost mesmerized, as a north-bound car pulled out of the inside lane into the path of an overtaking motor-cycle. The rider was thrown slithering to the other side of the road where his white helmet hit the kerb with a sickening thwack, and where the nearside wheel of a south-bound lorry, for all its squealing brakepower, ran over the man's pelvis with an audible crunch.

Others on that scene showed, perhaps for the first time in their lives, a desperate courage born of the hour: figures knelt by the dying man, and coats were laid over his crushed body; a young man with greasy shoulder-length hair took upon himself the duties of a traffic policeman; a doctor was on his way from the Summertown Health Centre on the corner; the ambulance and police were already being summoned.

But Morse felt his stomach tighten and twist in a spasm of pain. A light sweat had broken out on his forehead, and he thought he was going to vomit as he averted his eyes and hurried away. The sense of his inadequacy and cowardice disgusted him, but the physical sickness prowling in his bowels drove him on, farther and farther up the road, past the Summertown shops, and at last to his home. Even the Levite had taken a quick look before passing by on the other side.

What it was about road accidents that threw him so completely off balance, Morse had never quite been able to understand. Many a time he had been on the scene of a murder, and examined a brutally mutilated corpse. With an ugly distaste, certainly; but with nothing worse. Why was it, then? Perhaps it was something to do with the difference between death and the *process* of dying, certainly of dying in a writhing agony after a road accident. Yes, it was the *accidental* angle of things; the flukey, fortuitous nature of it all; the 'if only' of being just a few yards, just a few inches even, from safety; of being just a second, just a fraction of a second, earlier – or later. It was all that Lucretian business about the random concourse of the atoms, hurtling headlong through the boundless void, colliding occasionally like billiard balls, colliding like a car against a motor-bike. All so pointless, somehow; all so cruelly haphazard. Occasionally Morse considered the ever-decreasing possibility of having a family himself, and he knew that he might be able to face some terrible illness in those he loved; but never an accident.

In the distance sounded the urgent two-toned siren of an ambulance, like some demented mother wailing for her children.

Morse picked up his one pint of milk and shut the door of his bachelor flat behind him. Not the best of starts to a holiday! He selected Richard Strauss's *Vier Letzte Lieder*; but a sudden thought flashed through his mind, and he put the record down again. In the Randolph he had quickly read through cutting number four, the newspaper account of the inquest on Lawson; little of interest there, he'd thought. But had he been right? He read it through again now. The poor fellow had obviously been a terrible sight, his body violently crushed by his fall, his skull – Yes! That is what had clicked in Morse's mind as he had lifted the lid of the record-player. If he himself had been unwilling to look at the face of a dying motor-cyclist, had those two witnesses looked as closely as they should have done at that sadly shattered skull? All he needed now was a little information from the official report of the coroner's hearing; and, knowing the coroner very well, he could get that little information straight away – that very afternoon.

Ten minutes later he was asleep.

CHAPTER NINE

AVOIDING THE MAN'S look, Ruth Rawlinson finished her second Martini and stared at the slice of lemon at the bottom of her glass.

'Another?'

'No, I mustn't. Really. I've had two already.'

'Go on! Enjoy yourself! We only live once, you know.'

Ruth smiled sadly. It was just the sort of thing her mother kept saying: 'You're missing out on life, Ruthie dear. Why don't you try to meet more people? Have a good time?' Her mother! Her grumbling, demanding, crippled mother. But still her mother; and she, Ruth, her only child: forty-one years old (almost forty-two), a virgin until so recently, and then not memorably deflowered.

'Same again, then?' He was on his feet, her glass held high in his hand.

Why *not*? She felt pleasantly warm somewhere deep down inside her, and she could always go to bed for a few hours when she got home. Monday afternoon was her mother's weekly bridge session, and nothing short of a nuclear attack on north Oxford could ever disturb those four mean old women as they grubbed for penalty

66

points and overtricks at the small green-baize table in the back room.

'You'll have me drunk if you're not careful,' she said.

'What do you think I'm trying to do?'

She knew him fairly well now, and she watched him as he stood at the bar in his expensively cut suit: a few years older than herself, with three teenage children and a charming, intelligent, trusting wife. And he wanted *her*.

Yet for some reason she didn't want him. She couldn't quite bear the thought of being intimate with him – not (she reminded herself) that she really knew what intimacy was all about . . .

Her eyes wandered round the room once more, in particular to a point in the farthest corner of the room. But Morse had gone now, and for some unfathomable reason she knew she had wanted him to stay – just to *be* there. She'd recognized him, of course, as soon as she'd walked in, and she had been conscious of his presence all the time. Could she get into bed with *him?* It was his eyes that fascinated her; bluey-grey, cold – and yet somehow vulnerable and lost. She told herself not to be so silly; told herself she was getting drunk.

As she slowly sipped the third Martini, her companion was busily writing something on the back of a beer-mat.

'Here we are, Ruth. Be honest with me – please!'

She looked down at what he had written:

Tick the box which
in your opinion is nearest

to your inclinations. Will
you let me take you to bed
this week?   ❑
next week?   ❑
this year?   ❑
next year?   ❑
sometime?   ❑
never?   ❑

It made her smile, but she shook her head slowly and helplessly. 'I can't answer that. You know I can't.'

'You mean it's "never"?'

'I didn't say that. But – you *know* what I mean. You're married, and I know your wife. I respect her. Surely—'

'Just tick one of the boxes. That's all.'

'But—'

'But you'll disappoint me if you tick the last one, is that it? Go on, then. Disappoint me. But be honest about it, Ruth. At least I shall know where I stand.'

'I like you – you know that. But—'

'You've got plenty of choice.'

'What if none of the answers is the right one?'

'One of 'em must be right.'

'No.' She took out her own pen and wrote in a single word before 'sometime': the word 'perhaps'.

Unlike Morse, she didn't sleep that afternoon. She felt fresh and alive, and would have done a few odd jobs in the garden but for the persistent drizzle. Instead she revised the lines for her part in the play. Friday was looming frighteningly near, and the cast was rehearsing at 7.30 p.m. that evening. Not that a tuppenny-ha'penny play at a church social was all that grand; but she was never happy about doing even the smallest things half-heartedly – and they always had a good audience.

Morse himself woke up with a shudder and a grunt at 3 p.m., and slowly focused upon life once more. The newspaper cuttings still lay on the arm of his chair, and he collected them together and put them back in their envelope. Earlier in the day he had allowed things to get out of perspective. But no longer. He was on holiday, and he was going to *have* a holiday. From his bookshelf he hooked out a thick volume; and just as the Romans used to do it with the Sibylline Books, just as the fundamentalists still do it with the Holy Scriptures – so did Morse do it with the A.A. *Hotels of Britain.* He closed his eyes, opened the book at random, and stuck his index finger half-way down the left-hand page. There she was. Derwentwater: *Swiss Lodore Hotel.* Keswick, three miles S. along the . . . He rang the number immediately. Yes, they had a single room with private bath. How long for? Four or five nights, perhaps. All right. He'd be leaving straight away, and be there about – oh, about nine or ten. Good.

Evesham – about an hour, if he was lucky. Along the old Worcester Road. M5 and M6 – 80 m.p.h. in the fast lane. Easy! He'd be there in time for a slap-up meal and a bottle of red wine. Lovely. *That's* what holidays were all about.

CHAPTER TEN

THE REVEREND KEITH MEIKLEJOHN exuded a sort of holy enthusiasm as he stood at the door of the church hall. Obviously there was going to be a big audience, and in between the unctuous *Good evenings, how nice of you to comes*, he debated the wisdom of fetching some of the old chairs from the store-room. It was only 7.20 p.m., but already the hall was two-thirds full. He knew why, of course: it was the Sunday School infant classes' tap-dance troupe, with its gilt-edged guarantee of attracting all the mums and aunts and grandmas. 'Hello, Mrs Walsh-Atkins. How very nice of you to come. Just a few seats left near the front...' He despatched two reluctant choirboys for the extra chairs, and was ready with his beam of ecclesiastical bonhomie for the next arrival. 'Good evening, sir. How nice of you to come. Are you a visitor to Oxford or—?'

'No, I live here.'

The newcomer walked into the hall and sat down at the back, a slightly sour expression on his face. He gave five pence to the pretty pigtailed girl who came up to him and stuck the programme in his pocket. What a day! Almost six hours from Keswick to the Evesham exit: single-line traffic north of Stoke; a multiple pileup just after Birmingham, with all lanes closed for almost an hour on the south-bound carriageway; flood warnings flashing for the last thirty miles and the juggernaut lorries churning up spray like speed-boats . . . And what a so-called holiday! On fine days (he had little doubt) the view from his bedroom at the Swiss Lodore would have been most beautiful; but the mist had driven down from the encircling hills, and it was as much as he could do to spot the grass on the lawn below his window, with its white chairs and tables – all deserted. Some of his fellow-guests had taken to their cars and driven (presumably) in search of some less-bedraggled scenery; but the majority had just sat around and read paperback thrillers, played cards, gone swimming in the heated indoor pool, eaten, drunk, talked intermittently, and generally managed to look rather less miserable than Morse did. He could find no passably attractive women over-anxious to escape their hovering husbands, and the few who sat unattended in the cocktail-lounge were either too plain or too old. In his bedroom Morse found a leaflet on which was printed Robert Southey's 'How the Waters Come Down at Lodore'; but he felt that even a poet laureate had seldom sunk to such banality. And anyway, after three days, Morse knew only too well how the waters came down at Lodore: they came down in bucketfuls, slanting incessantly in sharp lines from a leaden sky.

On Friday (it was 7 April) *The Times* was brought into his room with his early-morning tea; and after looking at the weekend weather forecast he decided to leave immediately after breakfast. It was as he was taking out his chequebook at the reception desk that the folded white leaflet fluttered to the floor: he had pocketed it absent-mindedly from the literature set out on the table at the entrance to St Frideswide's, but it was only now that he read it.

CONCERT

At the Church Hall St Aldates
Friday, April 7th, at 7.30 p.m.

TAP-DANCE TROUPE (Sunday School)
GILBERT & SULLIVAN MEDLEY (Church Choir)
A VICTORIAN MELODRAMA (Drama Group)
Entrance Fee 20p. Programme 5p.

ALL WELCOME
(Proceeds in aid of the Tower Restoration Fund)

It was that last line, pregnant with possibilities, that had monopolized Morse's thoughts as he drove the Lancia south. Were the crenellations really crumbling after all? *Had* they crumbled, when Lawson looked his last over the familiar landmarks of the city? Whenever possible, juries were keen to steer away from 'suicide' verdicts, and if the tower had been at all unsafe the point would have been a crucial one. What Morse really needed was the coroner's report: it would all be there. And it was to the coroner's office that Morse had immediately driven when he finally reached Oxford at 4.30 p.m.

The report, apart from the detailed descriptions of Lawson's multiple mutilations, was vaguer than Morse had hoped, with no mention whatsoever of the parapet from which Lawson had plummeted to earth. Yet there was one section of the report that firmly gripped his interest, and he read it through again. 'Mrs Emily Walsh-Atkins, after giving formal evidence of identification, said that she had remained alone for some minutes in the church after the service. She then waited for about five minutes outside the church, where she had arranged to be picked up by taxi: the service had finished slightly earlier than usual. At about 8.10 a.m. she heard a terrible thud in the churchyard and had looked round to find Lawson's body spread-eagled on the railings. Fortunately two police officers had soon appeared on the scene and Mr Morris' (Morris!) 'had taken her back inside the church to sit down and recover . . .' Morse knew that he would have little mental rest until he had seen Mrs W.-A., and it was that lady who was the immediate cause of his attendance at the Church Concert. (Was she the *only* reason, Morse?) He had just missed her at the Home for Ageing Gentlefolk, but they knew where she had gone.

Meiklejohn had finished his long-winded, oily introduction, the lights had been switched off, and now the stage curtains were jerkily wound back to reveal the Tap-Dance Troupe in all its bizarre glory. For Morse the whole thing was embarrassingly amusing; and he was quite unprepared for the wild applause which greeted the final unsynchronized kneelings of the eleven little girls, plumed plastic headgear and all, who for three minutes or so had braved inadequate rehearsal, innate awkwardness, and the appallingly incompetent accompaniment of the pianist. To make matters worse, the troupe had started with a complement of twelve, but one small child had turned left instead of right at a crucial point in the choreography, and had promptly fled to the wings, her face collapsing in tearful misery. Yet still the audience clapped and clapped, and was not appeased until the appearance of the troupe's instructress, alias the piano player, leading by the hand the unfortunate, but now shyly smiling, little deserter – the latter greeted by all as if she were a prima ballerina from the Sadler's Wells.

The Gilbert and Sullivan selections were excellently sung, and Morse realized that the St Frideswide's choir contained some first-rate talent. This time, fortunately, the piano was in the hands of an infinitely more able executant – Mr Sharpe, no less, former deputy to Mr Morris (that name again!). Morris . . . the man who had been on the scene when Josephs was murdered; had been on the scene, too, when Lawson was – when Lawson was found. Surely, surely, it shouldn't be at all difficult to trace him? Or to trace Mrs Brenda Josephs? They must be somewhere; must be earning some money; must have insurance numbers; must have a house . . . With clinical precision the choir cut off the last chord from the finale of *The Mikado*, and their turn was complete – greeted by appreciative if comparatively short-lived applause.

It took a good five minutes for the Victorian melodrama to materialize; minutes during which could be heard the squeaking and bumping of furniture, during which the curtains were twice prematurely half opened, and during which Morse once more looked through the coroner's digest on Lawson's death. There was this fellow Thomas's evidence, for example: 'He had just parked his car in St Giles and was walking down towards Broad Street when he noticed someone on the tower of St Frideswide's. He could not recall seeing anyone standing there before, but it was not unusual to see people looking out over Oxford from St Mary's in the High, or from Carfax tower. He thought that the figure was dressed in black, looking down, his head leaning over the parapet . . .' That was all, really. Only later had he heard of the morning's tragedy and had reluctantly rung up the police – at his wife's suggestion. Not much there, but the man must have been the very last person (Morse supposed) to see Lawson alive. Or was he? He might just have been the first – no, the second – person to see Lawson *dead*. Morse found the key words again: 'looking down, his head leaning over the parapet . . .' How high *were* those parapets? No more than three feet or so, surely. And why bring Lawson's head into it? Why not just 'leaning over the parapet'? And why 'looking down'? Was a man about to leap to his death likely to be all that worried about the place he was going to land? A minister, surely – more than most of his fellow-mortals – might be expected to seek a little consolation from more ethereal realms, whatever the depths of his despair. But if . . . if Lawson had been dead already; if someone had—

The melodrama was under way at last, and in Morse's view a more crudely amateurish production could seldom have merited a public presentation. The play appeared to have been chosen to embrace the largest possible cast, and to allow to all of its participants the briefest possible exposure on the boards, in order to minimize their breathtaking incompetences. The bearded one-armed hero, who at least had learned his lines and spoke them audibly, clumped around in a pair of squeaky army boots, and at one point conducted a crucial telephone conversation by speaking into the ear-piece – of an incongruously modern-looking instrument at that; whilst one of the numerous housemaids was every other line reduced to referring to a copy of her part pasted on the underside of her dustpan. The only feature which prevented the whole thing from degenerating into a farcical shambles was the performance of the heroine herself, a young blonde who acted with a charm and sophistication hopelessly at variance with the pathetically inadequate crew around her. She appeared to know everyone else's part, and covered their lapses and stumbles with impressive aplomb. She even managed, at one stage, to prevent one of the butlers (blind fool! thought Morse) from tripping over an intervening chair as he carried in her ladyship's tea. Mercifully many of the lines (as originally written) must have been extremely amusing, and even voiced by these clowns could elicit a little polite laughter; and when the final curtain drew its veil over the proceedings there seemed to Morse not the slightest sign of embarrassed relief amongst the audience. Perhaps all church concerts were the same.

The Vicar had earlier announced that tea would be served at the end of the entertainment, and Morse felt certain that Mrs W.-A. would not be leaving without a cup. All he had to do was find out which one she was. He looked around in vain for Miss Rawlinson, but it seemed clear that she'd given the evening a miss – enough of a penance, no doubt, her scrubbing the pews. But he felt a certain disappointment ... People were leaving the hall fairly quickly now, but Morse decided to wait a minute or two. He took out his programme and looked at it vaguely, but with no real purpose other than that of seeming not to be lonely.

'I hope you'll have a cup of tea with us?' Even at this late stage Meiklejohn was not neglecting his pastoral duties.

Tea? It had never occurred to Morse that he might be drinking tea at 9 p.m. 'Yes; thank you. I wonder if you happen to know a Mrs Walsh-Atkins. I want—'

'Yes, yes. This way. Wonderful concert, wasn't it?'

Morse mumbled inaudibly and followed his guide into the crowded vestibule where a stout lady was coaxing a dark-brown liquid from a formidable urn. Morse took his place in the queue and listened to the conversation of the two women in front of him.

'You know, it's the fourth time now he's been in one of them. His dad would have been ever so proud of him.'

'No one would ever suspect he was blind, would they? Coming on the way he does and all that.'

'It's lots of rehearsal that does it, you know. You have to sort of picture where everything is—'

'Yes. You really must be proud of him, Mrs Kinder.'

'They've asked him to be in the next one, anyway, so he must be all right, mustn't he?'

So the poor devil *had* been blind after all. And learning a part and stepping out on to the stage had probably been about as much of an ordeal as for a sighted person walking through a swamp of crocodiles. Morse suddenly felt very moved, and very humbled. When it came to his turn, he slipped a fifty-pence piece on to the tea-money plate, and hoped that nobody had noticed. He felt oddly out of place there. These were good people, who rejoiced in the simple ties of family and Christian fellowship; who thought of God as a father, and who never in a month of Sabbaths could begin to understand the aberrations of the new theology which thought of Him (if it thought of Him at all) as the present participle of the verb 'to be'. Morse sipped his tea self-consciously, and once more took out his programme and looked for the name of Her Ladyship's butler, whose mother (with what sweet justification!) was feeling so happy and proud. But once again he was interrupted. Meiklejohn was at his shoulder, and with him a diminutive old lady munching a digestive biscuit.

'Mr – er?'

'Morse.'

'You said you wanted to meet Mrs Walsh-Atkins?'

Morse stood above her, acutely conscious of her smallness, and suggested they should sit down back in the hall. He explained who he was, why he was there, and what he wanted to know; and she readily told him of her own part in that dreadful day's events when she'd found Lawson dashed to pieces from the tower, repeating virtually verbatim the words she had used at the inquest.

Nothing! Morse had learned nothing. Yet he thanked her politely and asked if he could fetch her another cup of tea.

'One's enough for me these days, Inspector. But I must have left my umbrella somewhere. If you would be kind enough to . . .'

Morse felt his scalp tingling in the old familiar way. They were seated at a small table at the back of the hall, and there was the umbrella, large as life, lying diagonally across it. There could be little doubt about it: *the old lady must be going blind.*

'Do you mind me asking how old you are, Mrs Walsh-Atkins?'

'Can you keep a secret, Inspector?'

'Yes.'

'So can I,' she whispered.

Whether Morse's decision to patronize the cocktail-lounge of the Randolph was determined by his thirst, or by some wayward wish to find out if Miss Rawlinson might be there, he didn't stop to think. But he recognized no one, left after only one pint, and caught a bus outside the Taylorian. Back home, he poured himself a large neat whisky and put on *Vier Letzte Lieder*. Marvellous. 'Melismatic', as it said on the sleeve . . .

It was time for an early night, and he hung up his jacket in the hallway. The programme stuck out of one of the pockets and, third time lucky, he opened it and read it.

'Her Ladyship's Butler – Mr John Kinder.' And then his pulse raced as he looked at the top of the cast: 'Her Ladyship, the Hon. Amelia Barker-Barker – Miss Ruth Rawlinson.'

CHAPTER ELEVEN

MEDIUMS AND CLAIRVOYANTS claim enhanced scope for their talents if they can be physically present in a room where the absent ones – the missing or the plain dead – may have left a few stray emanations behind. Murderers, likewise, have the reputation of nursing an uncontrollable urge to revisit the scene of death, and on Sunday morning Morse found himself wondering whether the murderer of Josephs had ever set foot in St Frideswide's again since the day of his crime. He thought that the answer was probably 'yes', and it was one of the very few positive thoughts he had managed to generate since Friday evening. Somehow his mind had gone completely stale, and on the Saturday he had firmly resolved to abandon all idea of further investigation into a mysterious affair which was none of his business anyway. In the morning he had consulted the Sibyl once more, but had drawn the line at Inverness. In the afternoon he had wasted two idle hours in front of the television set watching the racing from Doncaster. He was restless and bored: there were so many books he could read, so many records he could play – and yet he could summon up no enthusiasm for anything. What *did* he want? His listless mood persisted through to Sunday morning, when not even the few erotic titbits in the *News of the World* could cheer him. He sprawled gloomily in his armchair, his eyes vaguely scanning the multi-coloured spines along the book-shelves. Baudelaire might match his mood, perhaps? What was that line about the prince in 'La Fleurs du Mal'? 'Riche, mais impuissant, jeune et pourtant très vieux . . .' And quite suddenly Morse felt better. Bloody nonsense! He was neither impotent nor senile – far from it! It was time for action.

He rang the number and she answered.

'Hello?'

'Miss Rawlinson?'

'Speaking.'

'You may not remember me. I – I met you in St Frideswide's last Monday.'

'I remember.'

'I was – er – thinking of going to church this morning—'

'Our church, you mean?'

'Yes.'

'You'd better get a move on – it starts at half-past ten.'

'Oh, I see. Well – er – thank you very much.'

'You're very interested in us all of a sudden, In-spector.' There was a suggestion of friendly amusement in her voice, and Morse wanted to keep her on the phone.

'Did you know I came to the social on Friday evening?'

'Of course.' Morse felt a silly juvenile joy about that 'of course'. Keep going, lad!

'I – er – I didn't see you afterwards. In fact I didn't realize that it was you in the play.'

'Amazing what a blonde wig does, isn't it?'

'Who is it?' Someone called behind her voice.

'Pardon?' said Morse.

'It's all right. That was my mother – asking who you are.'

'Oh, I see.'

'Well, as I say, you'd better hurry up if you're going—'

'Are *you* going? Perhaps I could give you—'

'No, not this morning. Mother's had one of her asthma attacks, and I can't leave her.'

'Oh.' Morse hid his disappointment beneath a cheerful farewell, and said 'Bugger it!' as he cradled the phone. *He* was going, though. It wasn't Ruth Rawlinson he wanted to see. He just wanted to get the feel of the place – to pick up a few of those stray emanations. He told himself that it didn't matter two hoots whether the Rawlinson woman was there or not.

Looking back on his first church attendance for a decade, Morse decided that it was quite an experience. St Frideswide's must, he thought, be about as 'spikey' as they come in the Anglican varieties. True, there was no Peter's Pence at the back of the church, no bulletin from the pulpit proclaiming the infallibility of his Holiness; but in other respects there seemed little that separated the church from the Roman fold. There'd been a sermon, all right, devoted to St Paul's humourless denunciation of the lusts of the flesh, but the whole service had really centred round the Mass. It had not started all that well for Morse who, two minutes late, had inadvertently seated himself in the pew reserved for the churchwarden, and this had necessitated an awkward, whispered exchange as the people knelt to confess their wrongdoings. Fortunately, from his vantage-point at the rear, Morse was able to sit and stand and kneel in concert with the rest, although many of the crossings and genuflections proved equally beyond his reflexes as his inclinations. What amazed him more than anything was the number of the cast assembled around the altar, each purposefully pursuing his part: the celebrant, the deacon, the sub-deacon, the incense-swinger and the boat-boy, the two acolytes and the four torch-bearers, and conducting them all a youngish, mournful-faced master of ceremonies, his hands sticking out horizontally before him in a posture of perpetual prayer. It was almost like a floor show, with everyone so well trained: bowing, crossing, kneeling, rising, with a synchronized discipline which (as Morse saw it) could profitably have been emulated by the Tap-Dance Troupe. To these manoeuvres the equally well-disciplined congregation would match its own reactions, suddenly sitting, as suddenly on its feet again, and occasionally giving mouth to mournful responses. The woman seated next to Morse had soon spotted him for the greenhorn that he was, and was continually thrusting the appropriate page of the proceedings under his nose. She herself sang in a shrill soprano, and was so refined in her diction that the long 'o' vowels issued forth as bleating 'ew's: thus, all the 'O Lords' became 'You Lords', and three times at the start of the service, whilst Meiklejohn walked briskly up and down the aisles sprinkling everything in sight with holy water, she had implored the Almighty to wash her from her sins and make her waiter yea waiter than snew. But there was one thing in Morse's favour – he knew most of the hymns; and at one point he thought he almost managed to drown the 'Hewly Hewly Hewly' on his right. And he learned something, too. From Meiklejohn's notices for the week's forthcoming attractions, it was clear that this Mass business was rather more complicated than he'd imagined. There must be three types, it seemed – 'low', 'high' and 'solemn'; and if, as Morse suspected, the low variety wasn't all that posh, if no choir was involved – no organist even? – then what in heaven's name was Morris doing in church when the unhappy Lawson dashed himself to pieces from the tower? People perhaps did sometimes go to church because they wanted to but ... Anyway, it might be worthwhile finding out a bit more about those different masses. And there was something else; something very suggestive indeed. With the exception of Morse himself, all the congregation partook of the blessed bread and the blessed wine, ushered quietly and firmly to the chancel-rails by that same churchwarden who had so nearly lost his seat, and who – doubtless by venerable tradition – *was himself the very last to receive the sacrament.* Josephs had been churchwarden. Josephs must have been the last to kneel at the chancel-rails on the evening of his death. Josephs had drunk some of the communion wine that same night. And Josephs – so the pathologist said – had finished up with some very queer things in his stomach. Was it possible? Was it possible that Josephs had been poisoned at the altar? From his observation of the final part of the ritual, it was clear to Morse that any celebrant with a chalice in his hands could wreak enormous havoc if he had the inclination to do so, for when he'd finished *he could get rid of every scrap of evidence.* Nor did he need any excuse for this, for it was part of the drill: rinse the cup and wipe it clean and stick it in the cupboard till the next time. Yes. It would be tricky, of course, with all those other stage-hands standing around, like they were now; but on the evening of Josephs' murder, the cast must surely have been very much smaller. Again, it was something worth looking into. There was another snag, though, wasn't there? It seemed that the celebrant himself was called upon to drain the dregs that were left in the chalice, and to do it in front of the whole congregation. But couldn't he just pretend to do that? Pour it down the piscina later? Or, again, there might have been nothing left in the chalice at all . . .

There were so very many possibilities . . . and Morse's fancies floated steeple-high as he walked out of the cool church into the sunlit reach of Cornmarket.

CHAPTER TWELVE

IT WAS SOME relief for Morse to recognize the fair countenance of Reason once more, and she greeted him serenely when he woke, clear-headed, on Monday morning, and told him that it would be no bad idea to have a quiet look at the problem itself before galloping off towards a solution. Basically there were only two possibilities: either Lawson had killed Josephs, and thereafter committed suicide in a not surprising mood of remorse; or else some unknown hand had killed Josephs and then compounded his crime by adding Lawson to his list. Of these alternatives, the first was considerably the more probable; especially so if Josephs had in some way been a threat to Lawson, if the dagger found in Josephs' back had belonged to Lawson, and if Lawson himself had betrayed signs of anxiety or distress in the weeks preceding Josephs' death, as well as in the days that followed it. The trouble was that Morse had no one to talk to. Yet someone, he felt sure, knew a very great deal about his three 'ifs', and at 9.45 a.m. he found himself knocking rather hesitantly on the door of number 14 Manning Terrace. Such hesitancy was attributable to two causes: the first, his natural diffidence in seeming on the face of it to be so anxious to seek out the company of the fair Ruth Rawlinson; the second, the factual uncertainty that he was actually knocking on the right door, for there were two of them, side by side; the one to the left marked 14B, the other 14A. Clearly the house had been divided – fairly recently by the look of it – with one of the doors (Morse presumed) leading directly to the upper storey, the other to the ground floor.

'It's open,' shouted a voice behind 14A. 'I can't get any farther.'

For once, Sod's Law had been inoperative, and he had chosen right. Two steps led up to the narrow carpeted passage which served as a hallway (the staircase was immediately behind the boarded-up wall to the left, and the conversion had left little room for manoeuvre here), and at the top of these steps sat Mrs Alice Rawlinson in her wheelchair, a rubber-tipped walking-stick held firmly across her lap.

'What d'you want?' Her keen eyes looked up at him sharply.

'I'm sorry to bother you – Mrs Rawlinson, isn't it?'

'I said what d'you want, Inspector.'

Morse's face must have betrayed his astonishment, and the old lady read his thoughts for him. 'Ruthie told me all about you.'

'Oh. I just wondered if—'

'No, she's not. Come in!' She worked her chair round in an expertly economical two-point turn. 'Close the door behind you.'

Morse obeyed quietly, and found himself pushed brusquely aside as he tried to help her through the door at the end of the passage. She waved him to an upright armchair in the neatly furnished sitting-room, and finally came to rest herself only about four feet in front of him. The preliminaries were now completed, and she launched into the attack immediately.

'If you want to cart my daughter off for a dirty week-end, you can't! We'd better get that straight from the start.'

'But Mrs Raw—' He was silenced by a dangerously close wave of the stick. (Belligerent old bitch! thought Morse.)

'I disapprove of many aspects of the youth of today – young men like yourself, I mean – especially their intolerable lack of manners. But I think they're quite right about one thing. Do you know what that is?'

'Look, Mrs Raw—' The rubber ferule was no more than three inches from his nose, and his voice broke off in mid-sentence.

'They've got enough sense to have a bit of sex together before they get married. You agree?'

Morse nodded a feeble acquiescence.

'If you're going to live with someone for fifty years—' She shook her head at the prospect. 'Not that I was married for fifty years . . .' The sharp voice had drifted a few degrees towards a more wistful tone, but recovered immediately. 'As I say, though. You can't have her. I need her and she's my daughter. I have the prior call.'

'I do assure you, Mrs Rawlinson, I hadn't the slightest intention of—'

'She's had men before, you know.'

'I'm not sur—'

'She was a very lovely girl, was my Ruthie.' The words were more quietly spoken, but the eyes remained shrewd and calculating. 'She's not a spring chicken any more, though.'

Morse decided it was wise to hold his peace. The old girl was going ga-ga.

'You know what her trouble is?' For a distasteful moment Morse thought her mind must be delving into realms of haemorrhoids and body-odour; but she sat there glaring at him, expecting an answer.

Yes, he knew full well what Ruth Rawlinson's trouble was. Too true, he did. Her trouble was that she had to look after this embittered old battle-axe, day in and day out.

'No,' he said. 'You tell me.'

Her lips curled harshly. 'You're lying to me, Inspector. You know her trouble as well as I do.'

Morse nodded. 'You're right. I don't think I could stick you for very long.'

Now her smile was perfectly genuine. 'You know, you're beginning to sound like the man Ruthie said you were.' (Perhaps, thought Morse, she's not so ga-ga after all?)

'You're a bit formidable sometimes, aren't you?'

'All the time.'

'Would Ruth have married – but for you?'

'She's had her chances – though I didn't think much of her choices.'

'Real chances?'

Her face grew more serious. 'Certainly one.'

'Well.' Morse made as if to rise, but got no farther.

'What was *your* mother like?'

'Loving and kind. I often think of her.'

'Ruthie would have made a good mother.'

'Not too old now, is she?'

'Forty-two tomorrow.'

'Hope you'll bake her a cake,' muttered Morse.

'What?' The eyes blazed now. 'You don't understand, either, do you? Bake? Cook? How can I do anything like that? I can't even get to the front door.'

'Do you try?'

'You're getting impertinent, Inspector. It's time you went.' But as Morse rose she relented. 'No, I'm sorry. Please sit down again. I don't get many visitors. Don't deserve 'em, do I?'

'Does your daughter get many visitors?'

'Why do you ask that?' The voice was sharp again.

'Just trying to be pally, that's all.' Morse had had his fill of the old girl, but her answer riveted him to the chair.

'You're thinking of Josephs, aren't you?'

No, he wasn't thinking of Josephs. 'Yes, I was,' he said, as flatly as his excitement would allow.

'He wasn't her sort.'

'And he had a wife.'

She snorted. 'What's that got to do with it? Just because you're a bachelor yourself—'

'You know that?'

'I know a lot of things.'

'Do you know who killed Josephs?'

She shook her head. 'I don't know who killed Lawson, either.'

91

'I do, Mrs Rawlinson. He killed himself. You'll find the information in the coroner's report. It's just the same as cricket, you know: if the umpire says you're out, you're out, and you can check it up in the papers next morning.'

'I don't like cricket.'

'Did you like Josephs?'

'No. And I didn't like Lawson, either. He was a homosexual, you know.'

'Really? I hadn't heard of any legal conviction.'

'You're surely not as naïve as you sound, Inspector?'

'No,' said Morse, 'I'm not.'

'I hate homosexuals.' The stick lifted menacingly, gripped tight in hands grown strong from long years in a wheelchair. 'I'd willingly strangle the lot of 'em.'

'And I'd willingly add you to the list of suspects, Mrs Rawlinson, but I'm afraid I can't. You see, if someone killed Lawson, as you're suggesting, that someone must have gone up the church tower.'

'Unless Lawson was killed in the church and *someone else* carried him up there.'

It was an idea; and Morse nodded slowly, wondering why he hadn't thought of it himself.

'I'm afraid I shall have to kick you out, Inspector. It's my bridge day, and I always spend the morning brushing up on a few practice hands.' She was winning every trick here, too, and Morse acknowledged the fact.

Ruth was fixing the lock on her bicycle when she looked up to see Morse standing by the door and her mother sitting at the top of the steps behind him.

'Hello,' said Morse. 'I'm sorry I missed you, but I've

had a nice little chat with your mother. I really came to ask if you'd come out with me tomorrow night.' With her pale face and her untidy hair, she suddenly seemed very plain, and Morse found himself wondering why she'd been so much on his mind. 'It's your birthday, isn't it?'

She nodded vaguely, her face puzzled and hesitant.

'It's all right,' said Morse. 'Your mother says it'll do you good. In fact she's very pleased with the idea, aren't you, Mrs Rawlinson?' (One trick to Morse.)

'Well, I – I'd love to but—'

'No buts about it, Ruthie! As the Inspector says, I think it would do you the world of good.'

'I'll pick you up about seven, then,' said Morse.

Ruth gathered up her string shopping bag, and stood beside Morse on the threshold. 'Thank you, Mother. That was kind of you. But' (turning to Morse) 'I'm sorry. I can't accept your invitation. I've already been asked out by – by someone else.'

Life was a strange business. A few seconds ago she'd looked so ordinary; yet now she seemed a prize just snatched from his grasp, and for Morse the day ahead loomed blank and lonely. As it did, if only he had known, for Ruth.

CHAPTER THIRTEEN

'WHAT THE 'ELL do *you* want?' growled Chief Inspector Bell of the City Police. A fortnight in Malaga which had coincided with a strike of Spanish hotel staff had not brought him home in the sweetest of humours; and the jobs he had gladly left behind him had (as ever) not gone away. But he knew Morse well: they were old sparring partners.

'The Spanish brothels still doing a roaring trade?'

'Had the wife with me, didn't I?'

'Tell me something about this Lawson business.'

'Damned if I will. The case is closed – and it's got nothing to do with you.'

'How're the kids?'

'Ungrateful little buggers. Shan't take 'em again.'

'And the Lawson case is closed?'

'Locked and bolted.'

'No harm in just—'

'I've lost the key.'

'All kids are ungrateful.'

'Especially mine.'

'Where's the file?'

'What d'you want to know?'

'Who killed Josephs, for a start.'

'Lawson did.'

'Morse blinked in some surprise. 'You mean that?'

Bell nodded. 'The knife that killed Josephs belonged to Lawson. The woman who charred for him had seen it several times on his desk in the vicarage.'

'But Lawson was nowhere near Josephs when—' Morse stopped in his tracks, and Bell continued.

'Josephs was just about dead when he was knifed: acute morphine poisoning, administered, as they say, at the altar of the Lord. What about that, Morse? Josephs was a churchwarden and he was always last at the altar-rail, and he finished up with some pretty queer things in his belly, right? It seems pretty obvious, then, that . . .' It was a strange experience for Morse. *Déjà vu.* He found himself only half-listening to Bell's explanation – no, not Bell's, his own explanation. '. . . rinse the utensils, wipe 'em clean, stick 'em in the cupboard till next time. Easy! Proof, though? No.'

'But how did Lawson—?'

'He's standing in front of the altar, waiting for the last hymn to finish. He knows Josephs is counting up the collection in the vestry as he always does, and Lawson's expecting him to be lying there unconscious; dead, probably, by now. But suddenly Josephs shouts for help, and Lawson comes swooping down the aisle in his batman outfit—'

'Chasuble,' mumbled Morse.

'—and covers him up under his what's-it; he keeps the others – there aren't many of 'em, anyway – away from the vestry, sends for help, and then when he's alone he sticks his knife in Josephs' back – just to make sure.'

'I thought the collection was pinched.'

Bell nodded. 'There was one of those down-and-out fellows at the service: Lawson had helped him occasionally – put him up at the vicarage, given him his old suits – that sort of thing. In fact, this fellow had been kneeling next to Josephs at the communion-rail—'

'So *he* could have put the stuff in the wine.'

Bell shook his head. 'You should go to church occasionally Morse. If he had done, Lawson would have been poisoned just like Josephs, because the minister has to finish off what's left of the wine. You know, I reckon your brain's getting addled in your old age.'

'Someone still pinched the collection,' said Morse feebly.

'Oh yes. And I'm sure it was this fellow – Swan, or something like that, his name was. He just saw the money in the vestry and – well, he just nicked it.'

'I thought you said Lawson kept all the others outside.'

'For a start, yes. He had to.'

Morse looked far from convinced, but Bell sailed happily on. 'A reasonably well-educated fellow, by all accounts. We put out a description of him, of course, but . . . They all look much of a muchness, those sort of fellows: none of 'em shave or get their hair cut. Anyway, he'd only be up for petty larceny if we found him. Two or three quid, at the outside – that's all he got. Funny, really. If he'd had a chance to go through Josephs' pockets, he'd have found nearly a hundred.'

Morse whistled softly. 'That means that Lawson couldn't have gone through his pockets, either, doesn't it? They tell me the clergy aren't exactly overpaid these days, and Lawson couldn't exactly have been rolling in—'

Bell smiled. 'Lawson was hellish lucky to get the chance to knife him – let alone go through his pockets. But that's neither here nor there. Lawson *was* rolling in it. Until a few weeks before he died, his deposit account at the bank stood at over £30,000.'

This time Morse's whistle was loud and long. 'Until a few weeks . . .?'

'Yes. Then he took his money out. Almost all of it.'

'Any idea—?'

'Not really.'

'What did the bank manager have to tell you?'

'He wasn't allowed to tell me anything.'

'What *did* he tell you?'

'That Lawson had told him he was going to make an anonymous donation to some charity, and that's why he wanted cash.'

'Some bloody donation!'

'Some people are more generous than others, Morse.'

'Did he take out all this cash before, or after, Josephs was murdered?'

For the first time Bell seemed slightly uneasy. 'Before, actually.'

Morse was silent for a short while. The new pieces of evidence were not fitting at all neatly. 'What was Lawson's motive for killing Josephs?'

'Blackmail, perhaps?'

'Josephs had some hold over him?'

'Something like that.'

'Any ideas?'

'There were a few rumours.'

'Well?'

'I prefer facts.'

'Was Lawson buggering the choirboys?'

'You always did put things so nicely.'

'What facts, then?'

'Lawson had made out a cheque for £250 to Josephs a couple of weeks earlier.'

'I see,' said Morse slowly. 'What else?'

'Nothing.'

'Can I look through the files?'

'Certainly not.'

Morse spent the next hour in Bell's office looking through the files.

Considering the limited number of personnel available, the investigations into the deaths of Josephs and Lawson had been reasonably thorough, although there were a few surprising omissions. It would have been interesting, for example, to read the evidence of every single member of the congregation present when Josephs died, but it seemed that several of them had been only casual visitors – two American tourists amongst them – and Lawson had quite innocently informed them that perhaps they needn't stay. Understandable, no doubt – but very careless and quite improper. Unless ... unless, thought Morse, Lawson wasn't over-anxious for all of them to tell the police what they'd seen? It was sometimes just those little details, just those little inconsistencies ... Of the statements that were available, all cleanly set out, all neatly typed, only one arrested Morse's attention: the one, duly signed in the dithery hand of Mrs Emily Walsh-Atkins, attesting to the identification of Lawson.

'Did you interview this old girl?' asked Morse, pushing the statement across the table.

'Not personally, no.'

So far Bell had shown himself a jump or two ahead all round the course, but Morse thought he now saw himself coming through pretty fast on the rails. 'She's as blind as a bloody bat, did you know that? What sort of identification do you think this is? I met her the other night and—'

Bell looked up slowly from the report he'd been reading. 'Are you suggesting that fellow we found draped over the railings *wasn't* Lawson?'

'All I'm suggesting, Bell, is that you must have been pretty hard up for witnesses if you had to rely on her. As I say, she's—'

'She's as blind as a bat – almost your own words, Morse; and, if I remember rightly, exactly the words of my own Sergeant Davies. But don't be too hard on the old dear for wanting to get into the act – it was the most exciting thing that ever happened to her.'

'But that doesn't mean—'

'Hold your horses, Morse! We only needed one identification for the coroner's court, so we only *had* one. Right? But we had another witness all ready, and I don't think *he's* as blind as a bat. If he is, he must have one helluva job when he play the organ in six sharps.'

'Oh, I see.' But Morse didn't see. What was Morris
doing at St Frideswide's that morning? Ruth Rawlinson
would know, of course. Ruth ... Huh! Her birthday
today, and she would be all dolled up for a date with
some lecherous lout ...

'Why was Morris at church that morning?'

'It's a free country, Morse. Perhaps he just wanted to
go to church.'

'Did you find out if he was playing the organ?'

'As a matter of fact, I did, yes.' Bell was thoroughly
enjoying himself again – something he'd seldom experienced in Morse's company before. 'He *was* playing the
organ.'

After Morse was gone, Bell stared out of his office
window for several minutes. Morse was a clever beggar.
One or two questions he'd asked had probed a bit
deeper than was comfortable; but most cases had a few
ragged ends here and there. He tried to switch his
mind over to another channel but he felt hot and sticky;
felt he might be sickening for something.

Ruth Rawlinson had lied to Morse – well, not exactly
lied. She did have an assignation on the evening of her
birthday; but it wouldn't last for long, thank goodness!
And then? And then she could meet Morse – if he still
wanted to take her out.

At 3 p.m. she nervously flicked through the *m*s in the
blue Oxford Area Telephone Directory, and found
only one 'Morse' in north Oxford: Morse, E. She didn't
know his Christian name, and she vaguely wondered

what the 'E' stood for. Irrationally, as she heard the first few rings, she hoped that he wasn't in; and then, as they continued, she prayed that he was.

But there was no answer.

Chapter Fourteen

From the City Police H.Q. Morse walked up past Christ Church to Cornmarket. To his left he noticed that the door of Carfax tower stood open, and beside it a notice inviting tourists to ascend and enjoy a panoramic view of Oxford. At the top of the tower he could see four or five people standing against the skyline and pointing to some of the local landmarks, and a teenage youth actually sitting on the edge, with one of his boots wedged against the next parapet. Morse, feeling a twinge of panic somewhere in his bowels, lowered his eyes and walked on. He joined the small bus-queue just outside Woolworth, thinking again of what he'd just been reading: the life-histories of Josephs and Lawson, the accounts of their deaths, the subsequent investigations. But for the moment the filters of his brain could separate out no new nugget of precious information, and he turned towards St Giles and looked up at the tower of St Frideswide's. No one up there, of course ... Just a minute! Had anyone been up there – recently? Suddenly a curious thought came into his mind – but no, it must be wrong. There'd been something in Bell's file about it: 'Each November a group of volunteers go up to sweep the leaves.' It had just been a thought, that's all.

A Banbury Road bus nudged into the queue, and Morse sat upstairs. As they passed St Frideswide's he looked up again at the tower and made a guess at its height: eighty, ninety feet? The trees ahead of him in St Giles had that long-distance look of green about them as the leaves began to open; and the bus, as it pulled into the lay-by outside the Taylorian Institute, was scraping against some of their budded branches, when something clicked in Morse's mind. How tall were the trees here? Forty, fifty feet? Not much more, certainly. So how in the name of gravity did the autumnal leaves ever manage to dance their way to the top of St Frideswide's tower? Wasn't there perhaps a simple answer, though? They *didn't.* The November leaf-sweeping brigade had no need to go up to the main tower at all: they just cleared the lower roofs over the aisle and the Lady Chapel. That must be it. And so the curious thought grew curiouser still: since the time of Lawson's death, when doubtless Bell's minions had sieved every leaf and every fragment of stone, had *anyone* been up to the roof of the tower?

The bell pinged for the bus to stop at the Summer-town shops; and simultaneously another bell rang in Morse's mind, and he joined the exodus. In Bell's notes (it was all 'bells' now) there'd been a few tactful mentions of Josephs' weakness for gambling on the horses, and the intelligent early suggestion (before Bell's visit to Josephs' bank manager) that the £100 or so found in the dead man's wallet might have had a fairly simple provenance – the licensed betting-office in Summertown.

Morse pushed open the door and immediately registered some surprise. It was more like a branch of Lloyds Bank than the traditional picture of a bookmaker's premises. A counter faced him along the far wall, with a low grille running the length of it, behind which two young women were taking money and stamping betting-slips. Round the three other walls the racing pages of the daily newspapers were pinned, and in front of them were placed black plastic chairs where clients could sit and study the form guides and consider their own fancies or the tipsters' selections. There were about fifteen people there, all men – sitting or standing about, their minds keenly concentrated on the state of the going, the weights and the jockeys, their ears intent on the loudspeaker which every few minutes brought them the latest news of the betting direct from the courses. Morse sat down and stared vacantly at a page of the *Sporting Chronicle*. To his right, a smartly dressed Chinaman twisted the knob on a small machine affixed to the wall and tore off a betting-slip. And from the corner of his eye Morse could see exactly what he wrote: '3.35 Newmarket – £20 win – The Fiddler'. Phew! Surely most of the punters here had to be satisfied with a modest fifty pence or so each way? He turned his head and watched the Chinaman at the pay-in counter, four crisp fivers fanned out neatly in his right hand; watched the girl behind the grille, as she accepted the latest sacrifice with the bland indifference of a Buddhist deity. Two minutes later the loudspeaker woke up again, and without enthu-

siasm an impersonal voice announced the 'off';
announced, after a period of silence, the order of the
runners at the four-furlong marker; then the winner,
the second, the third – The Fiddler not amongst them.
To Morse, who as a boy had listened to the frenetically
exciting race-commentaries of Raymond Glendenning,
the whole thing seemed extraordinarily flat, more like
an auctioneer selling a Cézanne at Sotheby's.

The Chinaman resumed his seat beside Morse, and
began to tear up his small yellow slip with the exaggerated delicacy of one who practises the art of origami.

'No luck?' ventured Morse.

'No,' said the Chinaman, with a polite oriental
inclination of the head.

'You lucky sometimes?'

'Sometime.' Again the half-smile, the gentle inclination of the head.

'Come here often?'

'Often.' And, as if to answer the query on Morse's
face, 'Me pretty rich man, you think so?'

Morse took the plunge. 'I used to know a fellow who
came in here most days – fellow called Josephs. Used to
wear a brown suit. About fifty.'

'Here now?'

'No. He died about six months ago – murdered,
poor chap.'

'Ah. You mean Harree. Yes. Poor Harree I know
heem. We often talk. He murdered, yes. Me verree
sorree.'

'He won quite a bit on the horses, I've heard. Still,
some of us are luckier than others.'

'You wrong. Harree verree unluckee man. Always just not there quite.'

'He lost a lot of money, you mean?'

The Chinaman shrugged. 'Perhaps he rich man.' His narrow eyes focused on the 4.00 card at Newmarket, his right hand reaching up automatically for the knob on the wall machine.

Probably Josephs had been losing money pretty consistently, and not the sort of money he could hope to recoup from the unemployment exchange. Yet he'd got money from somewhere, by some means.

Morse considered a little wager of his own on the Chinaman's next selection, but squint as he would he couldn't quite see the name, and he left and walked thoughtfully up the hill. It was a pity. A few minutes after Morse had let himself into his flat, the little Chinaman stood smiling a not particularly inscrutable smile at the pay-out counter. He hadn't really got his English syntax sorted out yet, but perhaps he'd coined as fitting an epitaph for Harry Josephs as any with those five disjointed adverbs: 'Always just not there quite.'

CHAPTER FIFTEEN

'No, I'm sorry, Inspector – he isn't.' It was ten past seven and Mrs Lewis regretted the interruption to *The Archers*: she hoped that Morse would either come in or go away. 'Oxford are playing tonight, and he's gone to watch them.'

The rain had been falling steadily since tea-time, and still pattered the puddles in the Lewises' front drive. 'He must be mad,' said Morse.

'It's working with you, Inspector. Are you coming in?'

Morse shook his head and a raindrop dripped from his bare head on to his chin. 'I'll go and see if I can find him.'

'You must be mad,' muttered Mrs Lewis.

Morse drove carefully through the rain up to Headington, the windscreen-wipers sweeping back and forth in clean arcs across the spattered window. It was these damned holidays that upset him! Earlier this Tuesday evening he had sat in his armchair, once again in the grip of a numbing lethargy that minute by minute grew ever more paralysing. The Playhouse offered him a Joe Orton farce, hailed by the critics as a comedy classic. No. The Moulin Rouge announced that the torrid

Sandra Bergson was leading a sexy, savage, insatiable all-girl gang in *On the Game*: an X trailer, no doubt, advertising a U film. No. Every prospect seemed displeasing, and even women, temporarily, seemed vile. Then he'd suddenly thought of Sergeant Lewis.

It had been no problem parking the Lancia in Sandfield Road, and Morse now pushed through the stiff turnstile into the Manor Road ground. Only a faithful sprinkling of bedraggled spectators standing along the west-side terrace, their umbrellas streaked with rain; but the covered terrace at the London Road end was tightly packed with orange-and-black-scarved youngsters, their staccato 'Ox-ford – clap-clap-clap' intermittently echoing across the ground. One row of brilliant floodlights was suddenly switched on, and the wet grass twinkled in a thousand silvery gleams.

A roar greeted the home team, yellow-shirted, blue-shorted, leaning forward against the slanting rain, and kicking and flicking a series of white footballs across the sodden pitch until they shone like polished billiard balls. Behind him, as Morse turned, was the main stand, under cover and under-populated; and he walked back to the entrance and bought himself a transfer ticket.

By half-time Oxford were two goals down, and in spite of repeated scrutinies of those around him, Morse had still not spotted Lewis. Throughout the first half, when the centre of the pitch and the two goal-mouths had churned up into areas of squelchy morass reminiscent of pictures of Passchendaele, Morse's thoughts had given him little rest. An improbable, illogical, intuitive notion was growing ever firmer in his mind –

a mind now focused almost mesmerically on the tower of St Frideswide's; and the fact that he himself was quite unable to check his forebodings served only to reinforce their probability. He needed Lewis badly – there could be no doubt of that.

Greeted by a cacophony of whistles and catcalls, his black top and shorts shining like a skindiver's suit, the referee came out to inspect the pitch again, and Morse looked at the clock by the giant scoreboard: 8.20 p.m. Was it really worth staying?

A firm hand gripped his shoulder from behind. 'You must be mad, sir.'

Lewis clambered over the back of the seat and sat himself down beside his chief.

Morse felt indescribably happy. 'Listen, Lewis. I want your help. What about it?'

'Any time, sir. You know me. But aren't you on—?'

'*Any* time?'

A veil of slow disappointment clouded Lewis' eyes. 'You don't mean—?' He knew exactly what Morse meant.

'You've lost this one, anyway.'

'Bit unlucky, weren't we, in the first half?'

'What are you like on heights?' asked Morse.

Like the streets around the football ground, St Giles was comparatively empty, and the two cars easily found parking-spaces outside St John's College.

'Fancy a beefburger, Lewis?'

'Not for me, sir. The wife'll have the chips on.'

Morse smiled contentedly. It was good to be back in harness again; good to be reminded of Mrs Lewis' chips. Even the rain had slackened, and Morse lifted his face and breathed deeply, ignoring Lewis' repeated questions about their nocturnal mission.

The large west window of St Frideswide's glowed with a sombre, yellow light, and from inside could be heard the notes of the organ, muted and melancholy.

'We going to church?' asked Lewis; and in reply Morse unlatched the north door and walked inside. Immediately on their left as they entered was a brightly painted statue of the Virgin, illumined by circles of candles, some slim and waning rapidly, some stout and squat, clearly prepared to soldier on throughout the night; and all casting a flickering kaleidoscopic light across the serene features of the Blessed Mother of God.

'Coleridge was very interested in candles,' said Morse. But before he could further enlighten Lewis on such enigmatic subject-matter a tall, shadowy figure emerged from the gloom, swathed in a black cassock.

'I'm afraid the service is over, gentlemen.'

'That's handy,' said Morse. 'We want to go up the tower.'

'I beg your pardon.'

'Who are you?' asked Morse brusquely.

'I am the verger,' said the tall man, 'and I'm afraid there's no possibility whatsoever of your going up to the tower.'

Ten minutes later with the verger's key, and the verger's torch, and the verger's warning that the whole

thing was highly irregular, Morse found himself on the
first few steps of the ascent – a narrow, steep, scalloped
stairway that circled closely upwards to the tower above.
With Lewis immediately behind he shone the torch
ahead of him, and, increasingly breathless from exer-
tion and apprehension, gritted his teeth and climbed.
Fifty-five, fifty-six, fifty-seven . . . On the sixty-third step
a narrow window loomed on the left, and Morse shut
his eyes, hugging the right-hand wall ever more closely;
and ten steps higher, steps still religiously counted, he
reached the inexorable conclusion that he would climb
one step higher, make an immediate U-turn, descend
to the bottom, and take Lewis for a pint in the Randolph. A cold sweat had broken out on his forehead,
and the planes registering the vertical and horizontal
realities were merging and sliding and slanting into a
terrifying tilt. He craved only one thing now: to stand
four-square on the solid ground outside this abom-
inable tower and to watch the blessedly terrestrial traffic
moving along St Giles. To stand? No, to sit there; to lie
there even, the members of his body seeking to embrace
at every point the solid, fixed contours of the flat and
comforting earth.

'Here you are, Lewis. You take the torch. I'm – I'm
right behind you.'

Lewis set off ahead of him, easily, confidently, two
steps at a time, upwards into the spiralling blackness;
and Morse followed. Above the bell chamber, up and
up, another window and another dizzying glimpse of
the ground so far below – and Morse with a supreme
effort of will thought only of one step upwards at a

111

time, his whole being concentrating itself into the purely physical activity of lifting each leg alternately, like a victim of locomotor ataxia.

'Here we are, then,' said Lewis brightly, shining the torch on a low door just above them. 'This must be the roof, I think.'

The door was not locked and Lewis stepped through it, leaving Morse to sit down on the threshold, breathing heavily, his back tight against the door-jamb and his hands tight against his clammy forehead. When finally he dared to look about him, he saw the tessellated coping of the tower framed against the evening sky and then, almost fatally, he saw the dark clouds hurrying across the pale moon, saw the pale moon hurrying behind the dark clouds, saw the tower itself leaning and drifting against the sky, and his head reeled vertiginously, his gut contracted, and twice he retched emptily – and prayed that Lewis had not heard him.

From the north side of the tower Lewis looked down and across the broad, tree-lined expanse of St Giles. Immediately below him, some eighty or ninety feet, he guessed, he could just make out the spiked railing that surrounded the north porch, and beyond it the moonlit graves in the little churchyard. Nothing much of interest. He shone the torch across the tower itself. Each of the four sides was about ten or twelve yards in length, with a gully running alongside the outer walls, and a flat, narrow walk, about a yard in width, between these walls and the leaded roof which rose from each side in a shallow pyramid, its apex some eight or nine feet high, on which a wooden post supported a slightly crooked weathervane.

He walked back to the door. 'You all right, sir?'

'Yes, fine. Just not so fit as you, that's all.'

'You'll get a touch of the old Farmer Giles sitting there, sir.'

'Find anything?'

Lewis shook his head.

'You looked all round?'

'Not exactly, no. But why don't you tell me what we're supposed to be looking for?' Then, as Morse made no reply: 'You *sure* you're all right, sir?'

'Go and – go and have a look all the way round, will you? I'll – er – I'll be all right in a minute.'

'What's wrong, sir?'

'I'm scared of bloody heights, you stupid sod!' snarled Morse.

Lewis said nothing more. He'd worked with Morse many times before, and treated his outbursts rather as he had once treated the saddeningly bitchy bouts of temper from his own teenage daughters. Nevertheless, it still hurt a bit.

He shone the torch along the southern side of the tower and slowly made his way along. Pigeon-droppings littered the narrow walk, and the gully on this side was blocked somewhere, for two or three inches of water had built up at the south-east corner. Lewis took hold of the outer fabric of the tower as he tried to peer round the east side, but the stonework was friable and insecure. Gingerly he leaned his weight against the slope of the central roofing, and shone the torch round. 'Oh Christ!' he said softly to himself.

There, stretched parallel to the east wall, was the body of a man – although even then Lewis realized that the only evidence for supposing the body to be that of a man was the tattered, sodden suit in which the corpse was dressed, and the hair on the head which was not that of a woman. But the face itself had been picked almost clean to the hideous skull; and it was upon this non-face that Lewis forced himself to shine his torch again. Twice in all – but no more.

Chapter Sixteen

At LUNCH-TIME ON the following day, Morse sat alone in the Bulldog, just opposite Christ Church, and scanned an early copy of the *Oxford Mail*. Although the main headline and three full columns of the front page were given over to COMPONENTS STRIKE HITS COWLEY MEN, 'Body Found on Church Tower' had been dramatic enough news to find itself halfway down the left-hand column. But Morse didn't bother to read it. After all, he'd been sitting there in Bell's office a couple of hours previously when one of the *Mail*'s correspondents had rung through and when Bell's replies had been guarded and strictly factual: 'No, we don't know who he is.' 'Yes, I did say a "he".' 'What? Quite a long time, yes. Quite a long time.' 'I can't say at the minute, no. They're holding the post-mortem this afternoon. Good headline for you, eh? P.M. THIS P.M.' 'No, I can't tell you who found him.' 'Could be a link-up, I suppose, yes.' 'No, that's the lot. Ring up tomorrow if you like. I might have a bit more for you then.' At the time Morse had felt that this last suggestion was a bit on the optimistic side, and he still felt so now. He turned to the back page and read the sports headline: UNITED COME UNSTUCK ON PITCH LIKE GLUE. But he didn't read that account, either. The truth was that he felt extremely puzzled, and needed time to think.

Nothing had been found in the dead man's pockets, and the only information imparted by the dark-grey suit, the underclothing, and the light-blue tie was 'Burton', 'St Michael' and 'Munro Spun' respectively. Morse himself had declined to view what Bell had called 'a sticky, putrescent mess', and had envied the perky *sang-froid* of the police surgeon who reported that whoever he was he wasn't quite such a gruesome sight as some of the bodies they used to fish out of the water at Gravesend. One thing was clear. It was going to be a tricky job to identify the corpse: tricky for Bell, that was. And Bell had not been in the best of humours as he'd glared across the table at Morse and reminded him that he *must* have some idea who the fellow was. It was Morse who had taken Lewis to the exact spot, wasn't it? And if he was pretty sure he was going to find a corpse he must have got a jolly good idea whose corpse it was!

But Morse hadn't – it was as simple as that. A peculiar combination of circumstances had concentrated his thoughts on to the tower of St Frideswide's, and all he'd done (whatever Bell suspected) was to obey a compelling instinct which had proved too strong even for his chronic acrophobia. But he'd not expected to find a corpse up there, had he? Or had he? When Lewis had shouted the grim discovery over the roof to him, Morse's mind had immediately jumped to the shadowy figure of the tramp and his miserably thin pickings from the collection-plate. All along he'd felt that it should have been comparatively easy for the police to pick up such a character. People like that had to depend almost entirely on charitable and welfare services of some kind, and were usually well known to the authorities wherever they went. Yet extensive enquiries had led nowhere, and might there not have been a very very simple reason for that?

Morse bought himself another pint and watched the glass as the cloudy sedimentation slowly cleared; and when he sat down again his brain seemed to have cleared a little, too. No; it wasn't the tramp they'd found, Morse felt sure of that. It was the clothes, really – especially that light-blue tie. Light-blue . . . Cambridge . . . graduates . . . teachers . . . Morris . . .

Bell was still in his office.

'What happened to Paul Morris?' asked Morse.

'Buggered off with Josephs' wife, like as not.'

'You don't *know*?'

Bell shook his head. He looked tired and drawn. 'We tried, but—'

'Did you find *her*?'

Again Bell shook his head. 'We didn't push things too far. You know how it is. What with Morris teaching at the same school as his son and—'

'His *what*? You didn't tell me Morris had a son!'

Bell sighed deeply. 'Look, Morse. Whadya want from me? You find me another body last night, and I'm deeply grateful, aren't I? That'll be another half-dozen of my lads out of circulation. And I've just had a call to say somebody's been fished out of the river at Folly Bridge, and we've got more trouble with some squatters down in Jericho.' He took out a handkerchief and sneezed heavily. 'And I'm sickening for the flu, and you want me to go chasing after some fellow who was known to be seein' Josephs' missus pretty regularly long before—'

'Really?' said Morse. 'Why didn't I read that in the report?'

'Come off it!'

'He could have killed Josephs. Jealousy! Best motive of the lot.'

'He was sittin' – playin' the bleedin' organ – when—' Bell sneezed noisily again.

Morse settled back in his chair, for some unfathomable reason looking very pleased with himself. 'You still think it really *was* Lawson you found on the railings?'

'I told you, Morse, we had two identifications.'

'Oh yes. I remember. One from a blind woman and one from the man who ran away with Brenda Josephs, wasn't it?'

'Why don't you go home?'

'You know,' said Morse quietly, 'when you've finished with your squatters, you'd better get a squad of lads to dig up old Lawson's coffin, because I reckon – just reckon, mind – that *you might not find old Lawson in it.*' Morse's face beamed with a mischievous pleasure, and he got up to go.

'That's a bloody fool's thing to say.'

'Is it?'

'Not all that easy, either.' It was Bell who was enjoying himself now.

'No?'

'No. You see, they cremated him.'

The news appeared to occasion little surprise or disappointment on Morse's face. 'I knew a minister once—'

'Well, well!' mumbled Bell.

'—who had one of his feet amputated in the First World War. He got it stuck in a tank, and they had to get him out quick because the thing was on fire. So they left his foot there.'

'Very interesting.'

'He was very old when I knew him,' continued Morse. 'One foot already in the grave.'

Bell pushed his own chair back and got up. 'Tell me about it some other time.'

'He was in a discussion one day about the respective merits of burial and cremation, and the old boy said he didn't mind two hoots what they did with him. He said he'd sort of got a foot in *both* camps.'

Bell shook his head in slow bewilderment. What the hell was *that* supposed to mean?

'By the way,' said Morse. 'What was the name of Paul Morris' son?'

'Peter, I think. Why—?'

'But Morse left without enlightening Bell on the point.

*

P.M. THIS P.M., Bell had said; and as he drove the Lancia up to Carfax the initials kept repeating themselves to his mind: post-mortem, post meridiem, prime minister, Paul McCartney, Post Master, putrifying mess, Perry Mason, Provost Marshal, Peter Morris ... The lights were red at the end of Cornmarket, and as Morse sat waiting there for them to change he looked up yet again at the tower of St Frideswide's looming overhead, and at the great west window which only last night had glowed in the dark when he and Lewis ... On a sudden impulse he pulled round the corner into Beaumont Street and parked his car outside the Randolph. A uniformed young flunkey pounced upon him immediately.

'You can't leave your car here.'

'I can leave the bloody car where I like,' snapped Morse. 'And next time you speak to me, lad, just call me "sir", all right?'

The north porch was locked, with a notice pinned to it: 'Due to several acts of wanton vandalism during the past few months, we regret that the church will now be closed to the public from 11 a.m. to 5 p.m. on weekdays.' Morse felt he would have liked to recast the whole sentence, but he satisfied himself by crossing through 'due' and writing 'owing'.

CHAPTER SEVENTEEN

MORSE RAPPED BRISKLY on the door marked 'Enquiries', put his head round the door, and nodded 'Hello' to a nice-looking school secretary.

'Can I help you, sir?'

'Headmaster in?'

'Is he expecting you?'

'Doubt it,' said Morse. He walked across the narrow office, tapped once on the study door and entered.

Phillipson, headmaster of the Roger Bacon School, was only too pleased to be of help.

Paul Morris, it seemed, had been a music master of the first water. During his short stay at the school he'd been popular both with his teaching colleagues and with his pupils, and his G.C.E. O Level and A Level results had been encouragingly good. Everyone had been mystified – for a start anyway – when he'd left so suddenly, without telling a soul; right in the middle of term, too, on (Phillipson consulted his previous year's diary) 26 October, a Wednesday. He had turned up for school perfectly normally in the morning and presumably gone off, as he often did on Wednesdays, to have lunch at home. And that was the last they'd seen of him. His son, Peter, had left the school just after lessons finished at a quarter to four, and that was the last they'd seen of *him*. The next day several members of staff had pointed out that both of them were absent from school, and no doubt someone would have gone round to the Morris residence if it hadn't been for a call from the Oxford City Police. It seemed that some anonymous neighbour had tipped them off that Morris and his son had left Kidlington and gone off to join a woman ('I suppose you know all about this, Inspector?') – a Mrs Josephs. Inspector Bell had called personally to see Phillipson and told him that a few enquiries had already been made, and that several of Morris' neighbours had seen a car answering the description of Mrs Josephs' Allegro parked somewhere nearby several times during the previous months. In fact, the police had learned from other sources that in all probability Morris and Mrs Josephs had been lovers for some time. Anyway, Bell had asked Phillipson to soft-pedal the whole thing; make up some story about Morris having to be away for the rest of the term – death of one of his parents – anything he liked. Which Phillipson had done. A temporary stand-in had taken over Morris' classes for the remainder of the autumn term, and a new woman appointed from January. The police had visited the house that Morris had rented furnished, and found that most of the personal effects had been taken away, although for some reason a fair number of books and an expensive record-player had been left behind. And that was all, really. Phillipson had heard nothing more from that day to this. To the best of his knowledge no one had received any communication from Morris at all. He had not applied for a reference, and perhaps, in the circumstances, was unlikely to do so.

Not once had Morse interrupted Phillipson, and when finally he did say something it was totally irrelevant. 'Any sherry in that cupboard, Headmaster?'

Ten minutes later Morse left the headmaster's study and leaned over the young secretary's shoulder.

'Making out a cheque for me, miss?'

'"Mrs"; Mrs Clarke.' She wound the yellow cheque from the typewriter carriage, placed it face downwards on her desk, and glared at Morse defiantly. His lack of manners when he'd come in had been bad enough, but—

'You look pretty when you're cross,' said Morse.

Phillipson called her through to his study. 'I've got to go out, Mrs Clarke. Take Chief Inspector Morse along to the first-year-sixth music group, will you? And wash up these glasses when you get back, please.'

Tight-lipped and red-cheeked, Mrs Clarke led the way along the corridors and up to the music-room door. 'In there,' she said.

Morse turned to face her and laid his right hand very gently on her shoulder, his blue eyes looking straight into hers. 'Thank you, Mrs Clarke,' he said quietly. 'I'm awfully sorry if I made you angry. Please forgive me.'

As she walked back down the steps, she felt suddenly and marvellously pleased with life. Why had she been so silly? She found herself wishing that he would call her back about something. And he did.

'When do the staff get their cheques, Mrs Clarke?'

'On the last Friday in the month. I always type them the day before.'

'You weren't typing them just now, then?'

'No. We're breaking up tomorrow, and I was just typing an expenses cheque for Mr Phillipson. He had a meeting in London yesterday.'

'I hope he's not on the fiddle.'

She smiled sweetly. 'No, Inspector. He's a very nice man.'

'You're very nice, too, you know,' said Morse.

She was blushing as she turned away, and Morse felt inordinately envious of Mr Clarke as he watched the secretary's legs disappearing down the stairs. Last Friday in the month, she'd said. That would have been 28 October, and Morris had left two days before his cheque was due. Very strange!

Morse knocked on the music-room door and entered.

Mrs Stewart stood up immediately and made as if to turn off the record-player; but Morse held up his right hand, waved it slightly, and sat down on a chair by the wall. The small class was listening to Fauré's *Requiem*; and with an almost instant ecstasy Morse closed his eyes and listened again to the ethereal sweep of the 'In Paradisum': *aeternam habeas requiem* . . . 'that thou mayest have eternal rest' . . . Too quickly the last notes died away into the silence of the room, and it occurred to Morse that rather too many people had all too recently had a premature dose of that eternal rest thrust forcibly upon them. The score stood at three at the minute; but he had a grim foreboding that soon it might be four.

He introduced himself and his purpose, and was

soon surveying the seven girls and the three boys who were in the first year of their A Level music course. He was making enquiries about Mr Morris; they'd all known Mr Morris; there were various business matters which had to be cleared up, and the police weren't sure where Mr Morris had gone to. Did any of them know anything at all about Mr Morris that might just possibly be of any help? The class shook their heads, and sat silent and unhelpful. So Morse asked them a lot more questions, and still they sat silent and unhelpful. But at least two or three of the girls were decidedly decorative – especially one real honey at the back whose eyes seemed to flash the inner secrets of her soul across the room at him. Morris must have looked at her lustfully just once in a while? Surely so . . .

But he was getting nowhere slowly, that was obvious; and he changed his tactics abruptly. His target was a pallid-looking, long-haired youth in the front row. 'Did you know Mr Morris?'

'Me?' The boy swallowed hard. 'He taught me for two years, sir.'

'What did you call him?'

'Well, I – I called him "Mr Morris".' The rest of the class smirked silently to each other, as if Morse must be a potential idiot.

'Didn't you call him anything else?'

'No.'

'You never called him "sir"?'

'Well, of course. But—'

'You don't seem to realize the seriousness of this

business, lad. So I'll have to ask you again, won't I? What else did you call him?'

'I don't quite see what you mean.'

'Didn't he have a nickname?'

'Well, most of the teachers—'

'What was his?'

It was one of the other boys who came to the rescue. 'Some of us used to call him "Dapper".'

Morse directed his gaze towards the new voice and nodded wisely. 'Yes. So I've heard. Why was it, do you think?'

It was one of the girls now, a serious-looking soul with a large gap between her front teeth. 'He alwayth drethed very nithely, thir.' The other girls tittered and twittered amongst themselves, and nudged each other knowingly.

'Any more contributions?'

It was the third boy who took up the easy theme. 'He always wore a suit, you see, sir, and most of the staff – well' (more sniggering) 'well, you know, most of 'em have beards, the men, I mean' (a great guffaw from the class now) 'and wear jeans and sweaters and all that. But Mr Morris, he always wore a suit and looked – well, smart, like.'

'What sort of suits did he wear?'

'Well' (it was the same boy) 'sort of dark, you know. Party suits, sort of thing. So, well, we called him "Dapper" – like we said.'

The bell rang for the end of the lesson, and several members of the class began to gather their books and file-cases together.

'What about his ties?' persisted Morse. But the psychological moment had passed, and the colour of Morris' ties seemed to have faded from the collective memory.

As he walked up the drive to his car, Morse wondered if he ought to talk to some of the staff; but he hadn't quite enough to go on yet, and decided it would be better to wait for the pathologist's report.

He had just started the engine when a young girl appeared at the driving-window. 'Hello, beautiful,' he said. It was the girl from the back row, the girl with the radar eyes, who leaned forward and spoke. 'You know you were asking about ties? Well, I remember one tie, sir. He often wore it. It was a light-blue tie. It sort of went with the suits he used to wear.'

Morse nodded understandingly. 'That's most helpful. Thank you very much for telling me.' He looked up at her and suddenly realized how tall she was. Strange how all of them looked about the same size when they were sitting down, as if height were determined not so much from the bottom to the shoulder as by the length of the legs – in this case by the length of some very beautiful legs.

'Did you know Mr Morris well?'

'Not really, no.'

'What's your name?'

'Carole – Carole Jones.'

'Well, thank you, Carole. And good luck.'

Carole walked thoughtfully back to the front entrance and made her way to the next lesson. She wondered why she so often felt so attracted to the older men. Men like this inspector fellow; men like Mr Morris . . . Her mind went back to the time they'd sat in the car together; when his hand had lightly touched her breasts, and when her own left hand had gently pushed its way between the buttons of his white shirt – beneath the light-blue tie he'd worn that day; the time when he'd asked her to his house, when he'd answered the door and told her that an unexpected visitor had just arrived and that he'd get in touch with her again – very soon.

But he never had.

Ch

MORSE WAS STILL ... bedside phone rang. ... the Thames Valley Police ...

'I've just had a call from ... still in bed?'

'No, no,' said Morse. 'Decorati ...

'I thought you were on holiday.'

'A man's got to use his leisure hours ...

'Like clambering over church roofs at ... night, you mean.'

'You heard?'

'Heard something else, too, Morse. Bell's got ... And since you seem to have taken over the case already I just wondered whether you'd like to sort of – take over the case. Officially, I mean.'

Morse shot upright in bed. 'That's good news, sir. When—?'

'From now. It'll be better if you work from St Aldates. All the stuff's there, and you can work from Bell's office.'

'Can I have Lewis?'

'I thought you'd already got him.'

Morse's face beamed with pleasure. 'Thank you, sir. I'll just slip a few clothes on and—'

ur pyjamas, Morse?'

ne, sir. Up with the lark—'

with the wren. Yes, I know. And it ad thing for morale here if you got to things, would it? So what about getting

tes later Morse got through to Lewis and ne good news. 'What are you doing today,

ay off, sir. I'm going to take the wife over to—'
e you?' The change of tense was not lost on , and he listened cheerfully to his instructions. l been dreading another visit to his ancient mother-aw.

The Lancia took only one and a half hours to cover the eighty-odd miles to Stamford in Lincolnshire, where the Lawson clan had lived for several generations. The speedometer had several times exceeded 85 m.p.h. as they drove along, up through Brackley, Silverstone and Towcester, then by-passing Northampton and twisting through Kettering before looking down from the top of Easton Hill on to the town of Stamford, its grey stone buildings matching the spires and towers of its many old churches. *En route* Morse had cheerfully sketched in the background of the St Frideswide's murders; but the sky had grown overcast and leaden, and the sight of thousands of dead elm trees along the Northampton-shire roads seemed a sombre reminder of reality.

'They say those trees commit suicide,' Lewis had

ventured at one point. 'They secrete a sort of fluid to try to—'

'It's not always easy to tell suicide from murder,' muttered Morse.

By late afternoon the two men had uncovered a fairly solid body of information about the late and (it seemed) little-lamented Lionel Lawson. There had been two Lawson brothers, Lionel Peter and Philip Edward, the latter some eighteen months the younger. Both had won scholarships to a public school some ten miles distant, and both had been weekly boarders, spending their Saturday evenings and Sundays during term-time with their parents, who ran a small local business specializing in the restoration of ancient buildings. Academically (it appeared) the two boys were more than competent, with Philip potentially the abler – if also the lazier and less ambitious. After leaving school each of them had spent eighteen months on National Service; and it was during his time in the Army that Lionel, always the more serious-minded of the two, had met a particularly persuasive psalm-singing padre, and been led to the conviction that he was called to the ministry. After demobilization, he had studied hard on his own for a year before gaining acceptance at Cambridge to read theology. During this period Philip had worked for his father for a few years, but seemingly with little enthusiasm; and finally he had drifted away from home, occasionally revisiting his parents, but with no firm purpose in life, no job, and with little prospect of discovering either. Five years ago Mr Lawson senior and his wife had been killed in the Zagreb air crash whilst returning from a holiday in southern Yugoslavia, and the family business had been sold, with each of the two sons inheriting about £50,000 net from the estate.

For most of the day Morse and Lewis had worked separately, each pursuing a different line of enquiry; and it was only on the last visit, to the ex-headmaster of the Lawson boys' public school, that they came together again.

Doctor Meyer's speech was that of an old schoolmaster, deliberate, over-latinized with an apparent dread of imprecision. 'He was a clever boy, young Philip. With a modicum of dedication and perseverance – who knows?'

'You've no idea where he is now?'

The old man shook his head. 'But Lionel, now. He worked like a Trojan – although exactly why the Trojans are proverbially accredited with a reputation for industriousness has always been a mystery to me. His ambition was always to win a scholarship to Oxford, but—' He broke off suddenly as if his memory could take him no farther along that avenue of recollection. But Morse was clearly anxious to push him past a few more trees.

'How long was Lionel in the sixth form?'

'Three years, as I recall it. Yes, that's right. He took his Higher School Certificate at the end of his second year, and got it all right. He took the Oxford entrance examination just after that, in the Michaelmas term, but I had little real hope for him. His mind was not quite – not quite alpha potential. They wrote to me about him, of course. They said they were unable to offer him a place, but the boy's work had not been without merit. They advised him to stay on for a further year in the sixth and then to try again.'

'Was he very disappointed?'

The old man eyed Morse shrewdly and relit his pipe before replying. 'What do you think, Inspector?'

Morse shrugged his shoulders as if the matter were barely of consequence. 'You said he was ambitious, that's all.'

'Yes,' replied the old man slowly.

'So he stayed on another year?'

'Yes.'

Lewis shuffled a little uncomfortably in his chair. At this rate of progress they wouldn't be home before midnight. It was as if Morse and Meyer were at the snooker table, each of them playing his safety shots. Your turn, Morse.

'He took his Higher again?'

Meyer nodded. 'He didn't do quite so well as in the previous year, if I remember rightly. But that is not unusual.'

'You mean he was more worried about preparing for his Oxford entrance?'

'That was probably the reason.'

'But he didn't make it to Oxford?'

'Er – no.'

Something seemed to be puzzling Morse, Lewis could

see that. Was he on to something? But it appeared not. Morse had got to his feet and was pulling on his coat. 'Nothing else you can tell me about him?'

Meyer shook his head and prepared to see his visitors out. He was a short man, and now well over eighty; yet there was still an air of authority in his bearing, and Lewis could well understand (what he'd heard earlier in the day) that Meyer had ruled his school with a rod of iron, and that pupils and staff alike had trembled at his coming.

'Nothing at all?' repeated Morse as they stood at the door.

'There's nothing more I can tell you, no.'

Was there slightly more emphasis on the 'can' than there need have been? Lewis wasn't sure. He was lost as usual anyway.

For the first part of their return journey, Morse seemed rapt in thought; and when he finally did say something Lewis could only wonder what those thoughts had been.

'What was the exact day when Lionel Lawson left school?'

Lewis looked through his notebook. 'November the eighth.'

'Mm.' Morse nodded slowly. 'Tell me when you spot a phone-box.'

When, ten minutes later, Morse got back into the car, Lewis could see that he was very pleased with himself.

'Are you letting me in on this one, sir?'

'Of course!' Morse looked sideways at his sergeant in mild surprise. 'We're partners, aren't we? We do things together, you and me. Or "you and I" as I've no doubt old man Meyer would say. You see, young Lionel Lawson was an ambitious little swot, right? He's not been over-endowed by the Almighty with all that much up top, but he makes up for it by sheer hard work. More than anything else he wants to go up to Oxford. And why not? It's a fine ambition. Let's just recap on Master Lionel, then. He tries once – and he fails. But he's a sticker. He stays on for another year – another year of grind on his set books and the rest of it, and all the time he's being groomed by his masters for his entrance exam. I shouldn't think he's too bothered about not doing so well in his other exams that summer – he's set his sights on higher things. Remember he's already done three years in the sixth form, and he goes back in the autumn term because that's when the entrance exams are always taken. He's all ready for the final furlong – agreed?'

'But he didn't make it.'

'No, you're right. But he didn't *fail* to get in, Lewis – and that's the interesting point. Lawson, L., left school on November the eighth, you tell me. And I'll tell *you* something. That year the entrance papers were sat in the first week of December – I just rang up the Registry at Oxford – *and Lawson, L., didn't sit the examination.*'

'Perhaps he changed his mind.'

'And perhaps somebody changed it for him!'

135

A light flickered dimly in the darkness of Lewis' mind. 'He was expelled, you mean?'

'That's about it, I reckon. And that's why old man Meyer was so cagey. He knew a good deal more than he was prepared to tell us.'

'But we have no real evidence—'

'Evidence? No, we haven't. But you've got to use a bit of imagination in this job, Lewis, haven't you? So let's use a bit. Tell me. Why do boys usually get expelled from public schools?'

'Drugs?'

'They had no drugs in those days.'

'I don't know, sir. I never went to a public school, did I? There was none of that Greek and Latin stuff for me. We had enough trouble with the three Rs.'

'It's not the three Rs we're worried about now, Lewis. It's the three Bs: bullying, beating and buggery! And Lawson, L., from what we've learned of him, was a quietly behaved little chap, and I doubt he got expelled for bullying or beating. What do you think?'

Lewis shook his head sadly: he'd heard this sort of thing before. 'You can't just – you can't just make up these things as you go along, sir. It's not fair!'

'As you wish.' Morse shrugged his shoulders, and the needle on the speedometer touched 90 m.p.h. as the Lancia skirted Northampton on the eastern bypass.

CHAPTER NINETEEN

BACK IN OXFORD at about 4.30 p.m. that same afternoon, two men were walking slowly down Queen Street from Carfax. The elder, and slightly the taller of the two, a growth of greyish stubble matting his long vacant face, was dressed in an old blue pin-striped suit which hung loosely on his narrow frame. In his right hand he carried a bull-necked flagon of Woodpecker cider. The younger man, bearded and unkempt, anywhere in age (it seemed) between his mid-forties and mid-fifties, wore a long army-issue greatcoat, buttoned up to the neck, its insignia long since stripped off or lost. He carried nothing.

At Bonn Square they turned into the circle of grass that surrounds the stone cenotaph, and sat down on a green-painted bench beneath one of the great trees girdling the tiny park. Beside the bench was a wire waste-paper basket, from which the younger man pulled out a copy of the previous day's edition of the *Oxford Mail*. The elder man unscrewed the liquor with great deliberation and, having taken a short swig of its contents, wiped the neck of the bottle on his jacket sleeve before passing it over. 'Anything in the paper?'

'Nah.'

Shoppers continuously criss-crossed one another in the pedestrian precinct in front of the park, many of them making their way down the covered arcade between the light-beige brickwork of the Selfridges building and the duller municipal stone of the public library. A few casual glances swept the only two people seated on the park benches – glances without pity, interest or concern. Lights suddenly blazed on in the multi-storeyed blocks around and the evening was ushered in.

'Let's look at it when you've finished,' said the elder man, and immediately, without comment, the paper changed hands. The bottle, too, was passed over, almost rhythmically, between them, neither man drinking more than a mouthful at a time.

'This is what they were talking about at the hostel.' The elder man pointed a thin grubby finger at an article on the front page, but his companion made no comment, staring down at the paving stones.

'They've found some fellow up the top of that tower, you know, just opposite—' But he couldn't quite remember what it was opposite to, and his voice trailed off as he slowly finished the article. 'Poor sod!' he said finally.

'We're all poor sods,' rejoined the other. He was seldom known to communicate his thoughts so fully, and he left it at that, hunching himself down into his greatcoat, taking a tin of shredded tobacco from one of its large pockets and beginning to roll himself a cigarette.

'P'haps you weren't here then, but a fellow got hisself murdered there last – when was it now? – last . . . Augh! Me memory's going. Anyway, a few days later the minister there, he chucks hisself off the bloody tower! Makes you think.'

But it was not apparent that the younger man was given cause to think in any way. He licked the white cigarette-paper from left to right, repeated the process, and stuck the ill-fashioned cylinder between his lips.

'What was his name? Christ! When you get older your memory . . . What was his name?' He wiped the neck of the bottle again and passed it over. 'He knew the minister there . . . I wish I could think of . . . He was some sort of relation or something. Used to stay at the vicarage sometimes. What *was* his name? You don't remember him?'

'Nah. Wasn't 'ere then, was I?'

'He used to go to the services. Huh!' He shook his head as if refusing credence to such strange behaviour. 'You ever go to church?'

'Me? Nah.'

'Not even when you was a lad?'

'Nah.'

A smartly dressed man carrying a briefcase and umbrella walked past them on his way from the railway station.

'Got a coupla bob for a cup o' tea, mister?' It was a long sentence for the younger man, but he could have saved his breath.

'I've not seen him around at all recently,' continued

the other. 'Come to think of it, I've not seen him since the minister chucked hisself . . . Were you there when the police came round to the hostel?'

'Nah.'

The elder man coughed violently and from his loose, rattling chest spat out a gob of yellowish phlegm on to the paving. He felt tired and ill, and his mind wandered back to his home, and the hopes of his early years . . .

'Gizz the paper 'ere!' said his companion.

Through thin purplish lips the elder man was now whistling softly the tune to 'The Old Folks at Home', lingering long over the melody like a man whose only precious pleasure now is the maudlin stage of drunkenness. 'Wa-a-ay down upon the—' Suddenly he stopped. 'Swan-something. *Swanpole* – that was it! Funny sort of name. I remember we used to call him Swanny. Did you know him?'

'Nah.' The younger man folded the *Oxford Mail* carefully and stuck it through the front of his coat. 'You oughta look after that cough o' yours,' he added, with a rare rush of words, as the elder man coughed up again – revoltingly – and got to his feet.

'I think I'll be getting along. You coming?'

'Nah.' The bottle was now empty, but the man who remained seated on the bench had money in his pockets, and there may have been a glint of mean gratification in his eyes. But those eyes were shielded from public view behind an incongruous pair of dark glasses, and seemed to be looking in the opposite direction as the elder man shuffled unsteadily away.

It was colder now, but the man on the bench was

gradually getting used to that. It was the first thing he'd discovered. After a time you learn to forget how cold you are: you accept it and the very acceptance forms an unexpected insulation. Except for the feet. Yes, except for the feet. He got up and walked across the grass to look at the inscriptions on the stone obelisk. Among the buglers and privates whose deeds were commemorated thereon, he noticed the odd surname of a young soldier killed by the mutineers in Uganda in 1897: the name was Death.

CHAPTER TWENTY

AT 4.30 P.M. ON the Friday of the same week, Ruth Rawlinson wheeled her bicycle through the narrow passageway and propped it against the side of the lawn-mower in the cluttered garden-shed. Really, she must tidy up that shed again soon. She took a white Sainsbury carrier bag from the cycle-basket, and walked back round to the front door. The *Oxford Mail* was in the letter-box, and she quietly withdrew it.

Just a little bit today, but still on page one:

CORPSE STILL UNIDENTIFIED

POLICE still have no positive clue about the identity of the body found on the tower-roof of St Frides-wide's Church. Chief Inspector Morse today repeated that the dead man was probably in his late thirties, and revealed that he was wearing a dark-grey suit, white shirt and light-blue tie. Anyone who may have any information is asked to contact the St Aldates Police Station, Oxford 49881. Enquiries have not as yet established any link with the still unsolved murder of Mr Harry Josephs in the same church last year.

Ruth's body gave an involuntary little jerk as she read the article. 'Anyone who may have . . .' Oh God! She had information enough, hadn't she? Too much information; and the knowledge was weighing ever more heavily upon her conscience. And was Morse in charge now?

As she inserted the Yale key, Ruth realized (yet again) how sickeningly predictable would be the dialogue of the next few minutes.

'Is that you, Ruthie dear?'

Who else, you silly old crow? 'Yes, Mother.'

'Is the paper come?'

You know it's come. Your sharp old ears don't miss a scratch, do they? 'Yes, Mother.'

'Bring it with you, dear.'

Ruth put the heavy carrier bag down on the kitchen-table, draped her mackintosh over a chair and walked into the lounge. She bent down to kiss her mother lightly on an icy cheek, placed the newspaper on her lap, and turned up the gas fire. 'You never have this high enough, you know, Mother. It's been a lot colder this week and you've got to keep yourself warm.'

'We've got to be careful with the bills, dear.'

Don't start on that again! Ruth mustered up all her reserves of patience and filial forbearance. 'You finished the book?'

'Yes, dear. *Very* ingenious.' But her attention was fixed on the evening paper. 'Anything more about the murder?'

'I don't know. I didn't know it was a murder anyway.'

'Don't be childish, dear.' Her eyes had pounced

upon the article and she appeared to read it with ghoulish satisfaction.

'That man who came here, Ruthie – they've put him in charge.'

'Have they?'

'He knows far more than he's letting on – you mark my words.'

'You think so?'

The old girl nodded wisely in her chair. 'You can still learn a few things from your old mother, you know.'

'Such as what?'

'You remember that tramp fellow who murdered Harry Josephs?'

'Who said he murdered—?'

'No need to get cross, dear. You know you're interested. You still keep all the newspaper clippings, I know that.'

You nosey old bitch! 'Mother, you must *not* go looking through my handbag again. I've told you before. One of these days—'

'I'll find something I shouldn't? Is that it?'

Ruth looked savagely into the curly blue line of flame at the bottom of the gas fire, and counted ten. There were some days now when she could hardly trust herself to speak.

'Well, that's who it is,' said her mother.

'Pardon?'

'The man up the tower, dear. It's the tramp.'

'Bit elegantly dressed for a tramp, wouldn't you say, Mother? White shirt and a—'

'I thought you said you hadn't seen the paper, dear.' The charge was levelled with a silky tongue.

Ruth took a deep breath. 'I just thought you'd like to find it for yourself, that's all.'

'You're beginning to tell me quite a few little lies, Ruthie, and you've got to stop it.'

Ruth looked up sharply. What was that supposed to mean? Surely her mother couldn't know about...? 'You're taking nonsense, Mother.'

'So you don't think it *is* the tramp?'

'A tramp wouldn't be wearing clothes like that.'

'People can change clothes, can't they?'

'You've been reading too many detective stories.'

'You could kill someone and then change his clothes.'

'Of course you couldn't.' Again Ruth was watching her mother carefully. 'Not just like that anyway. You make it sound like dressing up a doll or something.'

'It would be difficult, dear, I know that. But, then, life is full of difficulties, isn't it? It's not impossible, that's all I'm saying.'

'I've got two nice little steaks from Sainsbury's. I thought we'd have a few chips with them.'

'You could always change a man's clothes *before* you killed him.'

'What? Don't be so silly! You don't identify a body by the clothes. It's the face and things like that. You can't change—'

'What if there's nothing left of his face, dear?' asked Mrs Rawlinson sweetly, as if reporting that she'd eaten the last piece of Cheddar from the pantry.

Ruth walked over to the window, anxious to bring the conversation to a close. It was distasteful and, yes, worrying. And perhaps her mother wasn't getting quite so senile after all . . . In her mind's eye Ruth still had a clear picture of the 'tramp' her mother had been talking of, the man she'd known (though she'd never actually been told) to be Lionel Lawson's brother, the man who had usually looked exactly what he was – a worthless, feckless parasite, reeking of alcohol, dirty and degraded. Not quite always, though. There had been two occasions when she'd seen him looking more than presentable: hair neatly groomed, face shaven freshly, finger-nails clean, and a decently respectable suit on his back. On those occasions the family resemblance between the two brothers had been quite remarkable . . .

'. . . if they ask me, which doubtless they won't—' Mrs Rawlinson had been chattering non-stop throughout, and her words at last drifted through to Ruth's consciousness.

'What would you tell them?'

'I've *told* you. Haven't you been listening to me, dear? Is there something wrong?'

Yes, there's a lot wrong. You, for a start. And if you're not careful, mother dear, I'll strangle you one of these days, dress you up in someone else's clothes, carry your skinny little body up to the top of the tower, and let the birds have a second helping! 'Wrong? Of course there isn't. I'll go and get tea.'

Rotten, black blotches appeared under the skin of the first potato she was peeling, and she took another from the bag she had just bought – a bag marked with the words 'Buy British' under a large Union Jack. Red, white and blue ... And she thought of Paul Morris seated on the organ-bench, with his red hood, white shirt and blue tie; Paul Morris, who (as everyone believed) had run off with Brenda Josephs. But he hadn't, had he? Someone had made very, very sure that he hadn't; someone who was sitting somewhere – even now! – planning, gloating, profiting, in some way, from the whole dreadful business. The trouble was that there weren't many people left. In fact, if you counted the heads of those that *were* left, there was really only one who could conceivably ... Surely not, though. Surely Brenda Josephs could have nothing to do with it, could she?

Ruth shook her head with conviction, and peeled the next potato.

CHAPTER TWENTY-ONE

ALTHOUGH HER HUSBAND (unbeknown to her) had borrowed on the mortgage of their house in Wolvercote, Mrs Brenda Josephs was now comfortably placed financially, and the nurses' hostel in the General Hospital on the outskirts of Shrewsbury provided more than adequate accommodation. On Paul's specific instructions, she had not written to him once, and she had received only that one letter from him, religiously guarded under the lining of her handbag, much of which she knew by heart: '. . . and above all don't be impatient, my darling. It will take time, perhaps quite a lot of time, and whatever happens we must be careful. As far as I can see there is nothing to worry us, and we must keep it that way. Just be patient and all will be well. I long to see you again and to feel your beautiful body next to mine. I love you, Brenda – you know that, and soon we shall be able to start a completely new life together. Be discreet always, and do nothing until you hear from me again. Burn this letter – now!'

Brenda had been working since 7.30 a.m. on the women's surgical ward, and it was now 4.15 p.m. Her

Friday evening and the whole of Saturday were free, and she leaned back in one of the armchairs in the nurses' common room and lit a cigarette. Since leaving Oxford her life (albeit without Paul) had been fuller and freer than she could ever have hoped or imagined. She had made new friends and taken up new interests. She had been made aware, too, happily aware, of how attractive she remained to the opposite sex. Only a week after her appointment (she had given, as her referee, the name of the matron for whom she had worked prior to her nursing at the Radcliffe) one of the young married doctors had said to her, 'Would you like to come to bed with me, Brenda?' Just like that! She smiled now as she recollected the incident, and an unworthy thought, not for the first time, strayed across the threshold of her mind. Did she *really* want Paul all that badly now? With that son of his, Peter? He was a nice enough young boy, but ... She stubbed out her cigarette and reached for the *Guardian*. There was an hour and a half to wait before the evening meal, and she settled down to a leisurely perusal of the day's news. Inflation figures seemed mildly encouraging for a change; but the unemployment figures were not, and she knew only too well what unemployment could do to a man's soul. Middle East peace talks were still taking place, but civil wars in various parts of Africa seemed to be threatening the delicate balance between the superpowers. In the Home News, at the bottom of page three, there was a brief item on the discovery of a body on the tower of an Oxford church; but Brenda didn't reach it. The young doctor sat down beside her, unnecessarily but not distressingly close.

'Hello, beautiful! What about us doing the crossword together?'

He took the paper from her, folded it over to the crossword, and unclipped a biro from the top pocket of his white coat.

'I'm not much good at crosswords,' said Brenda.

'I bet you're good in bed, though.'

'If you're going to—'

'One across. Six letters. "Girl takes gun to district attorney." What's that, do you think?'

'No idea.'

'Just a minute! What about BRENDA? Fits, doesn't it? Gun – "bren"; district attorney – "D.A." Voilà!'

Brenda snatched the paper and looked at the clue: 'Girl in bed – censored.' 'You're making it up,' she laughed.

'Lovely word "bed", isn't it?' He printed the letters of 'Brenda' on the margin of the paper, and then neatly ringed the three letters 'b', 'e', 'd' in sequence. 'Any hope for me yet?'

'You're a married man.'

'And you ran away.' He underlined the three remaining letters 'r', 'a', 'n', and turned impishly towards her. 'No one'll know. We'll just nip up to your room and—'

'Don't be silly!'

'I'm not silly. I can't help it, can I, if I lust after you every time I see you in your uniform?' His tone was light and playful, but he suddenly became more serious as the door opened and two young nurses came in. He spoke softly now. 'Don't get cross with me if I keep trying, will you? Promise?'

'Promise,' whispered Brenda.

He wrote BANNED into the squares for 1 Across, and read out the clue for 1 Down. But Brenda wasn't listening. She didn't wish to be seen sitting so closely to the young doctor as this, and soon made up an excuse to go to her room, where she lay back on her single bed and stared long and hard at the ceiling. The door was locked behind her, and no one would have known, would they? Just as he'd said. If only ... She could hardly bring herself to read her own thoughts. If only he'd just walk up the stairs, knock on the door and ask her again in his simple, hopeful, uncomplicated way, she knew that she would invite him in, and lie down – just as she lay there now – gladly unresistant as he unfastened the white buttons down the front of her uniform.

She felt tired, and the room was excessively stuffy – the radiator too hot to touch. Gradually she dozed off, and when she awoke her mouth was very dry. Something had woken her; and now she heard the gently reiterated knock-knock at the door. How long had she slept for? Her watch told her it was 5.45 p.m. She fluffed her hair, straightened her uniform, lightly smeared on a little lipstick and, with a little flutter of excitement in her tummy, walked across to the door of her room, newly painted in dazzling white gloss.

It was lying by the same door that a member of the cleaning staff found her the next morning. Somehow

151

she had managed to crawl across from the centre of the small room; and it was clear that her fingers had groped in vain for the handle of the door, for the lower panels were smeared with the blood coughed up from her throat. No one seemed to know exactly where she came from, but the letter the police found beneath the lining of her handbag suggested strongly that she was, or had been, on the most intimate terms with a man called 'Paul', who had given his address only as 'Kidlington', and who had urged the recipient to burn the evidence immediately.

CHAPTER TWENTY-TWO

IT WAS ON Saturday morning, and in the middle of page two of the long-delayed post-mortem report on the corpse found on the tower, that Morse came to the conclusion he might just as well be reading the *Chinese People's Daily*. He appreciated, of course, the need for some technical jargon, but there was no chance whatsoever for a non-medical man to unjumble such a farrago of physiological labellings. The first paragraph had been fairly plain sailing, though, and Morse handed the report over to Lewis:

The body is that of an adult Caucasian male, brachycephalic. Height: 5 ft 8½ in. Age: not easy to assess with accuracy, but most likely between 35 and 40. Hair: light brown, probably cut a week or so before death. Eyes: colouring impossible to determine. Teeth: remarkably good, strongly enamelled, with only one filling (posterior left six). Physical peculiarities: none observable, although it cannot be assumed that there were no such peculiarities, since the largest patch of skin, taken from the lower instep (left), measures only . . .

Lewis passed the report back, for he had little wish to be reminded too vividly of the sight picked out so recently by the narrow beam of the verger's torch. Moreover, his next job promised to be quite gruesome enough for one morning, and for the next half-hour he sifted through the half-dozen transparent plastic bags containing the remnants of the dead man's clothes. Morse himself declined to assist in the unsavoury operation and expressed only mild interest when he heard a subdued whistle of triumph from his subordinate.

'Let me guess, Lewis. You've found a label with his name and telephone number.'

'As good as, sir.' In a pair of tweezers, he held up a small rectangular bus-ticket. 'It was in the breast-pocket of the jacket – 30p fare on 26 October. I reckon the fare from Kidlington to Oxford's about 30p—'

'Probably gone up by now,' muttered Morse.

'—and surely' (Lewis' eyes suddenly sparkled with excitement) 'that was the day when Paul Morris disappeared, wasn't it?'

'Never my strong point – dates,' said Morse.

For the moment, however, nothing was going to dampen Lewis' enthusiasm. 'Pity his teeth were so good, sir. He's probably not been near a dentist for years. Still, we ought to be able to—'

'You're taking an awful lot for granted, you know. We neither of us have the slightest proof about who the fellow is, agreed? And until—'

'No, we haven't. But there's not much sense in closing our eyes to the obvious.'

154

'Which is?'

'That the man we found is Paul Morris,' replied Lewis with firm confidence.

'Just because a young girl in one of his classes says he used to wear a dark suit—'

'And a blue tie.'

'—and a blue tie, all right, that makes him Paul Morris, you say? Lewis! You're getting as bad as I am.'

'Do you think I'm wrong?'

'No, no. I wouldn't say that. I'm just a little more cautious than you, shall we say?'

This was ridiculous. Morse, as Lewis knew only too well, was a man prepared to take the most prodigious leaps into the dark; and yet here he was now – utterly blind to the few simple facts that lay staring him in the face in broad daylight. Forget it, though!

It took Lewis no more than ten minutes to discover that Paul Morris had been a patient at the Kidlington Health Centre, and after a little quiet but urgent pressure the senior partner of that consortium was reading through the details on his medical card.

'Well?' asked Morse, as Lewis cradled the receiver.

'Fits pretty well. Thirty-eight years old, five feet nine inches, light-brown hair—'

'Fits a lot of people. Medium height, medium colouring, medium—'

'Don't you *want* to find out who he is?' Lewis stood up and looked down at Morse with unwonted exasperation in his voice. 'I'm sorry if all this doesn't fit in with any clever little theory you've thought up, but we've got to make some sort of start, haven't we?'

Morse said nothing for a few moments, and when he did speak his quiet words made Lewis feel ashamed of the tetchiness which had marked his own.

'Surely you can understand, can't you, Lewis, why I'm hoping that rotting corpse isn't Paul Morris? You see, if it is, I'm afraid we'd better start looking round pretty quickly, hadn't we? We'd better start looking round for yet another corpse, my old friend – a corpse aged about twelve.'

Like Bell, the landlord of 3 Home Close, Kidlington, had flu, but he gave Morse a sneezy blessing to look over the property, rented out (since Morris left) to a young married couple with one baby daughter. But no one answered Lewis' repeated knockings. 'Probably shopping,' he said as he sat down again next to Morse in the front of the police car.

Morse nodded and looked vaguely around him. The small crescent had been built some time in the early 1930s – a dozen or so red-brick, semi-detached properties, now beginning to look their age, with the supports of their slatted wooden fences virtually sopped and sapped away. 'Tell me, Lewis,' he said suddenly. 'Who do *you* think murdered Josephs?'

'I know it's not a very original idea, sir, but I should think it must have been this down-and-out fellow. Like as not he decided to pinch the collection-money, and Josephs got in his way, and he knifed him. Another possibility—'

'But why didn't Josephs yell the place down?'

'He did try to shout for help, sir, if you remember. Couldn't make himself heard above the organ, perhaps.'

'You could be right, you know,' said Morse, almost earnestly, as if he'd suddenly woken up to the fact that the obvious way of looking at things wasn't necessarily the wrong one. 'What about Lawson? Who killed him?'

'You know better than I do, sir, that the majority of murderers either give themselves up or commit suicide. There's surely not much doubt that Lawson committed suicide.'

'But Lawson didn't kill Josephs, did he? You just said—'

'I was going on to say, sir, that there was another possibility. I don't think Lawson himself actually killed Josephs, but I think he may have been *responsible* for killing him.'

'You do?' Morse looked across at his subordinate with genuine interest. 'I think you'd better take it a bit more slowly, Lewis. You're leaving me a long way behind, I'm afraid.'

Lewis allowed himself a mild grin of modest gratification. It wasn't often that Morse was the back-marker – just the opposite in fact: he was usually about three or four jumps ahead of his stable-companion. 'I think there's more than a possibility, sir, that Lawson got this down-and-out fellow to kill Josephs – probably by giving him money.'

'But why should Lawson want to kill Josephs?'

157

'Josephs must have had some hold over him.'

'And Lawson must have had some hold on this down-and-out fellow.'

'How right you are, sir!'

'Am I?' Morse looked across in a semi-bewildered way at his sergeant. He remembered how when he was taking his eleven-plus examination he was seated next to a boy renowned for his vacuous imbecility, and how this same boy had solved the tenth anagram whilst Morse himself was still puzzling over the third.

'As I see it,' continued Lewis, 'Lawson must have been looking after him all ways: meals, clothes, bed, everything.'

'He must have been like a sort of brother to him, you mean?'

Lewis looked at Morse curiously. 'Bit more than that, wasn't he, sir?'

'Pardon?'

'I said it was a bit more than being like a brother to him. He *was* a brother, surely.'

'You mustn't believe every piece of gossip you hear.'

'And you mustn't automatically disbelieve it, either.'

'If only we had a bit more to go on, Lewis!' And then the truth hit him, as it usually did, with a flash of blinding simplicity. Any corroboration he'd wanted had been lying under his nose since his visit with Lewis to Stamford, and a shiver of excitement ran along his scalp as at last he spotted it. 'Swanpole' had appeared several times in Bell's files as the probable name of the man who had been befriended by the Reverend Lionel

Lawson, the man who had so strangely disappeared after the murder of Josephs. But, if all the rumours were right, that man's real name was Philip Edward Lawson, and whether you were a rather timid little fellow trying your eleven-plus question-paper, or whether you were a souring middle-aged detective sitting in a panda-car, *Swanpole was an anagram of P. E. Lawson.*

'I reckon this'll be mother and infant,' said Lewis under his breath. And indeed the heavily pregnant, dowdily dressed young woman dragging a two-year-old child along the pavement duly announced that she herself was the present occupier of 3 Home Close and that this was her daughter, Eve. Yes, she said, since the landlord had no objections, they could come in and have a look round the house. With pleasure.

Morse declined the offer of a cup of tea, and went out into the back garden. Clearly someone had been very busy, for the whole plot showed every evidence of a systematic and recent digging-over; and in the small garden-shed the tines of the fork and the bottom half of the spade were polished to a silvery smoothness.

'I see your husband's keen on growing his own veg,' said Morse lightly, as he wiped his shoes on the mat by the back door.

She nodded. 'It was all grass before we came, but, you know, with the price of things these days—'

'Looks as if he's been doing a bit of double-digging.'

'That's it. Took him ages, but he says it's the only way.'

Morse, who hardly knew a sweet pea from a broad bean, nodded wisely, and gratefully decided he could forget about the garden.

'Mind if we have a quick look upstairs?'

'No. Go ahead. We only use two of the bedrooms – like the people who was here before us did. But – well, you never know . . .' Morse glanced down at her swollen belly and wondered how many bedrooms she might need before her carrying days were over.

Young Eve's bower, the smallest of the bedrooms, was redolent of urine, and Morse screwed up his nose in distaste as he cursorily bent down over the uncarpeted floorboards. A dozen Donald Ducks on the newly decorated walls seemed to mock his aimless investigations, and he quickly left the room and closed the door behind him.

'Nothing in either of the other rooms, sir,' said Lewis, joining Morse on the narrow landing, where the walls had been painted in a light Portland beige, with the woodwork cleanly finished off in white gloss. Morse, thinking the colours a good match, looked up at the ceiling – and whistled softly. Immediately above his head was a small rectangular trap-door, some 3 feet by $2\frac{1}{2}$ feet, painted as lovingly as the rest of the woodwork.

'You got a step-ladder?' Morse shouted downstairs.

Two minutes later Lewis was poking his head over the dusty beams and shining a torch around the rafters. Here and there a little of the early afternoon light filtered through ill-fitting joints in the tiles, yet the surprisingly large roof-space seemed dismal and darkly silent as Lewis took his weight on his wrists, gently levered himself up into the loft, and warily trod from beam to beam. A large trunk occupied the space between the trap-door and the chimney-stack, and as Lewis opened the lid and shone his torch on the slightly mildewed covers of the books inside a black, fat-bellied spider scurried its way out of reach. But Lewis was no arachnophobe, and quickly satisfying himself that the trunk was packed only with books he prodded around amid the rest of the débris: a furled Union Jack on a long blue pole, its colours faded now and forlorn; an old camp-bed probably dating from the Baden-Powell era; a brand-new lavatory-pan, patched (for some unfathomable purpose) with strips of gummed brown paper; an antiquated carpet-sweeper; two rolls of yellow insulation material; and a large roll of something else – surely? – pushed up tight between the beams and the roof-angle. Bending forward as low as he could, and groping in front of him, Lewis managed to reach the bundle, where his finger-tips prodded something soft and where his torch-light shone on to a black shoe sticking out of one end, the toe-cap filmed with a layer of grey dust.

'Anything there?' Lewis heard the quiet urgent voice from below, but said nothing. The string tying the bundle together broke as he tugged at it, and there unrolled before him a collection of good-quality clothes: trousers, shirts, underclothes, socks, shoes and half a dozen ties – one of them a light Cambridge blue.

Lewis' grim face appeared suddenly framed in the darkened rectangle. 'You'd better come up and have a look, sir.'

They found another roll of clothes then, containing very much the same sort of items as the first. But the trousers were smaller, as indeed were all the other garments, and the two pairs of shoes looked as if they might have fitted a boy of about eleven or twelve. There was a tie, too. Just the one. A brand-new tie, with alternate stripes of red and grey: the tie worn by the pupils of the Roger Bacon Comprehensive School.

CHAPTER TWENTY-THREE

A GOOD MANY of the gradually swelling congregation were acid-faced spinsters of some fifty or sixty summers, several of whom glanced round curiously at the two strangers who sat on the back row of the central pews, next to the empty seat now clearly marked CHURCH-WARDEN. Lewis both looked and felt extraordinarily uncomfortable, whilst Morse appeared to gaze round him with bland assurance.

'We do what everybody else does, understand?' whispered Morse, as the five-minute bell ceased its monotonous melancholy toll, and the choir set out in procession from the vestry and down the main aisle, followed by the incense-swinger and the boat-boy, the acolytes and torch-bearers, the master of ceremonies, and three eminent personages, similarly but not identically dressed, the last wearing, amongst other things, alb, biretta and chasuble – the ABC of ecclesiastical rig as far as Morse as yet had mastered it. In the chancel, the dramatis personae dispersed to their appropriate stations with practised alacrity, and suddenly all was order once more. Ruth Rawlinson, in a black, square choir-hat, took her place just beneath a stone-carved angel and the assembled choir now launched into the

163

Mass. During this time the churchwarden had slipped noiselessly into his seat, and handed Morse a little scrap of paper: 'Setting, *Iste Confessor* – Palestrina'; at which Morse nodded wisely before passing it on to Lewis.

At half-time, one of the eminent personages temporarily doffed his chasuble and ascended the circular steps of the pulpit to admonish his flock against the dangers and follies of fornication. But Morse sat throughout as one to whom the admonition was not immediately applicable. Once or twice earlier his eyes had caught Ruth's, but all the female members of the choir were now sheltered from view behind a stout octagonal pillar, and he leaned back and contemplated the lozenge-shaped panes of stained glass – deepest ruby, smoky blue and brightest emerald – his mind drifting back to his own childhood, when he had sung in the choir himself . . .

Lewis, too, though for different reasons, very soon lost all interest in fornication. Being, in any case, the sort of man who had seldom cast any lascivious glances over his neighbour's wife, he let his mind wander quietly over the case instead, and asked himself once more whether Morse had been right in his insistence that another visit to a church service would be certain to spark off a few flashes of association, 'to give the hooked atoms a shake', as Morse had put it – whatever that might mean . . .

It took some twenty minutes for the preacher to exhaust his anti-carnal exhortations; after which he descended from the pulpit, disappeared from view through a screen in the side of the Lady Chapel, before re-emerging, chasuble redonned, at the top of the main chancel. This was the cue for the other two members of the triumvirate to rise and to march in step towards the altar where they joined their brother. The choir had already picked up their Palestrina scores once more, and amid much genuflexion, crossing and embracing the Mass was approaching its climactic moment. 'Take, eat, this is my body,' said the celebrant, and his two assistants suddenly bowed towards the altar with a perfect synchronization of movement and gesture – just as if the two were one. Yes, just as if the two were one ... And there drifted into Morse's memory that occasion when as a young boy he'd been taken to a music-hall show with his parents. One of the acts had featured a woman dancing in front of a huge mirror, and for the first few minutes he had been unable to fathom it out at all. She wasn't a particularly nimble-bodied thing, and yet the audience had seemed enthralled by her performance. Then his mind had clicked: the dancer wasn't in front of a mirror at all! The apparent reflection was in reality another woman; dancing precisely the same steps, making precisely the same gestures, dressed in precisely the same costume. There were two women – not one. So? So, if there had been two dancers, could there not have been two priests on the night when Josephs was murdered?

The kittiwake was soaring once again ...

Five minutes after the final benediction, the church was empty. A cassocked youth had finally snuffed out the last candle in the galaxy, and even the zealous Mrs Walsh-Atkins had departed. *Missa est ecclesia.*

Morse stood up, slid the slim red *Order of Service* into his raincoat pocket, and strolled with Lewis into the Lady Chapel, where he stood reading a brass plaque affixed to the south wall.

In the vaults beneath are interred the terrestrial remains of Jn. Baldwin Esq., honourable benefactor and faithful servant of this parish. Died 1732. Aged 68 yrs. Requiescat in pace.

Meiklejohn smiled without joy as he approached them, surplice over his left arm. 'Anything else we can do for you, gentlemen?'

'We want a spare set of keys,' said Morse.

'Well, there *is* a spare set,' said Meiklejohn, frowning slightly. 'Can you tell me why—?'

'It's just that we'd like to get in when the church is locked, that's all.'

'Yes, I see.' He shook his head sadly. 'We've had a lot of senseless vandalism recently – mostly school-children, I'm afraid. I sometimes wonder . . .'

'We shall only need 'em for a few days.'

Meiklejohn led them into the vestry, climbed on to a chair, and lifted a bunch of keys from a hook underneath the top of the curtain. 'Let me have them back as soon as you can, please. There are only four sets now, and someone's always wanting them – for bell-ringing, that sort of thing.'

Morse looked at the keys before pocketing them: old-fashioned keys, one large, three much smaller, all of them curiously and finely wrought.

'Shall we lock the door behind us?' asked Morse. It was meant to be lightly jocular, but succeeded only in sounding facetious and irreverent.

'No, thank you,' replied the minister quietly. 'We get quite a lot of visitors on Sundays, and they like to come here and be quiet, and to think about life – even to pray, perhaps.'

Neither Morse nor Lewis had been on his knees throughout the service; and Lewis, at least, left the church feeling just a little guilty, just a little humbled: it was as if he had turned his back on a holy offering.

'C'm on,' said Morse, 'we're wasting good drinking time.'

At 12.25 p.m. the same day, a call from the Shrewsbury Constabulary came through to the Thames Valley Police H.Q. in Kidlington, where the acting desk sergeant took down the message carefully. He didn't *think* the name rang any bells, but he'd put the message through the appropriate channels. It was only after he'd put the phone down that he realized he hadn't the faintest idea what 'the appropriate channels' were.

CHAPTER TWENTY-FOUR

MORSE WAS LINGERING longer than usual, and it was Lewis who drained his glass first.

'You feeling well, sir?'

Morse put the *Order of Service* back in his pocket, and finished his beer in three or four gargantuan gulps. 'Never better, Lewis. Fill 'em up.'

'Your round, I think, sir.'

'Oh.'

Morse leaned his elbows beside the replenished pints and continued. 'Who murdered Harry Josephs? That's the key question really, isn't it?'

Lewis nodded. 'I had a bit of an idea during the service—'

'No more ideas, please! I've got far too many already. Listen! The prime suspect's got to be the fellow Bell tried to trace. Agreed? The fellow who'd stayed several times at Lawson's vicarage, who was at the church when Josephs was murdered, and who disappeared afterwards. Agreed? We're not *quite* certain about it, but there's every chance that this fellow was Lionel Lawson's brother, Philip Lawson. He's hard up and he's a wino. He sees some ready cash on the collection-plate and he decides to pinch it. Josephs tries to stop him,

168

and gets a knife in the back for his trouble. Any problems?'

'How did Philip Lawson come to have the knife?'

'He'd seen it lying around the vicarage, and he decided to pocket it.'

'Just on the off chance?'

'That's it,' said Morse, as he turned unblinking towards Lewis.

'But there were only a dozen or so people at the service, and the collection wouldn't have come to more than a couple of quid.'

'That's it.'

'Why not wait till one of the Sunday-morning services? Then he'd have the chance of fifty-odd quid.'

'Yes. That's true.'

'Why didn't he, then?'

'I dunno.'

'But no one actually *saw* him in the vestry.'

'He skipped it as soon as he'd knifed Josephs.'

'Surely someone would have seen him – or heard him?'

'Perhaps he just hid in the vestry – behind the curtain.'

'Impossible!'

'Behind the door to the tower, then,' suggested Morse. 'Perhaps he went up to the tower – hid in the bell-chamber – hid on the roof – I dunno.'

'But that door was locked when the police arrived – so it says in the report.'

'Easy. He locked it from the inside.'

'You mean he had – he had the key?'

169

'You say you read the report, Lewis. Well? You must have seen the inventory of what they found in Josephs' pockets.'

The light slowly dawned in Lewis' mind, and he could see Morse watching him, a hint of mild amusement in the inspector's pale-blue eyes.

'You mean – they didn't find any keys,' he said at last.

'No keys.'

'You think he took them out of Josephs' pocket?'

'Nothing to stop him.'

'But – but if he looked through Josephs' pockets, why didn't he find the money? The hundred quid?'

'Aren't you assuming,' asked Morse quietly, 'that that was all there was to find. What if, say, there'd been a *thousand*?'

'You mean—?' But Lewis wasn't sure what he meant.

'I mean that everyone, *almost* everyone, Lewis, is going to think what you did: that the murderer didn't search through Josephs' pockets. It puts everyone on the wrong scent, doesn't it? Makes it look as if it's petty crime – as you say, a few pennies off the collection-plate. You see, perhaps our murderer wasn't really much worried about *how* he was going to commit the crime – he thought he could get away with that. What he didn't want was anyone looking too closely at the *motive*.'

Lewis was growing increasingly perplexed. 'Just a minute, sir. You say he wasn't much worried about how he murdered Josephs. But how *did* he? Josephs was poisoned as well as stabbed.'

'Perhaps he just gave him a swig of booze – doctored booze.'

Again Lewis felt the disconcerting conviction that Morse was playing a game with him. One or two of the points the chief had just made were more like those flashes of insight he'd learned to expect. But surely Morse could do better than this? He could do better himself.

'Josephs could have been poisoned when he took communion, sir.'

'You think so?' Morse's eyes were smiling again. 'How do you figure that out?'

'I reckon the churchwarden is usually the last person to take communion—'

'Like this morning, yes.'

'—and so this tramp fellow is kneeling there next to him and he slips something into the wine.'

'How did he carry the poison?'

'He could have had it in one of those rings. You just unscrew the top—'

'You watch too much television,' said Morse.

'—and sprinkle it in the wine.'

'It would be a whitish powder, Lewis, and it wouldn't dissolve immediately. So the Rev. Lionel would see it floating on top. Is that what you're saying?'

'Perhaps he had his eyes closed. There's a lot of praying and all that sort of thing when—'

'And Josephs himself? Was he doing a lot of praying and all that sort of thing?'

'Could have been.'

'Why wasn't Lawson poisoned, then? It's the minister's

job to finish off any wine that's left and, as you say, Josephs was pretty certainly the last customer.'

'Perhaps Josephs swigged the lot,' suggested Lewis hopefully; and then his eyes irradiated a sudden excitement. 'Or perhaps, sir – or perhaps the two of them, the two Lawson brothers, were in it together. That would answer quite a lot of questions, wouldn't it?'

Morse smiled contentedly at his colleague. 'You know, Lewis, you get brighter all the time. I think it must be my company that does it.'

He pushed his glass across the table 'Your turn, isn't it?'

He looked around him as Lewis waited patiently to be served: it was half past one and Sunday lunch-time trade was at its peak. A man with a rough beard, dressed in a long ex-army coat, had just shuffled through the entrance and was standing apprehensively by the bar; a man in latish middle age, it seemed, wearing that incongruous pair of sunglasses, and grasping an empty flagon of cider in his hand. Morse left his seat and walked over to him.

'We met before, remember?'

The man looked slowly at Morse and shook his head. 'Sorry, mate.'

'Life not treating you so good?'

'Nah.'

'Been roughing it long?'

'Last back-end.'

'You ever know a fellow called Swanpole?'

'Nah. Sorry, mate.'

'Doesn't matter. I used to know him, that's all.'

'I knew somebody who did,' said the tramp quietly. 'Somebody who knew the fellah you was just talking about.'

'Yes?' Morse fumbled in his pockets and pushed a fifty-pence piece into the man's hand.

'The old boy I used to go round with – 'e mentioned that name recently. "Swanny" – that's what they called 'im, but 'e's not round these parts any more.'

'What about the old boy? Is he still around?'

'Nah. 'E's dead. Died o' pneumonia – yesterday.'

'Oh.'

Morse walked back thoughtfully to the table, and a few minutes later watched a little sadly as the landlord showed the tramp the way to the exit. Clearly there was no welcome for the poor fellow's custom here, and no cider slowly to be sipped on one of the city's benches that Sunday afternoon; not from this pub anyway.

'One of your pals?' grinned Lewis, as he placed two more pints on the table.

'I don't think he's got any pals.'

'Perhaps if Lawson were still alive—'

'He's just the man we've got to talk about, Lewis – suspect number two. Agreed?'

'You mean he suddenly disappeared from in front of the altar, murdered Josephs, and then came back and carried on with the service?'

'Something like that.'

The beer was good, and Lewis leaned back, quite happy to listen.

'Come on, sir. I know you're dying to tell me.'

'First, let's just follow up your idea about the

173

COLIN DEXTER

poisoned chalice. There are too many improbabilities
in the way you looked at it. But what if the Rev. Lionel
himself put the morphine in the wine? What then?
After his brother's had a swig, he can pretend that the
chalice is empty, turn round to the altar, slip in the
powder, pour in a drop more wine, give it a quick stir –
no problem! Or else he could have had two chalices –
one of 'em already doctored – and just put the one
down and pick up the other. Easier still! Mark my
words, Lewis. If it was either of the two brothers who
poisoned Josephs, I reckon the odds are pretty heavily
on the Rev. Lionel.'

'Let me get it straight, sir. According to you, Lionel
Lawson tried to kill Josephs, only to find that someone
had done a far neater job a few minutes later – with a
knife. Right?' Lewis shook his head. 'Not on, sir, is it?'

'Why not? The Rev. Lionel knows that Josephs'll go
straight to the vestry, and that in a few minutes he's
going to be very dead. There's one helluva dose of
morphine in the communion wine and the strong
probability is that Josephs is going to die all nice and
peaceful like, because morphine poisoning isn't a pain-
ful death – just the opposite. In which case, Josephs'
death may well pose a few problems; but no one's going
to be able to pin the murder on the Rev. Lionel. The
chalice has been carefully washed out and dried, in
strict accord with ecclesiastical etiquette – a wonderful
example of a criminal actually being encouraged to
destroy the evidence of his crime. Beautiful idea! But
then things began to go askew. Josephs must have
guessed that something was desperately wrong with

him, and before he collapsed in the vestry he just managed to drag himself to the curtains and shout for help – a shout that all the congregation heard. But someone, *someone*, Lewis, was watching that vestry like a hawk – the Rev. Lionel himself. And as soon as he saw Josephs there he was off down the aisle like an avenging Fury; and he was down there in the vestry before anyone else had the nous or the guts to move; and once inside he stabbed Josephs viciously in the back, turned to face the congregation, and told 'em all that Josephs was lying there – murdered.' (Morse mentally congratulated himself on an account that was rather more colourful and dramatic than Bell's prosaic reconstruction of exactly the same events.)

'He'd have got blood all over him,' protested Lewis.

'Wouldn't have mattered much if he'd been wearing the sort of outfit they were wearing this morning.'

Lewis thought back to the morning service and those deep-crimson vestments – the colour of dark-red blood ... 'But why finish Josephs off with a knife? He'd be almost dead by then.'

'Lionel was frightened that Josephs would accuse him of doing the poisoning. Almost certainly Josephs would have guessed what had happened.'

'Probably everyone else would, too.'

'Ah! But if you stabbed Josephs in the back as well, people are going to ask who did *that*, aren't they?'

'Yes. And they're going to think that was Lawson, too. After all, it was Lawson's knife.'

'No one knew that at the time,' said Morse defensively.

'Did Bell think that's how it happened?'

Morse nodded. 'Yes, he did.'

'And do *you*, sir?'

Morse seemed to be weighing the odds in the mental balance. 'No,' he said finally.

Lewis leaned back in his chair. 'You know, when you come to think of it, it's a bit improbable that a minister's going to murder one of his own congregation, isn't it? That sort of thing doesn't happen in real life.'

'I rather hope it does,' said Morse quietly.

'Pardon, sir?'

'I said I rather hope it *does* happen. You asked me if Lionel Lawson killed Josephs in a particular way, and I said I didn't think so. But I reckon it *was* Lionel Lawson who killed Josephs, though in a rather more simple way. He just walked down to the vestry, knifed poor old Harry Josephs—'

'And then he walked back!'

'You've got it!'

Lewis' eyes rolled towards the tobacco-stained ceiling and he began to wonder if the beer had not robbed the inspector of his wits.

'With all the congregation watching him, I suppose.'

'Oh, no. They didn't see him.'

'They didn't?'

'No. The service at which Josephs was killed was held in the Lady Chapel. Now, if you remember, there's an archway in the screen separating this chapel from the central chancel, and I reckon that after the bread and wine had been dished out Lawson took a few of the utensils across from the altar in the Lady Chapel to the main altar – they're always doing that sort of thing, these priests.' (Lewis was hardly listening any more, and the landlord was wiping the tables, collecting glasses and emptying the ashtrays.) 'You want to know how he performed this remarkable feat, Lewis? Well, as I see it, the Rev. Lionel and his brother had got everything worked out, and that night the pair of 'em were all dressed up in identical ecclesiastical clobber. Now, when the Rev. Lionel walked out of the Lady Chapel for a few seconds, it wasn't the Rev. Lionel who walked back! There are only a few prayerful old souls in the congregation, and for that vital period the man standing in front of the altar, kneeling there, praying there, *but never actually facing the congregation*, is brother Philip! What do you think, Lewis? You think anyone looking up could have suspected the truth?'

'Perhaps Philip Lawson was bald.'

'Doubt it. Whether you go bald depends on your grandfather.'

'If you say so, sir.' Lewis was growing increasingly sceptical about all this jiggery-pokery with duplicate chalices and chasubles; and, anyway, he was anxious to be off home. He stood up and took his leave.

Morse remained where he was, the forefinger of his left hand marrying little droplets of spilt beer on the table-top. Like Lewis, he was far from happy about his possible reconstructions of Josephs' murder. But one idea was growing even firmer in his mind: there must have been some collaboration somewhere. And, like as not, that collaboration had involved the two brothers.

But how? For several minutes Morse's thoughts were chasing round after their own tails. For the thousandth time he asked himself where he ought to start, and for the thousandth time he told himself that he had to decide who had killed Harry Josephs. All right! Assume it was the Rev. Lionel – on the grounds that *something* must have driven him to suicide. But what if it wasn't Lionel who had thrown himself from the tower? What if it was Philip who had *been* thrown? Yes, that would have been very neat ... But there was a virtually insuperable objection to such a theory. The Rev. Lionel would have to dress up his brother's body in his own clothes, his own black clerical front, his dog-collar – everything. And that, in such a short space of time after the morning service, was plain physically impossible! But what if...? Yes! What if Lionel had somehow managed to persuade his brother to change clothes? Was it possible? Phew! Of course it was! It wasn't just possible – it was eminently probable. And why? *Because Philip Lawson had already done it before.* He'd agreed to dress up in his brother's vestments so that he could stand at the altar whilst Josephs was being murdered! Doubtless he'd been wonderfully well rewarded for his troubles on that occasion. So why not agree to a second little charade? Of course he would have agreed – little thinking he'd be dressing up for his own funeral. But with one seemingly insuperable problem out of the way another one had taken its place: two people had positively identified the body that had fallen from the tower. Was that a real problem, though? Had Mrs Walsh-Atkins really had the stomach to look all that carefully at a face that was as smashed and bleeding as the rest of that mutilated body? Had her presence outside the church just been an accidental fluke? Because someone else had been there, had he not? Someone all ready to testify to the identity – the false identity – of the corpse: Paul Morris. And Paul Morris had subsequently been murdered because he knew too much: knew, specifically, that the Reverend Lionel Lawson was not only still in the land of the living, but was also a murderer, to boot! A double-murderer. A triple-murderer...

'Do you mind drinking up, sir?' said the landlord. 'We often get the police round here on Sunday mornings.'

CHAPTER TWENTY-FIVE

ON THE SAME day, just after eight o'clock in the evening, a middle-aged man, his white shirt open at the neck, sat waiting in a brightly lit, well-furnished room. He was lounging back on a deep sofa, its chintz covers printed in a russet-and-white floral design, from which, smoking a king-sized Benson & Hedges cigarette, he vaguely watched the television. She was a little late tonight; but he had no doubts that she would come, for she needed him just as much as he needed her. Sometimes, he suspected, even more so. A bottle of claret, already opened, and two wineglasses stood on the coffee-table beside him, and through the half-opened bedroom door he could see the hypotenuse of white sheet drawn back from the pillows.

Come on, girl!

It was eight-ten when the key (she had a key – of course she did!) scraped gently in the Yale lock and she entered. Although a steady drizzle persisted outside, her pale-blue mackintosh seemed completely dry as she slipped it from her shoulders, folded it neatly across its waist, and put it over the back of an armchair. The white cotton blouse she wore was drawn tight across her breasts, and the close-fitting black skirt clung to the curve of her thighs. She said nothing for a while; merely looked at him, her eyes reflecting no affection and no joy – just a simmering animal sensuality. She walked across the room and stood in front of him – provocatively.

'You told me you were going to stop smoking.'

'Sit down and stop moaning, woman. Christ! You make me feel sexy in that outfit.'

The woman did exactly as she was told, almost as if she would do anything he asked without demur; almost as if she thrived on the brusque crudity of his commands, There were no tender words of preliminary love-play on either side, yet she sat close to him as he poured two full glasses of wine, and he felt the pressure of her black-stockinged leg (good girl – she'd remembered!) against his own. In token of some vestigial respect they clinked their glasses together, and she leaned back against the sofa.

'Been watching the telly all night?' Her question was commonplace, uninterested.

'I didn't get back till half past six.'

She turned to look at him for the first time. 'You're a fool going out like that. Especially on Sundays. Don't you realize—?'

'Calm down, woman! I'm not a fool, and you know it. Nobody's seen me slipping out of here yet. And what if they did? Nobody's going to recognize me now.' He leaned across her and his fingers deftly unfastened the top button of her blouse. And then the next button.

As always with this man, the woman experienced that curious admixture of revulsion and attraction –

compulsive combination! Until so very recently a virgin, she was newly aware of herself as a physical object, newly conscious of the power of her body. She lay back passively as he fondled her far beyond the point which a few months previously would have been either pleasing or permissible; and she seemed almost mesmerized as he pulled her up from the sofa and led the way through to the bedroom.

Their coitus was not exceptionally memorable – certainly not ecstatic; but it was satisfactory and satisfying. It usually was. As usual, too, the woman now lay between the sheets silently, feeling cheap and humiliated. It was not only her body that was naked, but her soul, too; and instinctively she drew the top of the sheet up to her neck and prayed that for a little while at least he would keep his hands and eyes away from her. How she despised him! Yet not one half, not one quarter as much as she had learned to despise herself.

It had got to stop. She hated the man and the power he had come to wield over her – yet she needed him, needed the firm virility of his body. He had kept himself wonderfully fit ... but, then, that wasn't ... wasn't surprising ... not really ... not really ...

Briefly she fell asleep.

He spoke to her as she stood by the door, the mackintosh loosely over her shoulders. 'Same time on Wednesday?'

Once more the humiliation of it all settled heavily upon her, and her lip was shaking as she replied.

'It's got to stop! You know it has!'

'Stop?' His mouth was set in a conceited sneer. 'You couldn't stop. You know that as well as I do.'

'I can stop seeing you whenever I like, and there's nothing you or anybody else—'

'Isn't there? You're in this as deeply as I am – don't you ever forget that!'

She shook her head, almost wildly. 'You said you'd be going away. You promised!'

'And I shall be. I'll be going very soon now, my girl, and that's the truth. But until I do go I keep seeing you – understand? I see you when I want, as often as I want. And don't tell me you don't enjoy it, because you do! And you know you do.'

Yes, she knew it, and she felt her eyes prickling with hurt at his cruel words. How could she do this? How could she hate a man so much – and yet allow him to make love to her? No! it just couldn't go on like this! And the solution to all her troubles was so childishly simple: she just had to go and see Morse, that was all; tell him everything and face the consequences, whatever they were. She still had a bit of courage left, didn't she?

The man was watching her carefully, half-guessing what was going through her mind. He was used to taking swift decisions – he always had been; and he saw his next moves as clearly as if he were a grandmaster playing chess with a novice. He had known all along that he would have to deal with her sooner or later; and, although he had hoped it would be later, he realized now that the game must be finished quickly.

For him, sex had always come – would always come – a poor second to power.

He walked over to her, and his face for once seemed kind and understanding as he placed his hands so very lightly on her shoulders, his eyes looking searchingly into hers.

'All right, Ruth,' he said quietly. 'I'll not be a nuisance to you any more. Come and sit down a minute. I want to talk to you.' Gently he took her arm and led her unresisting to the sofa. 'I won't make any more demands on you, Ruth – I promise I won't. We'll stop seeing each other, if that's what you really want. I can't bear to see you unhappy like this.'

It had been many weeks since he had spoken to her in such a way, and for a while, in the context of her wider grief, she felt infinitely grateful for his words.

'As I say, I'll be going away soon and then you can forget me, and we can both try to forget what we've done. The wrong we've done – because it *was* wrong, wasn't it? Not about us going to bed together – I don't mean that. That was something lovely for me – something I shall never regret – and I'd hoped . . . I'd hoped it was lovely for you, too. But never mind that. Just promise me one thing, Ruth, will you? If you ever want to come to me – while I'm here, I mean – please come! Please! You know I'll be wanting you – and waiting.'

She nodded, and the tears trickled down her cheeks at the bitter-sweet joy of his words as he cradled her head against his shoulder and held her firmly to him.

She stayed there for what seemed to her a long, long time; yet for him it was little more than a functional interspace, his cold eyes staring over her shoulder at the hateful wallpaper behind the television. He would have to kill her, of course: that decision had been taken long ago anyway. What he was quite unable to understand was the delay. Surely the police were not so stupid as they seemed? Nothing so far – *why?* – about the Shrewsbury murder. Nothing definite about the body on the tower; Nothing at all about the boy . . .

'Your mother all right?' He asked it almost tenderly.

She nodded and sniffed. It was time she was back home with that mother of hers.

'Still cleaning the church?'

She nodded again, continued her sniffing, and finally broke away from him.

'Mondays, Wednesdays and Fridays?'

'Just Mondays and Wednesdays now. I'm getting a bit slack in my old age.'

'Still in the mornings?'

'Mm. I usually go about ten. And I've been going for a drink in the Randolph when I've finished, I'm afraid.' She laughed nervously, and blew her nose loudly into her sopping handkerchief. 'I could do with a quick drink now if—'

'Of course.' He fetched a bottle of Teacher's whisky from the sideboard and poured a good measure into her wineglass. 'Here you are. You'll feel better soon. You feel better *now*, don't you?'

'Yes, I do.' She took a sip of the whisky. 'You – you remember when I asked you whether you knew anything about – about what they found up on the church tower?'

'I remember.'

'You said you hadn't any idea at all—'

'And I hadn't – haven't. Not the faintest idea. But I expect the police will find out.'

'They just say they're – they're making enquiries.'

'They've not been bothering you again, have they?'

She breathed deeply and stood up. 'No. Not that I could tell them anything about *that*.'

For a moment she thought of Morse with his piercing eyes. Sad eyes, though, as if they were always looking for something and never quite finding it. A clever man, as she realized, and a nice man, too. Why, oh why, hadn't someone like Morse found her many years ago?

'What are you thinking about?' His voice was almost brusque again.

'Me? Oh, just thinking how nice you can be when you want. That's all.'

She wanted to get away from him now. It was as if freedom beckoned her from behind the locked door, but he was close behind her and his hands were once again fondling her body; and soon he had forced her to the floor where, within a few inches of the door; he penetrated her once again, snorting as he did so like some animal, whilst she for her part stared joylessly at a hair-line crack upon the ceiling.

CHAPTER TWENTY-SIX

'THEY TELL ME you can start a fibroblast from the commercial banger,' said Morse, rubbing his hands delightedly over the crowded plate of sausages, eggs and chips which Mrs Lewis had placed before him. It was half past eight on the same Sunday evening.

'What's a fibroblast?' asked Lewis.

'Something to do with taking a bit of tissue and keeping it alive. Frightening really. Perhaps you could keep a bit of somebody alive – well, indefinitely, I suppose. Sort of immortality of the body.' He broke the surface of one of his eggs and dipped a golden-brown chip into the pale-yellow yolk.

'You won't mind if I have the telly on?' Mrs Lewis sat down with a cup of tea, and the set was clicked on. 'I don't really care what they do to me when I'm gone, Inspector, just as long as they make absolutely certain that I'm dead, that's all.'

It was an old fear – a fear that had prompted some of the wealthier Victorians to arrange all sorts of elaborate contraptions inside their coffins so that any corpse, revivified contrary to the expectations of the physicians, could signal from its subterranean interment immediate intelligence of any return to consciousness. It was a fear, too, that had driven Poe to write about such things with so grisly a fascination; and Morse refrained from mentioning the fact that those whose most pressing anxiety was they might be lowered living into their graves could have their minds set at rest: the disturbing medical truth was they quite certainly *would* be so lowered.

'What's on?' mumbled Morse, his mouth full of food.

But Mrs Lewis didn't hear him. Already, Svengali-like, the television held her in its holy trance.

Ten minutes later Lewis sat checking his football pools from the *Sunday Express*, and Morse leaned back on the sofa and closed his eyes, his mind preoccupied with death and people being lowered ... lowered into their graves ...

Where – where was he?

Morse's head and shoulders jerked backwards, and he blinked himself awake. Lewis was still engrossed in the back page of the *Sunday Express*, and on the television screen a head butler was walking sedately down some stairs to a wine-cellar.

That was it! Silently Morse cursed himself for his own stupidity. The answer had stared him in the face that very same morning: 'In the vaults beneath are interred the terrestrial remains ...' A wave of excitement set his senses tingling as he stood up and drew back the edge of the curtain from the window. It was dark now, and the pane was spattered with fine drizzle.

Things could wait, surely? What on earth was going to be gained by another nocturnal visit to a dark, deserted church that couldn't wait until the light of the morning? But inevitably Morse knew that he couldn't wait and wouldn't wait.

'Sorry about this, Mrs Lewis, but I shall have to take the old man away again, I'm afraid. We shouldn't be long, though; and thanks again for the meal.'

Mrs Lewis said nothing, and fetched her husband's shoes from the kitchen. Lewis himself said nothing, either, but folded the newspaper away and resigned himself to the fact that his Lit-plan permutations had once more failed to land him a fortune. It was the 'bankers' that always let him down, those virtual certainties round which the plan had to be constructed. Like this case, he thought, as he pulled on his shoes: no real certainties at all. Not in his own mind anyway; and from what Morse had said at lunch-time no real certainties in *his* mind, either. And where the Dickens, he wondered, were they off to now?

As it happened, the church was neither dark nor deserted, and the main door at the north porch creaked open to reveal a suffused light over the quiet interior.

'Do you think the murderer's here, sir – confessing his sins?'

'I reckon somebody's confessing something,' muttered Morse.

His ears had caught the faintest murmurings and he pointed to the closed curtains of the confessional, set into the north wall.

Almost immediately an attractive young woman emerged, her sins presumably forgiven, and with eyes averted from the two detectives click-clacked her way out of the church.

'Nice-looking girl, sir.'

'Mm. She may have what you want, Lewis; but do you want what she's got?'

'Pardon, sir?'

The Reverend Canon Meiklejohn was walking silently towards them on his rubber-soled shoes, removing a long, green-embroidered stole from round his neck.

'Which of you wants to be first, gentlemen?'

'I'm afraid I've not been sinning much today,' said Morse. 'In fact there's many a day when I hardly get through any sinning at all.'

'We're all sinners, you know that,' said Meiklejohn seriously. 'Sin, alas, is the natural state of our unregenerate humanity—'

'Is there a crypt under the church?' asked Morse.

Meiklejohn's eyes narrowed slightly. 'Well, yes, there is, but – er – no one goes down there. Not as far as I know anyway. In fact I'm told that no one's been down there for ten years or so. The steps look as if they've rotted away and—'

Again Morse interrupted him. 'How can we get down there?'

Meiklejohn was not in the habit of being spoken to

so sharply, and a look of slight annoyance crossed his face. 'I'm afraid you can't, gentlemen. Not now anyway. I'm due at Pusey House in about—' He looked down at his wristwatch.

'You don't really need me to remind you what we're here for, do you, sir? And it's not to inspect your Norman font, is it? We're investigating a murder – a series of murders – and as police officers we've every right to expect a bit of co-operation from the public. And for the minute *you're* the public. All right? Now. How do we get down there?'

Meiklejohn breathed deeply. It had been a long day and he was beginning to feel very tired. 'Do you really have to talk to me as if I were a naughty child, Inspector? I'll just get my coat, if you don't mind.'

He walked off to the vestry, and when he returned Morse noticed the shabbiness of the thick, dark over-coat; the shabbiness, too, of the wrinkled black shoes.

'We shall need this,' said Mciklejohn, pointing to a twenty-foot ladder against the south porch.

With a marked lack of professionalism, Morse and Lewis manœuvred the long ladder awkwardly out of the south door, through the narrow gate immediately opposite, and into the churchyard, where they followed Meiklejohn over the wet grass along the south side of the outer church wall. A street lamp threw a thin light on to the irregular rows of gravestones to their right, but the wall itself was in the deepest gloom.

'Here we are,' said Meiklejohn. He stood darkly over a horizontal iron grille, about six feet by three feet, which rested on the stone sides of a rectangular shaft

191

cut into the ground. Through the grille-bars, originally painted black but now brown-flaked with rust, the torch-light picked out the bottom of the cavity, about twelve feet below, littered with the débris of paper bags and cigarette-packets. To the side of the shaft furthest from the church wall was affixed a rickety-looking wooden ladder, and parallel to it an iron hand-rail ran steeply down. Set just beneath the church wall was a small door: the entrance to the vaults.

For a minute or so the three men looked down at the black hole, similar thoughts passing through the mind of each of them. Why not wait until the sane and wholesome light of morning – a light that would dissipate all notions of grinning skulls and gruesome skeletons? But no. Morse put his hands beneath the bars of the grille and lifted it aside easily and lightly.

'Are you sure no one's been down here for ten years?' he asked.

Lewis bent down in the darkness and felt the rungs of the ladder.

'Feels pretty firm, sir.'

'Let's play it safe, Lewis. We don't really want any more corpses if we can help it.'

Meiklejohn watched as they eased down the ladder, and when it was resting firmly on its fellow Lewis took the torch and slowly and carefully made his way down.

'I reckon someone's been down here fairly recently, sir. One of the steps near the bottom here's broken, and it doesn't look as if it happened all that long ago.'

'Some of these hooligans, I expect,' said Meiklejohn to Morse. 'Some of them would do anything for what they call a "kick". But look, Inspector, I really must be going. I'm sorry if I – er . . .'

'Forget it,' said Morse. 'We'll let you know if we find anything.'

'Are you – are you expecting to find something?'

Was he? In all honesty the answer was 'yes' – he was expecting to find the body of a young boy called Peter Morris. 'Not really, sir. We just have to check out every possibility, though.'

Lewis' voice sounded once more from the black hollow. 'The door's locked, sir. Can you—?'

Morse dropped his set of keys down. 'See if one of these fits.'

'If it doesn't,' said Meiklejohn, 'I'm afraid you really will have to wait until the morning. My set of keys is just the same as yours and—'

'We're in, Meredith,' shouted Lewis from the depths.

'You get off, then, sir,' said Morse to Meiklejohn. 'As I say, we'll let you know if – er – if . . .'

'Thank you. Let's just pray you don't, Inspector. This is all such a terrible business already that—'

'Goodnight, sir.'

With infinite pains and circumspection Morse eased himself on to the ladder, and with nervously iterated entreaties that Lewis make sure he was holding 'the bloody thing' firmly he gradually descended into the shaft with the slow-motion movements of a trainee tight-rope walker. He noted, as Lewis had just done, that the third rung from the bottom of the original wooden ladder had been snapped roughly in the middle, the left-hand half of it drooping at an angle of some forty-five degrees. And, judging from the yellowish-looking splintering at the jagged fracture, someone's foot had gone through the rung comparatively recently. Someone fairly heavy; or someone not so heavy, perhaps – with an extra weight upon his shoulder.

'Do you think there are any rats down here?' asked Morse.

'Shouldn't think so. Nothing to feed on, is there?'

'Bodies, perhaps?' Morse thought yet again of leaving the grim mission until the morning, and experienced a little shudder of fear as he looked up at the rectangle of faint light above his head, half-expecting some ghoulish figure to appear in the aperture, grinning horridly down on him. He breathed deeply.

'In we go, Lewis.'

The door creaked whiningly on its rusted hinges as inch by inch Lewis pushed it open, and Morse played his torch nervously to one side and then to the other. It was immediately clear that the main supporting pillars of the upper structure of the church extended down to the vaults, forming a series of stone recesses and dividing the subterranean area into cellar-like rooms that seemed (at least to Lewis) far from weird or spooky. In fact the second alcove on the left could hardly have been less conducive to thoughts of some skeletal spectre haunting these nether regions. For within its walls, dry-surfaced and secure, was no more than a large heap of coke (doubtless for the church's earlier heating system) with a long-handled spatulate instrument laid across it.

'Want a bit of free coke, sir?' Lewis was leading the way, and now took the torch from Morse and shone it gaily around the surprisingly dry interior. But as they progressed deeper into the darkness it became increasingly difficult to form any coherent pattern of the layout of the vaults, and Morse was already hanging back a little as Lewis shone the torch upon a stack of coffins, one piled on top of another, their lids warped and loose over the shrunken, concave sides.

'Plenty of corpses here,' said Lewis.

But Morse had turned his back and was staring sombrely into the darkness. 'I think it'll be sensible to come back in the morning, Lewis. Pretty daft trying to find anything at this time of night.' He experienced a deeper shudder of fear as he grew aware of something almost tangibly oppressive in the dry air. As a young boy he'd always been afraid of the dark, and now, again, the quaking hand of terror touched him lightly on the shoulder.

They retraced their way towards the entrance, and soon Morse stood again at the entrance to the vaults, his forehead damp with cold sweat. He breathed several times very deeply, and the prospect of climbing the solid ladder to the ground above loomed like a glorious release from the panic that threatened to engulf him. Yet it was a mark of Morse's genius that he could take hold of his weaknesses and almost miraculously transform them into his strengths. If anyone were going to hide a body in these vaults, he would feel something (surely!), at least *something*, of this same irrational fear of the dark, of the dead, of the deep-seated terror that

195

forever haunted the subconscious mind? No one, surely, would venture too far, alone and under the cover of night, into these cavernous, echoing vaults? His foot kicked a cigarette-packet as he walked past the heap of coke, and he picked it up and asked Lewis to shine the torch on it. It was a golden-coloured empty packet of Benson & Hedges, along the side of which he read: 'Government health warning. Cigarettes can seriously damage your health. Middle tar.' When had the Government decided to stipulate such a solemn warning to cigarette addicts? Three, four, five years ago? Certainly not – what had Meiklejohn said? – ten years!

'Have a look under the coke, will you?' said Morse quietly.

Five minutes later Lewis found him. He was a young boy, aged about eleven or twelve, well preserved, just over five feet in height, and dressed in school uniform. Round his neck was a school tie, a tie tightened so viciously that it had dug deep into the flesh around the throat; a tie striped alternately in the regulation red and grey of the Roger Bacon School, Kidlington.

In the Pending file of the duty-sergeant's tray at Thames Valley H.Q., there still lay the handwritten message taken down from Shrewsbury.

CHAPTER TWENTY-SEVEN

LEWIS REACHED BELL'S office at 9.15 a.m. the following morning, but Morse had beaten him to it and was sitting behind the desk shouting into the phone with a livid fury.

'Well, get the stupid bugger, then. Yes! *Now.*' He motioned Lewis to take a seat, the fingers of his left hand drumming the desk-top in fretful impatience.

'You?' he bellowed into the mouthpiece at last. 'What the hell do you think you're playing at? It's been sitting under your bloody nose since yesterday lunchtime! And all you can do is to sit on that great fat arse of yours and say you're sorry. You'll be sorry, my lad – you can be sure of that. Now, just listen to me carefully. You'll go along to the Super's office as soon as I give you permission to put that phone down, and you tell him exactly what you've done and exactly what you've *not* done. Is that understood?'

The unfortunate voice at the other end of the line could only have mumbled something less than propitiatory, and Lewis sat almost fearfully through the next barrage of abuse.

'What are you going to tell him? I'll tell you what you're going to tell him, my lad. First, you tell him you deserve the bloody V.C. All right? Second, you tell him it's about time they made you chief constable of Oxfordshire. He'll understand. Third, you tell him you're guilty of the blindest bloody stupidity ever witnessed in the history of the force. That's what you tell him!' He banged down the phone and sat for a minute or so still seething with rage.

Sensibly Lewis sat silent, and it was Morse who finally spoke. 'Mrs Josephs was murdered. Last Friday, in a nurses' hostel in Shrewsbury.'

Lewis looked down at the threadbare carpet at his feet and shook his head sadly. 'How many more, sir?'

Morse breathed deeply and seemed suddenly quite calm again.

'I dunno.'

'Next stop Shrewsbury, sir?'

Morse gestured almost hopelessly. 'I dunno.'

'You think it's the same fellow?'

'I dunno.' Morse brooded in silence and stared blankly at the desk in front of him. 'Get the file out again.'

Lewis walked across to one of the steel cabinets. 'Who was on the other end of the rocket, sir?'

Morse's face broke into a reluctant grin. 'That bloody fool, Dickson. He was sitting in as duty-sergeant yesterday. I shouldn't have got so cross with him really.'

'Why did you, then?' asked Lewis, as he put the file down on the desk.

'I suppose because I ought to have guessed, really – guessed that she'd be next on the list, I mean. Perhaps I was just cross with myself, I dunno. But I know one thing, Lewis: I know that this case is getting out of hand. Christ knows where we are; I don't.'

The time seemed to Lewis about right now. Morse's anger had evaporated and only an irritable frustration remained to cloud his worried features. Perhaps he would welcome a little bit of help.

'Sir, I was thinking when I got home last night about what you'd been saying in the Bulldog. Remember? You said that Lawson, the Reverend Lawson, that is, might just have walked straight down—'

'For God's sake, Lewis, come off it! We're finding corpses right, left and centre, are we not? We're in the biggest bloody muddle since God knows when, and all you can do is to—'

'It was you who said it – not me.'

'I *know* – yes. But leave me alone, man! Can't you see I'm trying to think? *Somebody's* got to think around here.'

'I was only—'

'Look, Lewis. Just forget what I said and start thinking about some of the *facts* in the bloody case. All right?' He thumped the file in front of him viciously. 'The facts are all in here. Josephs gets murdered, agreed? All right. Josephs gets murdered. The Reverend Lionel Lawson jumps off the bloody tower. Right? He jumps off the bloody tower. Morris senior gets murdered and gets carted off to the same bloody tower. Right? Exit Morris senior. Morris junior gets strangled and gets carted off down the crypt. Right? Why not just accept these facts, Lewis? Why fart around with all that piddling nonsense about – Augh! Forget it!'

199

Lewis walked out, making sure to slam the door hard behind him. He'd had just about enough, and for two pins he'd resign from the force on the spot if it meant getting away from this sort of mindless ingratitude. He walked into the canteen and ordered a coffee. If Morse wanted to sit in peace – well, let the miserable blighter! He wouldn't be interrupted this side of lunch-time. Not by Lewis anyway. He read the *Daily Mirror* and had a second cup of coffee. He read the *Sun* and had a third. And then he decided to drive up to Kidlington.

There were patches of blue in the sky now, and the overnight rain had almost dried upon the pavements. He drove along the Banbury Road, past Linton Road, past Belbroughton Road, and the cherry- and the almond trees blossomed in pink and white, and the daffodils and the hyacinths bloomed in the borders of the well-tended lawns. North Oxford was a lovely place in the early spring; and by the time he reached Kidlington Lewis was feeling slightly happier with life.

Dickson, likely as not, would be in the canteen. Dickson was almost always in the canteen.

'I hear you got a bit of a bollocking this morning,' ventured Lewis.

'Christ, ah! You should have heard him.'

'I did,' admitted Lewis.

'And I was only standing in, too. We're so short here that they asked me to take over on the phone. And then this happens! How the hell was I supposed to know who she was? She'd changed her name anyway, and she only *might* have lived in Kidlington, they said. Huh! Life's very unfair sometimes, Sarge.'

'He can be a real sod, can't he?'

'Pardon?'

'Morse. I said he can be a real—'

'No, not really.' Dickson looked far from down-hearted as he lovingly took a great bite from a jam doughnut.

'You've not been in to the Super yet?'

'He didn't mean that.'

'Look, Dickson. You're in the force, you know that – not in a play-school. If Morse says—'

'He didn't. He rang me back half an hour later. Just said he was sorry. Just said forget it.'

'He didn't!'

'He bloody did, Sarge. We had quite a pally little chat in the end, really. I asked him if I could do anything to help, and d'you know what he said? Said he just wanted me to find out from Shrewsbury C.I.D. whether the woman was killed on Friday. That's all. Said he didn't give a monkey's whether she'd been knifed or throttled or anything, just so long as she was killed on Friday. Funny chap, ain't he? Always asking odd sort of questions – never the questions you'd think he'd ask. Clever, though. Christ, ah!'

Lewis stood up to go.

'It wasn't a sex murder, Sarge.'

'Oh?'

'Nice-looker, they said. Getting on a little bit, but it seems quite a few of the doctors had tried to get off with her. Still, I've always thought those black stockings are sexy – haven't you, Sarge?'

'Was she wearing black stockings?'

Dickson swallowed the last of his doughnut and wiped his fingers on his black trousers. 'Don't they all wear—?'

But Lewis left him to it. Once more he felt belittled and angry. Who was supposed to be helping Morse anyway? Himself or Dickson? Aurrgh!

It was 11.45 a.m. when Lewis re-entered St Aldates Police Station and walked into Bell's office. Morse still sat in his chair, but his head was now resting on the desk, pillowed in the crook of his left arm. He was sound asleep.

CHAPTER TWENTY-EIGHT

MRS RAWLINSON WAS getting more than a little
anxious when Ruth had still not arrived home at five
minutes to one. She suspected – knew, really – that
Ruth's visits to the Randolph were establishing themselves into a regular lunch-time pattern, and it was high
time she reminded her daughter of her filial responsibilities. For the moment, however, it was the primitive
maternal instinct that was paramount; and increasingly
so as the radio news finished at ten past one with still
no sign of her daughter. At a quarter past one the
phone rang, shattering the silence of the room with a
shrill, abrupt urgency, and Mrs Rawlinson reached
across for the receiver with a shaking hand, incipient
panic welling up within her as the caller identified
himself.

'Mrs Rawlinson? Chief Inspector Morse here.'

Oh my God! 'What is it?' she blurted out. 'What's
happened?'

'Are you all right, Mrs Rawlinson?'

'Yes. Oh, yes. I – I just thought for a moment . . .'

'I assure you there's nothing to worry about.' (But
didn't *his* voice sound a little worried?) 'I just wanted a
quick word with your daughter, please.'

'She's – she's not in at the moment, I'm afraid. She—' And then Mrs Rawlinson heard the key scratching in the front door. 'Just a minute, Inspector.'

Ruth appeared, smiling and fresh-faced, round the door.

'Here! It's for you,' said her mother as she pushed the receiver into Ruth's hand, and then leaned back in her wheelchair, luxuriating in a beautifully relieved anger.

'Hello?'

'Miss Rawlinson? Morse here. Just routine, really. One of those little loose ends we're trying to tie up. I want you to try to remember, if you can, whether the Reverend Lawson wore spectacles.'

'Yes, he did. Why—?'

'Did he wear them just for reading or did he wear them all the time?'

'He always wore them. Always when I saw him anyway. Gold-rimmed, they were.'

'That's very interesting. Do you – er – do you happen to remember that tramp fellow? You know, the one who sometimes used to go to your church?'

'Yes, I remember him,' replied Ruth slowly.

'Did he wear spectacles?'

'No-o, I don't think he did.'

'Just as I thought. Good. Well, that's about all, I think. Er – how are you, by the way?'

'Oh, fine; fine, thanks.'

'You still engaged on your – er – your good works? In the church, I mean?'

'Yes.'

'Mondays and Wednesdays, isn't it?'

'Ye-es.' It was the second occasion she'd been asked the same question within a very short time. And now (she knew) he was going to ask her what time she usually went there. It was just like hearing a repeat on the radio.

'Usually about ten o'clock, isn't it?'

'Yes, that's right. Why do you ask?' And why did she suddenly feel so frightened?

'No reason, really. I just – er – I just thought, you know, I might see you again there one day.'

'Yes. Perhaps so.'

'Look after yourself, then.'

Why couldn't *he* look after her? 'Yes I will,' she heard herself say.

'Goodbye,' said Morse. He cradled the phone and for many seconds stared abstractedly through the window on to the tarmacadamed surface of the inner yard. Why was she always so tight with him? Why couldn't she metaphorically open her legs for him once in a while?

'You ask some very odd questions,' said Lewis.

'Some very important ones, too,' replied Morse rather pompously. 'You see, Lawson's specs were in his coat pocket when they found him – a pair of gold-rimmed specs. It's all here.' He tapped the file on the death of the Reverend Lionel Lawson which lay on the desk in front of him. 'And Miss Rawlinson said that he always wore them. Interesting, eh?'

'You mean – you mean it wasn't Lionel Lawson who—'

'I mean exactly the opposite, Lewis. I mean it *was* Lionel Lawson who chucked himself off the tower. I'm absolutely sure of it.'

'I just don't understand.'

'Don't you? Well, it's like this. Short-sighted jumpers invariably remove their specs and put 'em in one of their pockets before jumping. So any traces of glass in a suicide's face are a sure tip-off that it wasn't suicide but murder.'

'But how do you know Lawson was short-sighted. He may have been—'

'Short-sighted, long-sighted – doesn't matter! It's all the same difference.'

'You serious about all this?'

'Never more so. It's like people turning their hearing-aids off before they have a bath or taking their false teeth out when they go to bed.'

'But the wife never takes hers out when she goes to bed, sir.'

'What's your wife got to do with it?'

Lewis was about to remonstrate against the injustice of such juvenile logic, but he saw that Morse was smiling at him. 'How do you come to know all this stuff about suicides anyway?'

Morse looked thoughtful for a few seconds. 'I can't remember. I think I read it on the back of a match-box.'

'And that's enough to go on?'

'It's something, isn't it? We're up against a very clever fellow, Lewis. But I just can't see him murdering

Lawson, and then very carefully taking off his specs and putting 'em back in their case. Can you?'

No, Lewis couldn't see that; couldn't see much at all. 'Are we making any progress in this case, sir?'

'Good question,' said Morse. 'And, as one of my old schoolmasters used to say, "Having looked that problem squarely in the face, let us now pass on." Time we had a bit o' lunch, isn't it?'

The two men walked out of the long three-storey stone building that forms the headquarters of the Oxford Constabulary, up past Christ Church, across Carfax, and turned into the Golden Cross, where Morse decided that, for himself at least, a modicum of liquid refreshment was all that would be required. He had always believed that his mind functioned better after a few beers, and today he once again acted on his customary assumption. He should, he realized, be off to Shrewsbury immediately; but the prospect of interviewing hospital porters and nurses and doctors about times and places and movements and motives filled him with distaste. Anyway, there was a great deal of routine work to be done in Oxford.

Lewis left after only one pint, and Morse himself sat back to think. The flashing shuttles wove their patterns on the loom of his brain, patterns that materialized in different shapes and forms, but patterns always finally discarded. After his third pint, there was nothing to show for his cerebrations except the unpalatable truth that his fanciful theories, all of them, were futile, his thinking sterile, his progress nil. Somewhere, though, if only he could think where, he felt convinced that he had missed something – something that would present him with the key to the labyrinth. Yes, that's what he needed: the key to the— He had the key to the *church*, though. Was it there, in the church itself, that he had overlooked some simple, obvious fact that even at this very second lay waiting to be discovered?

CHAPTER TWENTY-NINE

MORSE RELOCKED THE door in the north porch after him, conscious that he must try to look upon the interior of the church somehow differently. Previously he had gazed vaguely across the pews, his mind wafted away to loftier things by the pervasive sickly sweet smell of the incense and the gloomy grandeur of the stained-glass windows. Not so now. He fingered through half a dozen devotional tracts, neatly stacked side by side on a wall-ledge just inside the door to the left; he examined a sheaf of leaflets to be filled in by those who wished to be added to the electoral roll; he drew back a curtain just behind the font and noticed a bucket, a scrubbing-brush and two sweeping-brushes. This was much better – he felt it in his bones! He examined postcards (6p each), which carried exterior views of the church taken from several angles, large close-ups of the famous font (much admired, it seemed, by all save Morse), and full frontal photographs of one of the grinning gargoyles on the tower (how on earth had anyone taken those?); then he turned his attention to a stack of Guides to St Frides-wide's (10p each), and another stack of Parish Notes (2p each) in which details of the current month's activities were fully listed; then, beside the west wall, he noted again the heaps of prayer books with their dull-red covers and the heaps of hymn-books with their— He suddenly stopped, experiencing the strange conviction that he had already overlooked the vital clue that he'd been looking for. Was it something he'd just seen? Something he'd just heard? Something he'd just smelt? He went back to the door, retraced his few steps around the porchway, and then duplicated as far as he could his exact actions since entering the church. But it was no use. Whatever it was – if it was anything – was still eluding his grasp. Maddeningly. Slowly he paced his way up the central aisle and there stood still. The hymns from the previous evening's service were there, white cards with their red numbers, slotted into a pair of hymn-boards, one on either side of him. Odd! Why hadn't they been taken down? Was that one of Ruth Rawlinson's jobs? The bucket and the scrubbing-brush looked as if they had been used very recently, almost certainly by Ruth herself that very morning. Had she forgotten the hymn-boards? Or was that the job of the Vicar? Or one of the choir? Or one of the supernumerary assistants? For someone had to look after such matters. Come to think of it, someone had to decide the hymns, the psalms, the collects, epistles and gospels and the rest. Morse knew nothing about it, but he presumed that it was all laid down in some great holy book available for the guidance of the clergy. Must be. Like all those saints' days and other religious festivals. No one could carry all that stuff around in his head. What was more, someone would have to keep some sort of record of all the services every week – surely so! – especially when you had as many services as—*That* was it! He walked quickly back to the north porch and picked up a copy of the Parish Notes, and stared with curious excitement at the front page:

CHURCH OF ST FRIDESWIDE, OXFORD

SERVICES

Sundays Mass and Holy Communion 8 a.m.
10.30 a.m. (High) and 5.30 p.m.
Evening Service 6 p.m.
Weekdays Mass on Tuesdays and Fridays 7.30 a.m.
On Feast Days 7.30 a.m. and 7.30 p.m.
(Solemn)

CONFESSIONS

Tuesdays, Fridays and Saturdays, all at midday.
Or by arrangement with the clergy.

CLERGY

The Revd Canon K. D. Meiklejohn (Vicar),
St Frideswide's Vicarage.
The Revd Neil Armitage (Curate),
19 Port Meadow Lane.

APRIL

1st In Octave of Easter
2nd LOW SUNDAY. Preacher at 10.30 a.m.
     The Bishop of Brighton. Annual Parish
     Meeting 6.15 p.m.
3rd ST RICHARD OF CHICHESTER
     Mass at 8 a.m. and 7.30 p.m.

4th   Holy Hour 11 a.m.
5th   Mothers' Union 2.45 p.m.
6th   Deanery Synod 7.45 p.m.
8th   Holy Hour 5 to 6 p.m.
9th   EASTER II . . .

So it went on, through the whole month, with one major Feast Day (Morse noted) in two of the other three weeks. But so what? Was there anything here that was of the slightest interest or value? The name 'Armitage' was new to Morse, and he suspected that the Curate was probably a fairly recent acquisition, and had almost certainly been one of the three wise men in the purple vestments. Still, with all those services on the programme, there'd be need of a helping hand, wouldn't there? It would be a pretty hefty assignment for one poor fellow, who presumably was entrusted, in addition, with the pastoral responsibilities of visiting the lame and the sick and the halt and the blind. My goodness, yes! Meiklejohn would certainly need a co-labourer in such an extensive vineyard. And then a little question posed itself to Morse's mind, and for a second or two the blood seemed to freeze in his cheeks. *Did Lawson have a curate?* It should be easy enough to find out, and Morse had a peculiar notion that the answer might be important, though exactly *how* important he had, at this point, no real idea at all.

He pocketed the Parish Notes, and turned back into the church. A long tasselled rope barred access to the altar in the Lady Chapel, but Morse stepped irrever-

212

ently over it and stood before the heavily embossed and embroidered altar-cloth. To his immediate left was the arched opening to the main altar, and slowly he walked through it. In a niche to the left of the archway was an Early English piscina, and Morse stopped to look at it carefully, nodding slowly as he did so. He then turned left, made his way along the high carved screen which separated the Lady Chapel from the main nave, skipped lightly across the entrance to the Lady Chapel, and came to a halt outside the vestry. For some reason he looked quite pleased with himself and nodded his head again several times with a semi-satisfied smile.

He stood where he was for several minutes looking around him once more; and, indeed, had he but realized it, he was now within a few yards of the clue that would smash some of his previous hypotheses into a thousand pieces; but for the moment the Fates were not smiling upon him. The north door was opened and Meiklejohn entered, carrying a carton of electric light-bulbs, in the company of a young man balancing an extending ladder on his shoulder.

'Hello, Inspector,' said Meiklejohn. 'Discovered anything more yet?'

Morse grunted non-commitally, and decided that the investigation of the vestry could, without any cosmic ill-consequence, be temporarily postponed.

'We're just going to change the bulbs,' continued Meiklejohn. 'Have to do it, you know, every three or four months. Quite a few have gone already, I'm afraid.'

Morse's eyes travelled slowly up to the tops of the walls where, about forty feet above the floor he could

213

see a series of twin electric-light bulbs, each pair set about twenty feet apart. Meanwhile the ladder had been propped up beneath the nearest lights, and in a progressively more precarious stutter of elongations the two men were pushing the ladder even higher until the slimly converging top of the third extension now rested about two or three feet below the first pair of bulbs.

'I'm afraid,' said Morse, 'that I just haven't got the stomach to stop and witness this little operation any further.'

'Oh, it's not so bad, Inspector, as long as you're careful. But I must admit I'm always glad when it's over.'

'He's a better man than I am,' said Morse, pointing to the young man standing (rather nervously?) on the second rung and gently manœuvring the ladder on to a more firmly based vertical.

Meiklejohn grinned and turned to Morse quietly. 'He's about as bad as you are – if not worse. I'm afraid I have to do the job myself.'

And may the good Lord be with you, thought Morse, as he made his rapid exit, completely forgetting that he was debtor to church funds to the sum of 2p; forgetting, too, that there was a most important question he had yet to put to the daredevil incumbent of St Frideswide's.

In all there were twenty bulbs to change, and as always the job was taking an unconscionably long time to complete. To any observer of the scene, it would have appeared that the young man who stood dutifully with his foot placed firmly on the bottom rung of the ladder seemed quite incapable of raising his eyes above the strict horizontal as Meiklejohn repeatedly ascended to the dizzy heights above him where, standing on the antepenultimate rung, he would place his left hand for support against the bare wall, stretch up to twist out one of the old bulbs, place it carefully in his coat pocket, and then insert one of the new bulbs with an upward thrust of his right arm which virtually lifted his body into unsupported space. With the merest moment of carelessness, with the slightest onset of giddiness, the good vicar would have lost his precarious balance and plunged to his death on the floor so far below; but mercifully the task was now almost complete, and the ladder was in place below the last pair of bulbs when the door (which had remained unlocked) creaked open to admit a strange-looking man whose beard was unkempt, who was dressed in a long, shabby greatcoat, and who wore an incongruous pair of sunglasses. For a moment or two he looked about him, unaware of the presence of the other two men. The afternoon had grown dull and the electricity had been turned off whilst the bulbs were being changed.

'Can I help you?' asked Meiklejohn.

'What?' The man started nervously. 'Cor, you frightened me, guv.'

'Please do have a look around. You're most welcome.'

'Sorright. I just – I just wanted to – er . . .'

'I can show you around myself in a minute if you can—'

'Nah. Sorright, guv.' He shuffled out, and Meikle-john raised his eyebrows to the young man. The ladder was ready again now and he put his right hand up to the rung just above his head – and then stopped.

'You remember my predecessor here – poor Mr Lawson? He had a way with these down-and-outs, they tell me. Often used to have one or two of them staying with him for a few days. You probably know that anyway. Perhaps I should make more of an effort than I do. Still, we're all different, Thomas. Just as the good Lord made us.' He smiled, rather sadly, and began to climb. 'Perhaps poor Mr Lawson wasn't very good at changing light-bulbs, eh?'

Thomas managed a ghostly-weak smile in response and took up his guardian rôle on the bottom rung, his eyes once more averted from the fast-disappearing soles of the vicar's black shoes. Funny, really! He'd joined St Frideswide's church just over a year ago (he was an undergraduate at Hertford College) and he remem-bered the previous vicar very well indeed. He thought he remembered other things, too. For example, he thought he remembered the tramp who'd just walked in. Hadn't he seen him in church once or twice?

CHAPTER THIRTY

THE DECISION TO travel to Shrewsbury was taken, momentarily and arbitrarily, when Morse had walked out of the church on his way back to St Aldates; and as Lewis drove the police car round the Woodstock Road roundabout and headed out on to the A34 both men were mentally calculating the possible time schedule. It was already 4.20 p.m. Two hours, say, to get there – if the traffic was reasonable; two hours actually there; another two hours back. So, with a bit of luck, they could be back in Oxford by about 10.30 p.m.

Morse, as was his wont, spoke little in the car, and Lewis was quite happy to give his whole attention to the motoring. They had started in time to miss the diurnal mass exodus from Oxford which begins at about a quarter to five and continues its semi-paralytic progress for almost another hour. It was good fun, too, driving in a conspicuously marked POLICE car. As always other road-users immediately became punctilious about speed restrictions as they spied the pale-blue and white car in their mirrors, and ostentatiously shunned the slightest suspicion of sub-standard driving, behaving with a courtesy and care that were wildly at variance with their customary frenetic aggression.

So it was now.

Lewis turned left off the A34 through Chipping Norton, up through Bourton-on-the-Hill, through-Moreton-in-Marsh, and then, with the Vale of Evesham opening out in a vast panorama before them, down the long, steep hill into Broadway, its houses of mellowed Cotswold stone gleaming a warm yellow in the late afternoon sun. At Evesham, Morse insisted that they took the road to Pershore, in which town he enthused lovingly over the red-brick houses with their white-painted window-frames; and at Worcester he directed Lewis along the Bromyard Road.

'I've always thought,' said Morse, as they turned north from Leominster on to the A49, 'that this is one of the prettiest roads in England.'

Lewis sat silent. It was also a pretty long way round, and at this rate it would be about seven before they reached Shrewsbury. Yet as they drove past Church Stretton it seemed to Lewis that Morse was perhaps right; and even more so as they left the Long Mynd behind them, when the sun, still hovering over the Welsh hills far off on the western horizon, suffused the early evening sky with a fiery glow and turned the white clouds to the softest shade of purple.

It was half past seven when finally the two Oxford detectives were seated in the Superintendent's office at the Salop Police H.Q.; and it was half past eight when they emerged. Morse had said little, and Lewis less, and neither man felt that the meeting was of more than routine value. There were no grounds for suspecting anyone, and not the slightest whisper of a likely motive.

The dead woman had been quietly popular with her fellow-nurses, slightly less quietly popular with the surgeons and housemen, and it was difficult to believe that even Florence Nightingale herself could have found too many faults with her efficient and experienced nursing. One of the doctors had spoken to her the previous evening, had sat in the nurses' common room with her doing a crossword puzzle; but, although he was probably the last person (apart from the murderer) to see her alive, there was no reason whatsoever to suspect that he'd had anything to do with her death. But somebody had. Somebody had strangled her brutally with her own belt and left her for dead on the floor by the side of her bed, from where she had later managed to crawl to the door of her room to try desperately to call for help. But no one had heard her, and no one had come.

'I suppose we'd better see her?' said Morse dubiously, as they all trooped out of the Superintendent's office.

In the cream-tiled police morgue, a constable pulled out a sliding container from a stainless-steel structure, and turned back the sheet from the face – white, waxy-textured and washed, the lolling bloodshot eyes bearing their chilling witness to the agony of her death. At the base of her neck and running up to her right ear was the hideous groove left by the belt.

'Probably left-handed,' muttered Lewis, 'if he strangled her from the front, that is.' He turned towards Morse as he spoke, and noticed that the great man had his eyes shut.

Five minutes later Morse was looking immeasurably happier as he sat in the anteroom surveying the contents of the murdered woman's pockets and handbag.

'We should be able to check the handwriting easily enough,' said Lewis, as he saw Morse studying the letter from Kidlington.

'We hardly need to, do we?' said Morse, putting it to one side and turning to the other contents of the handbag. There were two pocket diaries, a lady's handkerchief, a leather purse, three luncheon vouchers, and the usual bric-à-brac of feminine toiletry: perfume, nail-file, comb, hand-mirror, eye-shadow, lipstick and tissues.

'Was she wearing much make-up when you found her?' asked Morse.

The Superintendent frowned slightly and looked less than comfortable. 'I think she was wearing some, but – er . . .'

'I thought you said she'd just come off duty. They don't let 'em slink round the wards all tarted up, surely?'

'You think she might have been expecting somebody?' Morse shrugged his shoulders. 'Possibility, isn't it?'

'Mm.' The Superintendent nodded thoughtfully, and wondered why he hadn't thought of that himself; but Morse had brushed aside the cosmetics as if whatever interest they might momentarily have exercised over him was now a thing of the past.

The purse contained six one-pound notes, about fifty pence in small change, and a local bus timetable. 'No driving licence' was Morse's only comment, and the

Superintendent confirmed that as far as they knew she'd had no car since coming to work at the hospital.

'She was pretty anxious to cover up her tracks, Super. Perhaps,' he added quietly, 'perhaps she was frightened that somebody would find her.' But again he seemed to lose interest in the line of thought upon which he had embarked, and proceeded to turn his attention to the two slim diaries, one for the current, one for the previous year.

'She wasn't exactly a Samuel Pepys, I'm afraid,' said the Superintendent. 'The odd jotting here and there, but not much to go on as far as I can see.'

Mrs Brenda Josephs had certainly started off the two years with admirable intentions, and the first few days of each of the two Januarys were fairly fully documented. But, even then, such *aide-mémoire* entries as her 'Six fish fingers' or '8.30 Nurses' Social' seemed hardly likely to lead the Salop or the Oxon constabulary very much nearer to the apprehension of her murderer. The expression on Morse's face was mildly sour as he flicked rather aimlessly through the pages, and in truth he found little to hold his attention. On the day of Brenda's death he noticed the single entry 'Periods due'; rather pathetic, but of little consequence.

Lewis, who hitherto had felt his contribution to the visit to have been less than positively constructive, picked up the diary for the previous year and examined it with his usual exaggerated care. The writing was neatly and clearly charactered, but for the most part so small that he found himself holding the diary at arm's length and squinting at it lop-sidedly. Against virtually every Sunday throughout the year up to mid-September were the letters 'SF', and these same letters were repeated at irregular intervals and on irregular week-days throughout the the same period. 'SF'? The only thing he could think of was Science Fiction, but that was obviously wrong. There was something else, though. From July up until late September there was a series of 'P's, written (almost imperceptibly) in pencil in the ruled blue lines which separated the days of the month from each other. And the day was always a Wednesday.

'What does "SF" stand for, sir?'

'Saint Frideswide's,' said Morse without a moment's thought.

Yes. That must be it. Harry Josephs (as Lewis now recalled) had been disqualified from driving, and it was his wife's duty to take him down to the church in her own car. That fitted all right. Sunday mornings for the big service of the week, and then, at intermittent intervals, the mid-week days whenever some prestigious saint or other held an anniversary. That was it. No doubt about it.

'What does "P" stand for, sir?'

Morse reeled them off with the fluency of a man who had devoted too many hours of his life to the solving of crosswords: 'soft', 'president', 'prince', 'page', 'participle'.

'Nothing else?'

'Phosphorus?'

Lewis shook his head. 'Probably the initial of some-one's name. It's a capital "P".'

222

'Let's have a look, Lewis.'

'Could be "Paul", sir? Paul Morris?'

'Or Peter Morris – if she's a paedophile.'

'Pardon?'

'Nothing.'

'Always on Wednesdays, though, sir. Perhaps she suddenly decided she wanted to see him more often—'

'And her old man was in the way and so she bumped him off?'

'I've heard of odder things. She said she'd nipped off to the pictures that night, didn't she?'

'Mm.' Morse's interest appeared to be engaged at last. 'How much does it cost to go to the pictures these days?'

'Dunno, sir. A quid? One-fifty?'

'Expensive for her, wasn't it? She couldn't have been there much more than an hour, at the most.'

'*If* she went, sir. I mean, she mightn't have gone to the pictures at all. She might have just crept quietly back into the church and—'

Morse nodded. 'You're quite right. She probably had the best motive of the lot of 'em. But you're forgetting something. The door creaks like hell.'

'Only the north door.'

'Really?' But Morse had clearly lost all interest in creaking doors, and Lewis found himself once more wondering why they'd bothered to come all this way. Nothing had been learned. No progress had been made.

'There's another "P", isn't there?' said Morse suddenly. 'We've forgotten Philip Lawson.'

Yes, Lewis had forgotten Philip Lawson; but where on earth was *he* supposed to fit into this particular picture?

The constable packed up Brenda Josephs' possessions, replaced them in their plastic bags, and redeposited the bags in a labelled cabinet. Morse thanked the Superintendent for his co-operation, shook hands with him, and got into the car beside Lewis.

It was on the Kidderminster road about six or seven miles south of Shrewsbury that a wave of chilling excitement, starting from the bottom of the back, gradually crept up to the nape of Morse's neck. He tried to conceal the agitation of his mind as he questioned Lewis. 'Did you say that Brenda Josephs marked off the days when she took her husband to church?'

'Looked like it, sir. And quite a few times apart from Sundays.'

' "SF", you said. She put "SF"?'

'That's about it, sir. As you said, it's "St Frideswide's". Not much doubt about that.' He turned suddenly and glanced at Morse, who was staring with extraordinary intensity into the outer darkness of the night. 'Unless, of course, you think it stands for something else?'

'No, no. It doesn't stand for anything else.' And then, very quietly, he said, 'Turn round, please. We're going back.'

The luminous dial on the fascia board showed half past ten, just gone, and things were running way behind even the most pessimistic schedule. But Lewis turned round at the earliest possible opportunity. He also was a man under authority.

The constable in the police mortuary reopened the cabinet and shook out the contents of the plastic bags once more. They were always a funny lot – these fellows from other forces.

Morse managed to keep his hand from shaking as he picked up the earlier of the two diaries and turned to the one specific page. And as he looked at the page the blood seemed to congeal in his jowls, and a slow smile of joyous satisfaction formed about his mouth.

'Thank you very much, Constable. Thank you very much. You don't think I could take this diary?'

'I don't know about that, sir. The Super's gone off now and—'

Morse held up his right hand like a priest delivering the benediction. 'Forget it! Doesn't matter!' He turned quickly to Lewis. 'See that?' He pointed to the space for Monday, 26 September, the day on which Harry Josephs had been murdered; and Lewis' forehead creased into a frown as he looked at it, and then looked at it again. The space was completely blank.

'You remember your Sherlock Holmes, Lewis?' But whether or not Lewis was familiar with the works of that great man was not immediately apparent, for clearly Morse himself had a good many passages of Holmesian dialogue by heart, and before Lewis could reply he proceeded to recite one:

'"Is there any point to which you would wish to draw my attention?"

'"To the curious incident of the dog in the night-time."

'"The dog did nothing in the night-time."

' "That was the curious incident." '

'I see,' said Lewis, seeing not.

'How fast will she go?' asked Morse as he clambered into the police car once more.

'About ninety – bit more – on the straight.'

'Well, put the flasher on and start the siren up. We must get back to Oxford quickly, all right?'

The car sped through the darkened countryside, down through Bridgnorth and Kidderminster, along the old Worcester Road to Evesham, and then in an almost incredibly short time back to Oxford. An hour and a half – almost to the minute.

'Back to the station, is it?' asked Lewis as he turned into the Northern Ring Road.

'No. Take me straight home, Lewis. I'm tired out.'

'But I thought you said—'

'Not tonight, Lewis. I'm dead beat.' He winked at Lewis and slammed the door of the Ford behind him. 'Good fun, wasn't it? Sleep tight! We've got work to do in the morning.'

Lewis himself drove off home happily. His honest soul had very few vices – but fast driving was certainly one of them.

CHAPTER THIRTY-ONE

PERHAPS THE EVENTS of the past few days had disturbed the Reverend Keith Meiklejohn rather less than they should have done; and being an honest man the realization of this was worrying to him. It was true that, inducted as he had been only in the previous November, he had not known the Morris family personally, and could not therefore be expected to react too keenly to the tragic discoveries of what (if rumour were to be believed) were the bodies of father and son. Yet as he sat in his study at 9.30 a.m. on Tuesday morning he knew that his compassion should have been engaged more deeply, and he wondered about himself; wondered about his church, too.

Meiklejohn was a robust, well-built man, forty-one years of age and happily unmarried. His childhood had been spent in a family household brimming with evangelical piety, and one forever frequented by inveterate god-botherers and born-again Baptists. From his earliest years the promises of eternal life and the terrors of the lake that burneth with fire and brimstone had been as real to him as liquorice allsorts and the landscape of his Dorset home. In his early youth, whilst his classmates discussed the prospects of their favourite football teams

or the merits of their new racing bikes, young Keith
had grown zealous over matters ecclesiastical and theological and by the age of sixteen the way ahead was
quite clear: he was destined to take holy orders. As a
young curate he had at first been moderately low-
church in his views on the liturgy and the sacraments;
but gradually he had been more and more attracted
towards the doctrines of the Oxford Movement, and at
one point he had come within a communion wafer of
conversion to the Roman Church. But all that was in
the past. With a new-found balance, he discovered he
could tread the tight-rope of High Anglicanism with
security and confidence, and it was pleasing to him that
his congregation appeared to think well of him for
doing so. His predecessor, Lionel Lawson, had not (it
seemed) found universal favour with an ecclesiastical
stance that was decidedly more middle-and-leg than
middle-and-off. In fact, when Lawson's curate, some
five years earlier, had been promoted to a parish of his
own there had been no request to the Bishop for a
replacement, and Lawson himself had coped single-
handed with the manifold duties of St Frideswide's
parish. Inevitably, of course, there had been cuts in
services, and it was Meiklejohn's resolve to restore as
soon as possible the daily masses at 11.15 a.m. and 6.15
p.m. which were a wholly necessary feature (as he saw
things) of a church that was dedicated to the glory of
God.

Yet, as he sat at the ancient roll-top desk, the page
over which his pen had been poised for several minutes
remained blank. It was high time he preached again on

transubstantiation: a tricky issue, of course, but one that was vital for the spiritual health of the brethren. But could that sermon wait, perhaps? His limp-leather copy of the Holy Writ lay open before him at the book of Hosea. A marvellous and memorable piece of writing! It was almost as if the Almighty himself had not really known what to do with his people when their goodness and mercy were as evanescent as the mists or the early dews that melted away in the morning sun. Was the Church in danger of losing its love? For without love the worship of God and the care of the brethren was little more than sounding brass and tinkling cymbals ... Yes, a possible sermon was just beginning to shape itself nicely. Not too forcefully expressed: nothing to smack too strongly of the stamping pulpit-thumper. But then another verse caught his eye from an earlier chapter of the same prophecy: 'Ephraim is joined to idols; let him alone.' Another striking verse! Idolaters were, after all, those within the Church – not those outside it. Those who worshipped, but who worshipped a false representation of God. And not just the golden calf, either. There was always a danger that other representations could get in the way of true worship: yes – he had to admit it! – things like incense and candles and holy water and crossings and genuflections, and all the sheer apparatus of ceremonial which could perhaps clog up the cleansing power of the Holy Spirit. It was possible, too – only too easy, in fact – to be blinded to the spiritual health of the Church by the arithmetical aggregation of its membership, especially when he considered (as he did with pride) the undoubted increase in the numbers attending divine worship since his own arrival. The records showed that there had been times under Lawson's régime when attendance had been just a little disappointing; and indeed some occasions in mid-week when it had been difficult to muster much of a congregation at all! But God didn't just count heads – or so Meiklejohn told himself; and he pondered again the central problem that had dominated his earlier thinking: should he not be more concerned than he was about the spiritual health of his church?

He was still undecided about the text of his next sermon, the page still blank beneath his pen, the disturbing words of the prophet Hosea still lying before him, when the door-bell rang.

Had it been the will of Providence that he had been pondering the state of St Frideswide's soul? At the very least, it was an uncanny coincidence that his visitor was soon asking him the very same questions he had been asking himself; asking them pretty bluntly, too.

'You had a big congregation last Sunday, sir.'

'About usual, Inspector.'

'I've heard that you get even more people than Lawson did.'

'Perhaps so. Certainly in the week, I think.'

'The crowds are flocking back, so to speak?'

'You make it sound like a football match.'

'Bit more interesting than the last football match I saw, I hope.'

'And one doesn't have to queue up at the turnstiles, Inspector.'

'You keep a fairly accurate record of the congrega-
tions, though?'

Meiklejohn nodded. 'I've continued my predecessor's practice in that respect.'

'Not in all respects?'

Meiklejohn was aware of the Inspector's blue eyes
upon him. 'What are you trying to say?'

'Was Lawson lower-church in his views than you are?'

'I didn't know him.'

'But he was?'

'He had views, I believe, which were – er . . .'

'Lower-church?'

'Er – that might be a way of putting it, yes.'

'I noticed you had three priests in church on Sunday
morning, sir.'

'You've still got quite a lot to learn about us, Inspector. There were myself and my curate. The sub-deacon
need not be in holy orders.'

'Three's a bit more than the usual ration, though,
isn't it?'

'There are no ration-books when it comes to divine
worship.'

'Did Lawson have a curate?'

'For the first part of his time here, he did. The
parish is a large one, and in my view should always have
a curate.'

'Lawson was on his own, then – for the last few
years?'

'He was.'

'Did you ever hear, sir, that Lawson might have been
a fraction too fond of the choirboys?'

'I – I think it quite improper for you or for me to—'

'I met his former headmaster recently,' interrupted Morse, a new note of authority in his voice. 'I felt he was concealing something, and I guessed what it was: the fact that Lionel Lawson had been expelled from school.'

'You're sure of that?'

Morse nodded. 'I rang the old boy up today and put it to him. He told me I was right.'

'Expelled for homosexuality, you say?'

'He refused to confirm that,' said Morse slowly. 'He also refused to deny it, I'm afraid, and I'll leave you to draw your own conclusions. Look, sir. I want to assure you that whatever you may have to tell me will be treated in the strictest confidence. But it's my duty as a police officer to ask you once again. Have you heard any rumours that Lawson was at all inclined to that sort of thing?'

Meiklejohn looked down at his feet and picked his words with uneasy care. 'I've heard one or two rumours, yes. But I don't myself think that Lawson was an active homosexual.'

'Just a passive one, you mean.'

Meiklejohn looked up, and spoke with quiet conviction: 'It is my view that the Reverend Mr Lawson was not a homosexual. I am, of course, sometimes wrong, Inspector. But in this case I think I am right.'

'Thank you,' said Morse, in the tone of a man who says 'Thank you for nothing'. He looked round the room at the bookshelves, lined with rows of theological works, the spines of most of them either dark-blue or brown. It was in this dark and sombre room that Lawson himself would have sat, probably for several hours each day, during his ten-year ministry at St Frideswide's. What had *really* gone wrong here? What strange tales of the human heart and the deep abyss of human consciousness could these walls and these books tell, if only they had tongues to speak to him? Could Meiklejohn tell him any more? Oh, yes, he could. There was just that one final question, the most vital question he would ask in the whole case. It was the question which had suddenly sprung to life in his mind the previous evening on the road just a few miles south of Shrewsbury.

He took from his pocket the now-crumpled Parish Notes for April.

'You print one of these every month?'

'Yes.'

'Do you' – this was it, and his mouth seemed suddenly to grow dry as he asked it – 'do you keep copies of them from previous years?'

'Of course. It's a great help in compiling the Parish Notes to have the previous year's copy. Not so much with the Easter period, of course, but—'

'Can I look at last year's Notes, please, sir?'

Meiklejohn walked over to one of the bookshelves and took out a loose-leafed folder. 'Which month's copy do you want?' His eyes reflected a shrewd intelligence. 'September, perhaps?'

'September,' said Morse.

'Here we are, yes. July, August . . .' He stopped and looked a little puzzled. 'October, November . . .' He turned back to January and went very carefully through the issues once more. 'It's not here, Inspector,' he said slowly. 'It's not here. I wonder . . .'

Morse was wondering, too. But – please! – it wouldn't be too difficult to find a copy somewhere, would it? They must have printed a few hundred – whoever 'they' were.

'Who prints these for you, sir?'

'Some little man in George Street.'

'He'd surely keep the originals, wouldn't he?'

'I'd have thought so.'

'Can you find out for me – straight away?'

'Is it that urgent?' asked Meiklejohn quietly.

'I think it is.'

'You could always check up from the church register, Inspector.'

'The *what*?'

'We keep a register in the vestry. Every service – I think it *is* a service you're looking for? – every service is recorded there. The time, the type of service, the minister officiating, the offertory – even the number of the congregation, although I must admit that's a bit of a rough guess sometimes.'

Morse allowed himself an exultant grin. His hunch had been right, then! The clue for which he'd been searching was where he'd always thought it would be – under his very nose inside the church itself. The next time he had a hunch, he decided, he would pursue it with a damned sight more resolution than he had done this one. For the moment, however, he said nothing. He was there – almost there anyway – and he felt the thrill of a man who knows that he has seven draws up on the football pools and is just going out to buy a sports paper to discover the result of the eighth match.

The two men walked down the wide staircase and into the hallway, where Meiklejohn took his coat from the clothes-stand, stained dark brown like almost every other item of furniture in the large, echoing vicarage.

'A lot of room here,' said Morse they stepped out into the street.

Again the Vicar's eyes flashed with intelligence. 'What you mean to say is that I ought to turn it into a hostel, is that it?'

'Yes, I do,' replied Morse bluntly. 'I understand your predecessor used to take in a few waifs and strays now and then.'

'I believe he did, Inspector. I believe he did.'

They parted at George Street, and Morse, in a state of suppressed excitement, and already fingering the heavy church-keys in his raincoat pocket, walked on down Cornmarket to St Frideswide's.

CHAPTER THIRTY-TWO ·

JUST AS MEIKLEJOHN had said, the bulky, leather-bound register stood on its shelf in the vestry, and Morse felt the same amalgam of anxiety and expectation with which as a schoolboy he had opened the envelopes containing his examination results: any second – and he would know. The pages of the register were marked in faded blue lines, about a third of an inch apart, with each line, stretched across the double page, quite sufficient to accommodate the necessary information. On the left-hand page were written the day, the date, and the time of the service, followed by some brief specification of the particular saint's day, feast day, et cetera; on the right-hand page the record was continued with details of the type of service cele-brated, the number present in the congregation, the amount taken at the offertory, and lastly the name (almost always the signature) of the minister, or minis-ters, officiating. Doubtless in a church permeated by a more fervent evangelicalism, there would have been the biblical reference of the text which the preacher had sought to propound; but Morse was more than delighted with the information he found in front of him. The register had fallen open at the current month and he noted the last entry: 'Monday, 3rd April. 7.30 p.m. St Richard of Chichester. Low Mass. 19. £5.35. Keith Meiklejohn M.A. (Vicar).' Then he turned back a thickish wadge of the book's heavy pages. A little too far, though: July, the previous year. On through August, and his heart suddenly seemed to sink within him as the thought flashed into his mind that someone might well have torn out the page he was seeking. But no! There it was now, staring him in the face: 'Monday, 26th Sept. 7.30 p.m. The Conversion of St Augustine. Solemn Mass. 13. – . Lionel Lawson M A. (Vicar).' For several minutes Morse stared at the entry with a blank fixity. Had he been wrong after all? For there it was, all printed out in Lawson's own hand – the precise details of the service at which Josephs had been murdered: the date and time, the occasion, the type of service (which, of course, accounted for Paul Morris' presence); the number in the congregation, the offertory (the sum quite naturally unknown and unrecorded, except perhaps for a few brief seconds in Josephs' brain before he met his death), and then Lawson's signature. All there. All in order. What had Morse hoped to find there? Surely he had not expected the amount of the offertory to be recorded? That would have been an elementary mistake of such monumental stupidity on Lawson's part that if repeated in other aspects of his crime would have led to an arrest within a few hours by any even moderately competent detective. No. Morse had not been looking for any such mistake. The simple truth of the matter was that *he'd expected there to be no entry at all.*

The door at the north porch creaked open, and Morse felt a sudden brief surge of primitive fear as he stood alone in the silent church. Somewhere, perhaps somewhere very near, there was a murderer still at large, watching every latest development with a vicious, calculating mind; watching even now, perhaps, and sensing that the police might be hovering perilously close to the truth. Morse walked on tiptoe to the heavy red curtain which cloaked the entrance to the vestry and cautiously peered through.

It was Meiklejohn.

'This is what you want, Inspector,' he said breezily. 'You must excuse me, if you will. We've got a service here at eleven.'

He handed to Morse a single sheet of paper, printed on both sides in faded black ink, with rows of asterisks dividing up the Parish Notes for the previous September into a series of closely typed paragraphs, of which the first, in double columns, gave full details of that month's forthcoming (and, in one case, fatal) functions. Morse sat down in the back pew and looked down intently at the sheet.

He was still looking down at the sheet several minutes later when Mrs Walsh-Atkins made her careful way down the central aisle, passing her left hand from pew-head to pew-head as she progressed, until finally settling herself in her accustomed seat where she knelt down, her forehead resting on the crook of her left arm, for a further protracted audience with the Almighty. A few other faithful souls had come in, all of them women, but Morse had not heard their entrances, and it was clear to him that the hinges on the door at the south porch had received a more recent oiling than those of its fellow at the north porch. He registered the point, as if it might be of some importance.

Morse sat through the devotional service – literally 'sat'. He made no pretence to emulate the gestures and movements of the sprinkling of ageing ladies; but a neutral observer would have marked a look of faintly smiling contentment on his features long before Meiklejohn's solemn voice at last, at very long last, intoned the benediction.

'It *was* what you wanted, I hope, Inspector?' Meiklejohn was leaning forward over the low table in the vestry, writing down the details of the service in the register with his right hand, his left unfastening the long row of buttons down his cassock.

'Yes, it was, and I'm most grateful to you. There's just one more thing, sir. Can you tell me anything about St Augustine?'

Meiklejohn blinked and looked round. 'St Augustine? Which St Augustine?'

'You tell me.'

'There were two St Augustines. St Augustine of Hippo, who lived about A.D. 400 or thereabouts. He's chiefly famous for his *Confessions* – as you'll know, Inspector. The other one is St Augustine of Canterbury, who lived a couple of hundred years or so later. He's the one who brought Christianity to Britain. I've got several books you could borrow if—'

'Do you know when either of 'em was converted?'

'Converted? Er – no, I'm afraid I don't. In fact I

239

wasn't aware that there was any such biographical data – certainly not about our own St Augustine anyway. But as I say—'

'Which one of 'em do you celebrate here, sir?' Upon Meiklejohn's answer, as Morse now knew, hung all the law and prophets, and the light-blue eyes that fixed the Vicar were almost hostile in their unblinking anticipation.

'We've never celebrated either of them,' said Meiklejohn simply. 'Perhaps we should. But we can't have an unlimited succession of special days. If we did, none of them would be "special", if you follow me. "When everyone is somebody, then no one's anybody."'

Phew!

After Meiklejohn had left, Morse hurriedly checked the three previous years' entries for September in the register, and almost purred with pleasure. The institution of any celebration to mark the conversion of one or other of the great Augustines had only begun – if it had begun at all – in the September of the previous year. Under the Reverend Lionel Lawson!

As Morse was about to leave the church, he saw that Mrs Walsh-Atkins had finally risen from her knees, and he walked back to help her.

'You're a faithful old soul, aren't you?' he said gently.

'I come to all the services I can, Inspector.'

Morse nodded. 'You know, it's surprising really that you weren't here the night when Mr Josephs was murdered.'

The old lady smiled rather sadly. 'I suppose I must have forgotten to look at the Parish Notes that week.

That's one of the troubles of growing old, I'm afraid – your memory just seems to go.'

Morse escorted her to the door and watched her as she walked away up to the Martyrs' Memorial. Had he wished, he could have told her not to worry too much about forgetting things. At the very least there had been no error of memory on her part over the Parish Notes for the previous September. For in those same notes, the notes which Meiklejohn had just found for him, *there was not a single word about the service at which Josephs would be murdered.*

Chapter Thirty-Three

Lewis had spent a busy morning. He had co-ordinated arrangements with the Coroner's Sergeant for the forth-coming inquests on the Morrises, *père et fils*; he had written a full report on the Shrewsbury trip; and he had just come back from acquainting a rapidly recovering Bell with the latest developments in the case when Morse himself returned from St Frideswide's, looking tense yet elated.

'What time does the *Oxford Mail* go to press, Lewis?'

'First edition about now, I should think.'

'Get me the editor on the blower, will you? Quick! I've got some news for him.'

Morse very hastily scribbled a few notes, and when Lewis handed him the phone he was ready.

'I want this in tonight's *Mail*, is that clear? Absolutely vital. And what's more it's got to go on the front page somewhere. Got your pencil ready? Here goes. Head-line: ARREST IMMINENT IN ST FRIDESWIDE'S MURDER HUNT. Got that? Good. Now, here's your copy. Exactly as I tell you. I don't want any sub-editor buggering about with so much as a comma. "The Oxford police today reported that their long investigation into the murder last September of Mr Harry Josephs is now

242

virtually complete stop The further deaths at St Frideswide's reported in these columns last week are now
known to be connected with the earlier murder comma
and the bodies discovered comma one on the tower
and one in the crypt of the church comma have been
positively identified as those of Mr Paul Morris comma
formerly music-master of the Roger Bacon School
Kidlington comma and of his son Peter Morris comma
former pupil of the same school and a member of the
church choir stop The police confirmed also that a
woman found murdered last week in a nurses' genitive
plural hostel in Shrewsbury was Mrs Brenda Josephs
comma wife of Mr Harry Josephs stop Chief Inspector
Morse capital M-o-r-s-e of the Thames Valley Constabulary told reporters today that public response to earlier
appeals for information had been extremely encouraging comma and that evidence is now almost complete."
No. Change that last bit: "and that only one more key
witness remains to come forward before the evidence is
complete stop In any case an arrest is confidently
expected within the next forty hyphen eight hours
stop" End of copy. You got all that? Front page, mind,
and give it a good big headline – about the same size
type you use when Oxford United win.'

'When did that last happen?' asked the editor.

Morse put down the phone and turned to Lewis.
'And here's a little printing job for you. Get it typed
and stick it on the outside of the south door at St
Frideswide's.'

Lewis looked down at what Morse had written:
'Because of imminent danger from falling masonry

immediately above the inside of the porch, this door must on no account be opened until further notice'.

'Come back as soon as you've done that, Lewis. There are a few things I've got to tell you.'

Lewis stood up and tapped the note with his fingers. 'Why don't we just lock the door, sir?'

'Because there's only one lock on it, that's why.'

For once Lewis refused to rise to the bait, put a clean white sheet of paper into the typewriter carriage, and turned the ribbon to 'red'.

The hump-backed surgeon put his head round the door of Bell's office just after 3 p.m., and found Morse and Lewis in earnest conversation.

'Won't interrupt you, Morse. Just thought you ought to know we're not much forrader with that fellow you found up the tower. I dunno as we're ever going to be certain, you know.'

Morse seemed neither surprised nor overmuch interested. 'Perhaps you're getting too old for the job.'

'Not surprising, Morse, old son. We're all ageing at the standard rate of twenty-four hours *per diem*, as you know.'

Before Morse could reply, he was gone, and Lewis felt glad that the interruption was so brief. For once in the case he knew exactly (well, almost exactly) where they were and why they were there.

*

It was just after half past four when one of the paper-boys from the Summertown Newsagents turned into Manning Terrace on his racing-bicycle, the drop handlebars (in one of the stranger perversions of fashion) turned upward. Without dismounting he took a copy of the *Oxford Mail* from the canvas bag thrown over his shoulder, folded it expertly in one hand, rode up to the door of number 7, and stuck it through the letter-box. Four doors in a row next, all on the right-hand side, starting with number 14A, where Ruth Rawlinson was just inserting her Yale key after an afternoon's shopping in Oxford.

She took the paper from the boy, put it under her right arm, and carried the two fully laden shopping bags into the house.

'Is that you, Ruthie dear?'

'Yes, Mother.'

'Is the paper come?'

'Yes, Mother.'

'Bring it with you, dear.'

Ruth put her carrier bags down on the kitchen table, draped her mackintosh over a chair, walked into the lounge, bent down to kiss her mother lightly on the cheek, placed the newspaper on her lap, turned up the gas fire, almost commented on the weather, wondered why she hadn't already gone mad, realized that to-morrow was Wednesday – oh God! How much longer would she be able to stand all this – her mother, and him? Especially *him*. There was little enough she could do about her mother, but she could do something

245

about him. She just wouldn't go – it was as simple as that.

'Ruth! Come and read this!' said her mother.

Ruth read through the front-page article. Oh my God!

The man seated on the deep sofa, its chintz covers designed in the russet-and-white floral pattern, was not surprised by the factual material reported in the front-page article, but he was deeply worried by its implications. He read the article through many, many times and always would his eyes linger on the same lines: 'only one more key witness remains to come forward before evidence is complete. In any case an arrest is confidently expected within the next forty-eight hours.' It was the piece about the 'key witness' which he found the more disturbing. Himself he could look after without help from anyone, but . . . In a flash, as always, the decision was taken. Yes, it had to be tomorrow – tomorrow morning. It *would* be tomorrow morning.

It was not only Ruth Rawlinson, therefore, who had decided to miss the regular Wednesday-evening rendez-vous. Someone else had now made exactly the same decision for her.

CHAPTER THIRTY-FOUR

AT FIVE MINUTES past ten the next morning, Ruth Rawlinson was not so wholly preoccupied with other things that she failed to notice and to admire the baskets of daffodils that bedecked the lamp-standards all the way along St Giles. But, if the morning was bright and sunny, her own mood was full of dark foreboding, for affairs were getting terrifyingly out of hand. Having been informed of the identities of the two bodies found at St Frideswide's, having learned of the death of Brenda Josephs, and knowing in any case far more than the police could know, her thoughts were in constant and grievous agitation. What was to stop her, at this very second, from cycling straight on through Cornmarket and down St Aldates to the Oxford City Police H.Q.? In any case, it was her duty to do so. It had always been her moral duty, but it was something more than that now: it was a personal cry for help as the walls began to close in around her. Five minutes earlier, when she had left Manning Terrace, her firm resolve had been to go to see Morse immediately and tell him the whole tragic tale. But that resolution was now crumbling, and she told herself that she needed a chance to think things out a little more clearly; a chance to brace herself emotionally, before plunging her own life, and thereby her mother's life, too, into utter ruin and desolation. Yes. She needed time – just a little more time. She propped her bicycle against the wall of the south porch, fastened the lock through the rear wheel, and then saw the notice on the door, pinned rather too high and typed in red capitals. Registering no particular surprise, Ruth Rawlinson walked round to the door at the north porch. It was open.

From the sub-manager's office on the top floor of the large store almost opposite, Lewis followed Ruth's progress with his binoculars – just as he had followed the progress of the others who had entered the church since 8.45 a.m., when the door at the north porch had first been unlocked. But they had been few, and his task had been far easier than he could have imagined. A flamboyantly dressed group of what looked from above like American tourists had gone in at 9.10 a.m.: ten of them. And at 9.22 a.m. ten of them had emerged into the sunlight and drifted off towards Radcliffe Square. At 9.35 a.m. a solitary white-haired lady had gone in, and had come out, her morning devotions completed, about ten minutes later. During the same time, a tall, bearded youth, carrying an extraordinarily large transistor radio, had gone in, only to make his exit some twenty seconds later, doubtless (as it appeared to Lewis) having mistaken the place for somewhere else. That was all – until Lewis recognized

Ruth Rawlinson. He'd accepted the offer of a cup of coffee five minutes after she'd gone in, but had kept his binoculars trained on the north entrance, even refusing to turn round to express his thanks. This, if Morse were right (and Lewis thought he was), could be the vital time. Yet half an hour later it hardly seemed as if it were going to be so. There had been no further visitors, if one discounted, that is, an innocent-looking white-haired terrier which had urinated against the west wall.

Some of the daffodils on the sides of the altar steps were now well past their prime, and Ruth picked them out, neatly rearranging the remainder, and mentally deciding to buy some more. She then walked boustrophedon along the pews on either side of the main aisle, replacing on their hooks whatever loose hassocks had been left on the floor, flicking the pew-ledges with a yellow duster, and at the same time collecting a few stray hymn-books and prayer-books. At one point she peered curiously up at the stonework above the south porch, but was unable to identify any visible signs of impending collapse.

Morse watched her with mixed emotions. He watched her large eyes and her full sensitive lips, and he realized once again how attractive she could have been to him. Even her little mannerisms were potentially endearing: the way she would blow a stray wisp of hair away from her face; the way she would stand, her hands on her waist, with something approaching pride on her face after completing one of her humble tasks. And yet, at the same time, he was conscious that she was in far more imminent danger than the masonry above the south porch was ever likely to be. If he was right (which after 10.20 a.m. he was beginning to doubt somewhat), Ruth Rawlinson was not likely to die in her nightdress, but in the very church in which he was now sitting, carefully concealed behind the dull-red curtain of the confessional. His intermittent fears that she would decide to spring-clean his own observation-post had hitherto proved groundless; but now, arms akimbo, she was looking searchingly around her. Did it matter all that much, though, if she did find him? He could explain as best he could – even take her over to the Randolph for a drink, perhaps. Yet he was glad when he heard the tell-tale clatterings and the drumming of cold water into the bottom of the scrubbing-bucket.

Several members of the public had entered the church during this time, and at each clinking of the latch and creaking of the door Morse felt the tension rise within him – only to fall again as the visitors stared rather vacantly around them, fumbled through the church literature, and without exception departed again within ten minutes of their arrival. Lewis had seen them go in; seen them leave, too – the coffee long since cold at his elbow. But Morse's own vigilance was becoming progressively less keen, and he began to feel just a little bored. The only book within arm's reach was a stiff-backed bible, whose pages he now turned desultorily, thinking back as he did so to his youth. Something had gone sadly wrong somewhere with his own spiritual development, for he had almost completely lost his early ebullient faith and he now had to confess that when faced with the overwhelming difficulties of forming any coherent philosophy of life and death he had come to regard the teachings of the Church as so much gobbledegook. He could be wrong, of course. Probably *was* wrong – just as he was probably wrong about this morning. Yet it had seemed such a logical time – certainly the time *he* would have chosen had he found himself in the murderer's shoes.

At some point in his musings, he thought he had heard a twanging metallic noise, but only now did it register fully. Could it have been the north door being locked? If so, it must surely have been locked from the outside. Yes. Blast it! He'd forgotten that notice about the recent vandalism, and someone must have come and locked the place up. But surely that someone would have looked into the church first? There was Ruth in there, for a start, although she probably had a key herself. *Did* she have a set of keys? What about any others who were in the church? If Ruth hadn't got a key, they'd all be shut up in there, wouldn't they?

Morse was only too conscious how woolly and confused his thinking was becoming – when he suddenly froze in his seat. He heard a man's voice, very close to him. It said, 'Hello, Ruth!' That was all. Quite a pleasant voice by the sound of it, but it seemed to turn Morse's blood to ice. Someone must have locked the door all right. *From the inside.*

251

CHAPTER THIRTY-FIVE

'WHAT ARE YOU doing in here?' she asked sharply. 'I didn't hear you come in.'

'No, you wouldn't would you? I've been here a long time. Up on the tower. It's cold up there; but you get a wonderful view, and I like looking down on things – and people.'

(Oh, Lewis! If only your eyes had not been focused quite so closely on the door!)

'But you must go! You can't stay here! You shouldn't be out at all!'

'You *worry* too much.' He laid a hand on her shoulder as they stood together in the central aisle, and pulled her towards him.

'Don't be silly!' she whispered harshly. 'I've told you – we agreed—'

'The door's locked, my beauty, have no fear. I locked it myself, you see. There's only the two of us here, so why don't we sit down for a little while?'

She pushed his hand from her. 'I've told you. It's got to finish.' Her lips were quivering with emotion, and she was very close to tears. 'I can't take any more of this. I just can't! You've got to go away from here. You've got to!'

'Of course I have. That's exactly what I've come to see you for – can't you understand that? Just sit down, that's all. Not too much to ask, is it, Ruth?' His voice was silkily persuasive.

She sat down and the man sat next to her, no more than ten feet or so from the confessional. (The man's heavy brown shoes, as Morse could now see, were of good quality, but appeared not to have been cleaned for many weeks.) For some time neither of them spoke as the man's left arm rested across the back of the pew, the hand lightly gripping her shoulder. (The fingernails, as Morse could now see, were clean and well manicured, reminding him of a clergyman's nails.)

'You read the article,' she said flatly. It was not a question.

'We both read the article.'

'You must tell me the truth – I don't care what you say, but you must tell me the truth. Did you – ' (her voice was faltering now) ' – did you have anything to do with all that?'

'Me? You must be joking! You can't honestly believe that – surely you can't, Ruth!' (The man, as Morse could now see, wore a pair of dingy grey flannels, and above them a large khaki-green jumper, with leather shoulder-patches, reaching up to the neck in such a way that it was not clear whether or not he wore a tie.)

Ruth was leaning forward, her elbows on the top edge of the pew in front of her, her head in her hands. From the look of her she might well be praying, and Morse guessed that she probably was. 'You're not telling me the truth. You're *not*. It was *you* who killed them! All of them! I *know* you did.' She was a lost soul now, uncaring in the bitter depths of her misery as she buried her head in her hands. Morse, as he watched her, felt a profound and anguished compassion welling up within him; yet he knew that he must wait. The previous day he had guessed at the truth behind the grim succession of tragedies, and here and now that very same truth was working itself out, not more than a few yards away from him.

The man made no denial of the charges spoken against him, but his right hand seemed to be working round his throat, his face momentarily turned away. (The face, as Morse had already noticed, was that of a man in his late forties – or early fifties perhaps, for both the long, unkempt, blackish hair and the beard which covered his face were heavily streaked with white and grey.)

Here it all was, then – in front of him. It was all so very simple, too – so childishly simple that Morse's mind, as always, had refused to believe it and had insisted instead on trying to find (and, indeed, almost finding) the weirdest, most complex solutions. Why, oh, why, just for once in a while was he not willing to accept and come to terms with the plain, incontrovertible facts of any case – the facts that stared him point-blank in the face and simply shrieked out for a bit of bread-and-butter common sense and application? The man sitting here now, next to Ruth Rawlinson? Well, Morse? Of course it was! It was Lionel Lawson's brother – *Philip Lawson*; the man so despised in the stories of clever detection, the man so despised by Morse himself; the man who committed a not-very-clever crime for the very meanest of rewards; the layabout, the sponger and the parasite, who had bedevilled his long-suffering brother's life from their earliest schooldays together; the cleverer boy, the more popular boy, the favourite – the boy who had grown up without a thread of moral fibre in his being, the boy who had wasted his considerable substance on riotous living, and who had come back to prey once more upon his wretched brother Lionel; come back, with a complete knowledge of his brother's life and his brother's weaknesses; come back with threats of betrayal and public exposure – threats which Lionel had paid off with help and kindness and compassion and, doubtless, with money, too. And then – yes, and then came the time when Lionel himself, for once in his life, had desperately needed the help of his worthless brother, and was more than prepared to pay for it; the time when the two brothers had planned the execution and arranged the subsequent cover-up of Harry Josephs' murder, a murder planned meticulously at the very moment when Paul Morris had just opened the diapason stop on the organ, and was doubtless drowning the church with the last verse of 'Praise to the Holiest in the Height' or something. *fff.*

These were the thoughts that flashed across Morse's mind in that instant, with the multiple murderer sitting there just in front of him, his left arm still resting along the back of the pew, his right hand still fumbling with something round his neck; and Ruth still bending forward in her posture of semi-supplication, still so pathetically vulnerable.

Then, even as he watched, Morse felt his every muscle tense in readiness as the adrenalin coursed through his body. The fingers of the man's left hand were holding the narrower end of a tie; a dark navy-blue tie with broad diagonal scarlet stripes bordered by very much thinner ones of green and yellow; and as Morse watched the scene being enacted immediately before his eyes his mind came to a dead stop in its tracks, seemed to turn a reverse somersault and to land in a state of complete stupefaction.

But the time for thought was past; already the man's left hand had looped the tie round the woman's neck; already the right hand was moving to meet it – and Morse acted. It was ill luck that the low door of the confessional opened inwards, for he had to clamber awkwardly in the narrow space and by the time he was out the element of surprise was gone; and as the tourniquet was already tightening about Ruth's throat she cried a terrible cry.

'Keep your distance!' snarled the man, springing to his feet and dragging Ruth up with him, the tie cutting cruelly into her neck. 'You heard me! Keep it there! Not a step farther or else.'

Morse hardly heard him. He lunged desperately at the pair of them, and Ruth fell heavily in the central aisle as Morse seized the man's right arm and tried with all his considerable strength to twist it behind his back. But with almost ridiculous ease his adversary shook himself clear and stood there, a vicious hatred blazing in his eyes.

'I know you,' said Morse, panting heavily. 'And you know who I am, don't you?'

'Yes, I know you, you bastard!'

'There's no sense in trying anything – I've got my men all round the church—' (the words were coming out in a series of breathless snatches) 'there's no way for you to get out of here – no way at all – now – now please be sensible – I'm going to take you from here – there's nothing to worry about.'

For a while the man stood quite motionless, only his eyes roving about in their sockets as if weighing the situation with a frenetic logicality, as if searching for some desperate remedy. Then something seemed to snap in the man, as if the glaze that suddenly dilated the eyes had effaced the very last vestiges of any rational thought. He turned swiftly, almost athletically, on his heel, and with his descending peal of maniacal laughter echoing under the vaulted roof he ran to the back of the church and disappeared behind the curtains of the vestry.

At that point (as Lewis later protested) Morse could have chosen several more logical courses of action than the one which he in fact pursued. He could have gone to the door at the north porch and signalled Lewis immediately; he could have led Ruth from the church and locked the door behind him, with his quarry cornered and powerless; he could have sent Ruth, if sufficiently recovered, to get help, and himself stayed where he was, performing no more than a watchdog brief until that help arrived. But Morse did none of these things. He felt that strangely compelling and primitive instinct of the hunter for the hunted, and he walked almost boldly to the vestry where in a sudden flurry he flung the curtains aside on their rollers. No one was there. The only other doorway from the vestry led to the tower, and Morse walked across the parquet floor and tried the door. Locked. He took out his keys, selected the right one first time, unlocked the door and, standing cautiously to one side, pulled it open. On the lowest of the circular stone steps, he saw a man's greatcoat, long, shabby and dirty; and, placed neatly on top of it, a pair of dark sunglasses.

CHAPTER THIRTY-SIX

TRACERIES OF BLACKENED cobwebs lined the under-lintels of the stone steps above his head as step by step Morse ascended the circular stairway. He was conscious of no fear: it was as if his paranoiac acrophobia was temporarily suspended, subsumed by the saner, more immediate danger from the man somewhere above him. Up and up he climbed, the door to the bell-chamber just appearing on his right when he heard the voice from high above him.

'Keep going, Mr Morse. Lovely view from the top.'

'I want to talk to you,' shouted Morse. He put his hands out to the walls on either side of him and looked upwards towards the tower. For a second his balance threatened to desert him as he caught sight, through the small low window to his left, of the shoppers walking along Cornmarket, far, far below him. But a raucous laugh from above served only to restore his equilibrium.

'I only want to talk to you,' repeated Morse, and climbed another six steps. 'I only want to *talk* to you. As I told you, my men are outside. Be sensible, man. For Christ's sake, be sensible!'

But there was no reply.

Another window, again to his left, and the angle

down on to the stream of shoppers was now virtually vertical. Strangely, however, Morse realized that he could now look down without that wave of incipient panic. What for the life of him he was unable to do was to look across at the store almost opposite, where he knew that the faithful Lewis would still be watching the door at the north porch with his wonted, unwavering vigilance.

Another six steps. And another six steps.

'The door's open, Mr Morse. Not much farther.' Then again the almost insane laugh, but softer this time – and more menacing.

On the second step from the top of the tower and with the door (as the man had asserted) wide open, Morse stopped.

'Can you hear me?' he asked. He was breathing heavily, and he realized sadly how ill-conditioned he had allowed his body to become.

Again, there was no reply.

'It must have been heavy work carting a body up here.'

'I've always kept fit, Mr Morse.'

'Pity the ladder collapsed, though. You could have hidden 'em both in the crypt then, couldn't you?'

'Well, well! How observant we are!'

'Why did you have to kill the boy?' asked Morse. But if there was a reply a sudden tugging gust of wind cut across the words and whipped them away.

It was clear to Morse that the man was not concealed behind the tower door and after taking one further step he could now see him, standing facing him at the northern wall of the tower, about thirty feet away, on the narrow gully that divided the sides of the tower from the shallow central eminence. With a peculiarly detached inconsequentiality, Morse noticed how very large the weather-vane was, and for a second or two he wondered whether he would soon be waking from a terrifying dream.

'Come down. We can't talk here. Come on.' Morse's tone was gentle and persuasive. He knew the whole truth at last, and his one remaining duty was to get this man down safely. 'Come on. Come down. We can talk then.' Morse climbed the final stop, and felt the wind pulling at his thinning hair.

'We'll talk now, Mr Morse, or we won't talk at all. Do you understand what I mean?' The man hitched himself up and sat on the coping between two of the crenellations, his feet dangling loosely above the tower floor.

'Don't do anything stupid!' shouted Morse, his voice betraying a sudden panic. 'That solves nothing. That's no way out for you. Whatever else you are, you're not a coward.'

The last word seemed to strike a chord which could still vibrate with something of its former attunement, for the man jumped lightly down and his voice was steady now. 'You're right, Mr Morse. Dangerous sitting there like that, especially in the wind.'

'Come on!' Morse's mind was racing now. This was the time when it mattered so desperately that he said and did exactly the right things. He felt sure that there must be some suitable phrases in the psychiatrist's hand-book that would soothe the raging of a maddened

261

lion; but his own brain was quite incapable of formu-
lating any such irenic incantations. 'Come on,' he said
again; then, as a minor variant, 'Come along.' And, in
spite of the bankruptcy of these banal exhortations,
Morse felt that he was adopting the right sort of
approach, for there now seemed some hesitation in the
other's manner, some indication of a slightly saner
attitude.

'Come along,' repeated Morse, and took one slow
step towards the man. Then another step. Then
another. And still the man stood motionless, his back
to the north wall of the tower. Only five or six yards
now separated them, and Morse took yet a further step
towards him. 'Come along.' He held out his hand as if
to lend support to one who has passed the dangers of a
long walk along a tight-rope, and now is only a few feet
from final safety.

With a snarl on his bearded lips, the man launched
himself at Morse and pinned him round the shoulders
with a vicious vice-like power. 'No one's ever called me
a coward,' he hissed. 'No one!'

Morse managed to grab hold of the man's beard
with both hands and to force his head back inch by
inch until they both lost their balance and fell heavily
against the leaded slope of the central roofing. Morse
felt himself pinned beneath the other man's body, his
legs and shoulders utterly powerless. He felt strong
hands at his throat, the thumbs digging deep into the
flesh; and his own hands were now frantically gripping
the man's wrists, temporarily staying the irresistible
thrust, his lips stretched to their widest extremity over

his gritted teeth, his eyes closed with a desperate tight-
ness, as though somehow this might lend him a few
extra seconds of time, an extra ounce of strength. The
blood thudded in his ears like someone pounding
against a heavy door that would admit no entrance, and
from somewhere he heard what sounded like the tinkling crash of a broken milk bottle; and the noise registered coolly and clinically in his brain, as if his mind
was now outside himself, contemplating events with an
objective detachment that was wholly devoid of panic
or fear. He saw the scene with such clearly focused
clarity. He was driving through the night along the fast,
straight, narrow stretch of road from Oxford to Bices-
ter, a long stream of cars coming towards him, ever
coming towards him, their twin headlights staggered
slightly in a continuous double line of yellow circles,
ever approaching – and then flashing past him. And
now there was another vehicle coming straight towards
him, coming on the wrong side of the road, its offside
blinker flashing as it closed upon him. Yet (amazingly!)
his hands remained firm and steady on the driving-
wheel ... Perhaps that was one of death's most
guarded secrets? Perhaps the fear of dying, perhaps
even death itself, was nothing but a great deception
after all ... The headlights turned to spinning yellow
circles in his brain, and then as he opened his eyes he
could see only the dull sky above him. His knees were
drawn up under the man's stomach: but so oppressive
was the weight upon him that he could gain no leverage
at all. If only he could find the strength to co-ordinate
his arms and his knees, there might just be the chance

of unbalancing the man and turning him sideways, and thus for a few seconds relieving the overpowering pressure of the hands at his throat. But his strength was almost gone, and he knew that his body, any second now, would almost gladly capitulate as the aching muscles in his arms screamed out for rest. He was relaxing already, his head resting almost comfortably now against the cold surface of the central roofing. That weather-vane really was enormous! How on earth could anyone have carried such a weight up here, up the circling staircase, up and up and up, with such a great weight upon his shoulder?

The full realization of his situation registered for the last time, and for a few seconds longer his grip on the man's wrists held firm as he dredged up the very last drop of his energy. But he had nothing more to offer. His grip on the steering-wheel slowly relaxed and as he closed his eyes the lights from the oncoming cars were dazzlingly bright. He thought of the final words of Richard Strauss's last song: 'Ist dies etwa der Tod?'

CHAPTER THIRTY-SEVEN

MORSE REALIZED THAT something miraculous had occurred. The body so inexorably pressing down upon him had become, in the self-same moment of time, both heavier and lighter; the grip at his throat both tighter and looser. The man groaned as if in some intolerable agony, and as he did so Morse's knees thrust him away, almost lightly and easily. The man reeled away towards the side of the tower where he frantically reached out to the nearest crenellation to stay himself. But his impetus was too great. The stonework crumbled away as his right hand jarred into it for support; and head first the man plunged over the parapet. Then was to be heard the diminuendo of a terrifying 'Yaooh' as the man's body fell somersaulting to the ground far below, and finally a deadly thump followed by the terrified shrieks of those passing by at the foot of the tower.

Lewis stood there still clutching the top end of a long brass candlestick. 'You all right, sir?'

Morse remained where he was, blissfully breathing in the heady air in mighty gulps. The pain in his arms was like raging toothache, and he spread them out beside him, lying there on the gently sloping roof like a man who is crucified.

265

'Are you all right?' It was another voice now, a gentler, softer voice, and slim, cool fingers pressed themselves against his wet forehead.

Morse nodded, and looked up at her face. He saw that there was a slight down of very fair hair upon her cheeks and light-brown freckles on either side of her nose. She was kneeling beside him, her large eyes brimming with happy tears. She held his head in her arms and pressed him closely to her for what to Morse seemed many days and many hours.

They said nothing to each other. When they slowly descended from the tower, she leading but only so little a way in front that their hands could remain firmly clasped, they still said nothing. When a few minutes later Lewis saw them they were sitting in the back pew of the Lady Chapel, her tear-stained face resting happily on his shoulder. And still they said nothing.

Lewis had seen the two men on the tower, had almost broken his own neck clambering down the five flights of stairs, had knocked several young ladies out of the way as he had run through the ground-floor cosmetic department, and finally, like some frustrated Fury, had hammered and hammered with his fists against the north door. The woman was still in there, he knew that, but it occurred to him that something might have happened to her; and in desperation he had hurled a large stone through the lowest and most convenient window with the dual purpose of making himself heard and of creating a possible means of entry. And the woman had heard him. The door was unlocked and, grabbing a candlestick from the shrine of the Blessed Virgin, he had taken the tower staircase three steps at a time and once on the roof he had smashed the candlestick with all his force across the middle of the back of Morse's bearded assailant.

Two duty-policemen were already on the scene when Lewis emerged. A ring of people, standing some four or five yards off, surrounded the dead body, and an ambulance, already summoned, was whining its way down St Giles from the Radcliffe Infirmary. Lewis had plucked a cassock from one of the hooks in the vestry, and now draped it over the dead man.

'Do you know who he is?' asked one of the policemen.

'I think so,' said Lewis.

'You all right?' The hump-backed police surgeon was the third person to have asked the same question.

'Fine. Few weeks on the Riviera and I'll be fine. Nothing serious.'

'Huh! That's what they all say. Whenever I ask my patients what their parents died of, they all say the same – "Oh, nothing serious".'

'I'd tell you if I wasn't all right.'

'You know, Morse, don't you, that every single person ever born has at least one serious illness in life – the last one?'

Mm. It was a thought.

Lewis came back into the church: things were almost ready outside. 'You all right, sir?'

'Oh, for Christ's sake!' said Morse.

Ruth Rawlinson still sat on the rear pew of the Lady Chapel, her eyes staring blankly ahead of her – composed, silent and passive.

'I'll see her home,' said Lewis quietly. 'You just—'

But Morse interrupted him. 'She can't go home, I'm afraid. You'll have to take her down to the station.' He breathed heavily and looked away from her. 'She's under arrest, and I want you personally to take her statement.' He turned to Lewis with inexplicable anger in his voice. 'Is that clear? You! Personally!'

Unspeaking and unresisting Ruth was led away to a police car by one of the constables; and after she was gone Morse, Lewis and the police surgeon followed.

The crowd outside, now standing three or four deep around the covered body, watched their emergence with deep interest, as if the principal protagonists in a drama had just walked on to the stage: the hump-backed, rather elderly man, who looked (had he been around in 1555) as if he might have viewed unmoved the sight of Ridley and Latimer as they had burned to death in front of Balliol, only a few hundred yards away; next, the placid-looking, rather thick-set man, who earlier had seemed to be in charge of all the operations but who now appeared to fade a little into the background as if he were in the presence of his superiors; and finally a slimmer, balding, pale-faced man with piercing eyes, in whose sombre mien – if in any of the trio's – lay the look of a natural authority.

They stood there, these three, over the covered body.

'You want to look at him, Morse?' asked the police surgeon.

'I've seen enough of him,' muttered Morse.

'His face is all right – if you're feeling squeamish.'

The surgeon pulled back the top of the cassock from the dead man's face, and Lewis looked down at it with great interest and intensity.

'So that's what he looked like, sir.'

'Pardon?' said Morse.

'Lawson's brother, sir. I was just saying that—'

'That's not Lawson's brother,' said Morse quietly; so quietly in fact that neither of the other men seemed to hear him.

The Book of Ruth

Chapter Thirty-Eight

Statement given by Miss Ruth Rawlinson, 14A Manning Terrace, Oxford, dictated by Miss Rawlinson, signed by the same, and witnessed by Sergeant Lewis, Thames Valley Police (C.I.D.)

Perhaps it is easier to start twenty years ago. I was then in the first-year sixth at Oxford High School studying for my A Levels in English and History and Economics. The headmistress came into the class one morning and called me outside. She told me that I must be a brave girl because she had some very sad news for me. My father who worked as a printer with Oxford University Press had suffered a massive coronary thrombosis and had died within an hour of being admitted to the Radcliffe Infirmary. I remember a feeling of numbness more than anything and little real grief. In fact for the next few days I felt almost a sense of pride as the mistresses and the other girls treated me with a kindness I had never really known before. It was just as if I were a heroine who had suffered much misfortune with great fortitude. But that wasn't the case at all really. I didn't dislike my father but we had never been close to each other. A perfunctory kiss when I went up to bed or a pound note sometimes when I'd done well in examinations but he had shown little real interest and no real love. Perhaps it wasn't his fault. My mother had been struck down with multiple sclerosis and although at that time she was still reasonably mobile my father's first and every thought was for her welfare and happiness. He must have loved her very dearly and his death was a terrible blow to her. Almost from that day onwards she seemed to change. It was as if the woman she had been could never come to terms with such bereavement and therefore had to become a different person. Something happened to me too. I suddenly began to lose all pride in my school work and I began to lose all love for my mother. I suspected that she exaggerated her physical handicaps and all the cooking and washing and cleaning and shopping I did for her were accepted with less and less gratitude. I stayed on at school and took my A Levels the next year but I didn't apply for a university place although oddly enough my mother wanted me to. Instead I took a year's course at the Marlborough Secretarial College in the High and soon found that I had a real aptitude for the work. Even before I left the college I had been offered three posts and I finally accepted a very good offer from Oxford University Press as a personal and confidential secretary to a man who had known my father slightly. He was a very kind boss and a very clever man and the five years I spent with him were the happiest of my life. He was a bachelor and a year or so after starting with him he began to ask me out for an occasional meal or a visit to the Playhouse and I accepted. He never tried to take the slightest advantage of me and only when he used to take my arm through his as we walked to the car was there the slightest physical contact between us. Yet I fell in love with him – quite hopelessly as I thought. Then two things happened almost within a few days of each other. My boss asked me if I would marry him and there was a sudden sharp deterioration in my mother's condition. Whether these two things were connected it is impossible for me to say. I had told her about the proposal of marriage and she had told me what she thought about it in typically forthright terms. He was just a dirty old man looking for a bit of regular sex and look at the huge difference in our ages. Ridiculous! I should find myself some nice young man about my own age – that is if I had finally decided to leave her to rot away in some lonely home for chronic invalids. She worked herself up into a most distraught state and I realize that I am perhaps being less than fair in doubting her genuine shock at the news I had brought her. Anyway her G.P. told me that she was very poorly indeed and would have to go into hospital immediately. Then two more things happened almost at once. My mother returned home now needing a great deal of daily attention and I told my boss that I couldn't accept his proposal and that in the circumstances it would be better for me to leave. I remember the look of childlike sadness and disappointment in his eyes. When I left three weeks later he took me out for a marvellous meal at the Elizabeth and he talked quite happily all the evening. When he took me home and we sat in the car trying to say our very awkward farewells I turned to him and kissed him freely and lovingly on the mouth. From that day I grew my own shell round me just as my mother had grown hers. Doubtless I am much more like my mother than I would want to believe. Anyway mother had probably been quite right. When I left work I was twenty-four and my boss was forty-nine. I met him once or twice after that just casually in the street. We asked the usual polite questions and went our ways. He never married. Two years afterwards he died of a brain haemorrhage and I went to his funeral. Looking back on it I feel no deep regrets that we didn't marry but I shall always regret that I never offered to become his mistress. These facts may seem irrelevant but I mention them only in the hope that someone may be able to understand why things began to go wrong and not in order to exonerate myself in any degree for my own part in the terrible business that was to come.

I must now talk about money. With my own quite handsome little salary now cut off, our financial situation had to be considered carefully and my mother thought that my own C-grade pass in A Level Economics was a sure guarantee of prudence and wizardry in monetary matters. Soon therefore I came to have a very full knowledge of all our financial affairs and it wasn't long before my mother gladly handed over all the responsibility to me. There was no problem with the house since my father had taken out a combined mortgage and life-insurance policy on it. It was far too big for the two of us but its market value was now about ten times greater than when my father had bought it twenty-five years earlier and with his death it was ours. At that time too my mother had realizable assets of about £2,000 in various stock-market equities and my own deposit account with Lloyds stood at over £800. In addition my mother had a small widow's pension accruing from a policy my father had taken out with the Press and from this time I also began to claim a dependency allowance from the Department of Social Security. For the next ten years or so I took on quite a lot of typing duties at home – mostly theses for doctorates and manuscripts for hopeful authors and that sort of thing. So we lived with a reasonable degree of comfort and security. And then two years ago came the stock-market slump and I was persuaded to realize my mother's stock capital for less than £500. If only I had held on for another six months all would have been well or at least not half so disastrous but there were great fears at the time of a complete collapse in the market. As the shares plummeted even lower in the weeks that followed it seemed that I had been wise to act as I had done but the truth was that I had been badly advised and that I had acted disastrously. I kept all this from my mother as best I could and this was not difficult. She had no real knowledge about financial affairs. Whilst my father was alive he had managed his small resources with a shrewd competence and would never let my mother worry about such things or enquire too closely into them. Since his death the burden of responsibility had fallen on my own slimmer shoulders and my mother fully expected that all was still well. I was too ashamed of my own incompetence to let her think otherwise. I decided then (and remember this was only two years ago) to put all our remaining assets into my one idea of a sound investment. I've already mentioned that our house was far too big for the two of us and I had my plans for it. We would divide the house into two with mother and myself living on tho ground floor and another family on the first floor. My idea was to partition the front hall so that the stairs to the upper floor led directly to a completely self-contained residence. The bathroom and toilet were already on that floor anyway and the only major reconstruction necessary was a kitchen sink upstairs and a small bathroom downstairs with a second front door so that there need be no sharing of keys or door-bells and no postal complications. A friend from St Frideswide's (yes I shall be coming to that soon) drew up some neat little plans for me and after finding out that no planning permission was required I asked for estimates. They all seemed to me surprisingly high but I decided we could just manage the lowest estimate of £1,500. So I went ahead and the work began a few months later with heaps of sand and piles of bricks and builders' planks appearing in the front driveway. Everything was going well until a year last February when my mother received a letter from an old friend of hers who had heard of a marvellous clinic in Switzerland which specialized in the treatment and care of multiple sclerosis. No magical cures were promised but there were glowing reports from satisfied clients and the brochure included with the letter gave full details of the three-week course together with technicolour pictures of the clinic itself overlooking Lake Thun with the snowy summits of the Alps behind and the foothills alive with saxifrage and eidelweiss. The cost was £630 which included the return air fare from Heathrow to Basel and transport to and from the clinic. Never before this time had I fully understood the terrible tyranny of money. If I had it my mother could go. If I didn't she couldn't go. There were no gradations of merit or need. I was rather sceptical about any treatment for my mother's illness but the clinic was obviously a reputable one and I knew that a period abroad would do my mother some good. She had not stirred out of the house for more than eighteen months and often couldn't even be bothered to get out of bed and into her wheelchair. But now for the first time in years she had taken a firm decision herself. She wanted to go and was excited at the prospect. She went. Although I spent the three weeks of her absence working as hard and as long as I could as a temporary typist by day and as a waitress in the evenings I found the time exhilarating and I once more discovered some of the joy of living. But things were not working out at all well. The builders were finding unexpected snags and I received a letter from the head of the firm saying that if the work was to be properly carried out the estimate would have to be increased by £350. My mother's return did nothing to help of course and when it was discovered that the waste pipes on the ground floor would quite definitely have to be replaced I was compelled to ask the builders to lay off work for a few weeks since I was unable to meet the next monthly instalment. By the middle of the summer I was at my wits' end. It was then I went to see the Reverend Lionel Lawson.

CHAPTER THIRTY-NINE

Statement given by Miss Ruth Rawlinson (continued)

The first time I had been in St Frideswide's was as a girl in the High School choir when we had sung the Stainer Crucifixion with the Oxford augmented choirs. Several of us sang there again especially when the choir was short of sopranos and contraltos for the Palestrina masses. So I got to know some of the people there and began to feel quite at home. Soon I became a regular member of the choir not because I had any deep conviction about High Anglicanism but because I enjoyed having a different ambit of action and acquaintances. There was an old woman there who cleaned the church every morning of the week – a woman so crippled with arthritis that the carrying of mops and buckets was in itself a positive affirmation of her faith and will. I got to know her well and one day I asked her about herself and she said ever so simply and happily that she hoped God would one day reward her for what she was doing but that if He decided she was not worthy then she still wished to praise and glorify Him for the blessings he had given her. Instead of feeling surprised or cynical about this I felt myself most profoundly moved and when she died I vowed that I would try to take upon myself at least some part of her good works. And so I found myself scrubbing and polishing and the rest and discovering just a little bit of the fulfilment in life that the old woman had experienced. In the course of this self-imposed pennance I naturally got to know Lionel Lawson quite well and as I say it was to him that I went for help and advice when I could no longer cope with our financial crisis. I had one of the great surprises of my life when he told me that if all I was worrying about was money I could and should forget my worries immediately. He asked me what I needed and when I told him he sat down at his desk (where I noticed a paper-knife in the form of a crucifix) and wrote out a cheque for £500. It was just like a miracle and when I told him that I had no idea of when I could repay him or how I could thank him enough he just said that he might be in trouble himself one day and if he was he'd like to know that I would try to help him in any way I could. Of course I promised that I would do absolutely anything for him, and I remember clearly how at the time I hoped and prayed that I would one day be able to do some really big favour for him in return. As I was leaving the vicarage that day I saw a man coming out of the kitchen downstairs. For a moment I didn't recognize him although his face looked familiar. He was rather shabbily dressed but he was freshly shaven and his hair had been recently trimmed. I knew that Lionel had a few of the men from the Church Army Hostel to stay with him for a day or two and sometimes he would persuade them to come along to church services. Then I recognized him. He was much the same age and build as Lionel but the last time I'd seen him he'd had a week or so's growth of stubble on his face and his hair had been long and dirty. It was only later that I learned that this man was Lionel's brother Philip.

It was shortly after this time that Harry Josephs came into my life. One way and another tensions were growing between various members of the church at the end of last summer. It was then that I first heard a nasty rumour about Lionel possibly liking the company of choirboys rather more than he should but I couldn't bring myself to believe it. Even now I am quite convinced that if Lionel was in some way homosexually inclined his weakness was a very gentle and a completely passive one. But there was another rumour almost everyone seemed to have heard about to the effect that Paul Morris the church organist was very much too fond of Harry Josephs' wife Brenda who almost always brought Harry to the services. Harry himself had been disqualified from driving for some reason. Brenda was often seen talking to Paul although she herself would rarely stay in the church for a service and one of the women in the congregation told me she had once seen them holding hands. I must admit that although I had no direct evidence to go on I began to suspect more and more that this second rumour might be true. And then I knew it was true because Harry Josephs told me so. The first time he had called at my home there were the three of us because mother happened to be up that day and he was very pleasant and polite and he stayed for about two hours. After that he called quite regularly always in the morning and we took to sitting together in the lounge when mother was in bed. In some ways he reminded me a bit of my old boss because he made no attempt at all to take the slightest advantage of me. Not then anyway. But he couldn't hide the fact that he was a lonely and disappointed man and before long he told me that he knew all about his wife's affair with Paul Morris. At first I think he must have come to see me just to find a little sympathy because he never once asked my opinion of what he should do. But then one day as we walked to the front door he just turned to me and told me that he found me attractive and that he would love to go to bed with me. Of course I felt a little bit flattered and certainly I had no moral scruples about the situation. We had been drinking sherry together and I was feeling rather more vivacious and daring than I normally do. What was I to say? I was still a virgin. I was forty-one. I had turned down the only man I had so far fallen in love with. I knew that life was passing me by and that if I didn't get to know something about sex fairly soon I never would. Not that I said any of this to Harry. In other circumstances I think I would have reminded him that he was married and that I liked and respected his wife too much to think of anything between us. As it was I think I just smiled and told him not to be so silly. He didn't say anything else but he looked so dejected and humiliated as he stood at the front door that I suddenly felt terribly sorry for him. Immediately to our right was the newly installed door to 14B which had just been painted Cambridge blue. I had the key in my pocket and I asked him if he'd like to have a look at the flat. He made love to me on the mattress of the unmade bed in the back room. It wasn't a particularly happy initiation for me but I experienced little regret. In fact I almost felt a sense of satisfaction and for the next few months we made love together once a week. As I became a little more practised in the physical side of it all I found myself enjoying the act of sex itself more and more. But I knew that something was sadly wrong because I felt so shoddy and cheap after it was over and I began to hate myself for wanting sex at all. I tried to stop it but looking back I think my try was half-hearted. The man seemed to have some power over me and I began living more and more on my nerves. I started worrying about my mother finding out although she seemed to suspect nothing. I started worrying about the neighbours too but goodness knows why because the houses on either side of us were multi-occupied with an ever-changing stream of temporary tenants or under-graduates. Above all I was worried about myself. The truth was that I now needed Harry more than he needed me and he knew this. Whatever agonies of self-reproach I suffered after he was gone I knew that I would be thinking all the time about our next meeting. I began to hate him as well as myself. He was like a drug to which I was fast becoming an addict.

It is perhaps important for you to know all this if you are to understand what happened to me later.

CHAPTER FORTY

Statement given by Miss Ruth Rawlinson (continued)

One Wednesday morning in early September my mother had a bad attack and I decided I had to put off my cleaning visit from the Wednesday morning to the Wednesday evening. But I had keys to the church and could get in whenever I wanted to so a break in my regular routine didn't matter. I locked the door behind me (I almost always used the south door because I could leave my bicycle in the porch there) and I was cleaning the confessional when I heard the north door being unlocked. Paul Morris and Lionel Lawson's brother (as I now knew) Philip came in. For some reason I felt frightened and I sat quietly where I was. I couldn't hear anything they said but it was clear to me that Paul was being blackmailed and that he couldn't and wouldn't pay up very much longer. I didn't understand too much of what was going on and I felt confused and worried. I just kept sitting where I was and I'm not sure exactly what happened next. But a few minutes later it was clear to me that Paul must have gone and that Lionel himself had come into the church because I could now hear the two brothers talking to one another. Again I didn't catch too much of what they were saying but the little I managed to pick up hit me like a thunderbolt. They were talking about murdering Harry Josephs. I was so astounded that the scrubbing-brush I was holding fell clattering to the floor – and they found me. Philip Lawson left almost immediately and then Lionel talked to me for a long long time. I am not prepared even now to disclose everything he told me then but the simple fact is that he begged me for my co-operation. He reminded me of course of my earlier promise to him and he offered to write me a cheque for £5,000 immediately (£5,000!) if I would do as he asked. He said that this payment was for me to keep the upstairs flat free so that his brother Philip could live there for what was likely to be no more than a month at the outside. I felt completely dumbfounded and could hardly begin to realize the implications of all this. At home things were going from bad to worse. The £500 loan from Lionel had all gone and although the flat was now virtually ready our own part of the house was living on borrowed time. According to the builders the whole of the ground floor badly needed rewiring and the water tank was corroded and likely to burst any day. To cap it all the gas central-heating had broken down completely only that very week after a few days of fitful functioning. I had not taken into account either the decoration of the con-verted kitchen upstairs and the only estimate I'd had on that was a horrifying £200. Just imagine my feelings then! But there was something else. I should have mentioned it much earlier but since it is the one thing in the whole case which inescapably incriminates me you will perhaps understand my reluctance – my refusal almost – to mention it. Lionel explained to me that I could now discharge my obligation to him and that this would involve me in the telling of one lie. No. Even now I am not being quite truthful. He made me swear on my most solemn honour I would tell this one lie. He emphasized repeatedly that it would only be one lie – it would involve me in nothing more than that and he insisted that it would be perfectly simple for me to carry out. I didn't care! I was desperately glad to be able to help him and I agreed without a second's hesitation. My mind was in a complete whirl as I left the church that evening. Of Harry Josephs I tried not to think at all. I suppose I almost managed to persuade myself that I had misheard the whole thing. But of course I hadn't. I knew that for some reason or other Harry Josephs was going to die and that my own commitment to tell one simple lie was quite certainly going to be associated with that (for me) not unwelcome event. Where did Philip Lawson fit in? I couldn't then be sure but if money was involved with me surely it would be involved with him too. The conviction gradually grew in my mind that Lionel had hired his brother to murder Harry Josephs and if this was the case my own part in the business – my own lie – would have something to do with being with a certain person at a certain time. An alibi. Yes. I began to feel convinced that such was the case – and again I didn't care! During this time I felt no burden of conscience. It was money now that played the tyrant. Sex was no longer the dominating force and even if it had been I had plenty of opportunity. Several times I had met a man in the Randolph cocktail-bar who showed he was obviously attracted towards me. He was a sales consultant for some prestigious firm and I had little doubt that the room he had in the Randolph would leave little to ask for in terms of physical comfort. I suspect he had taken up with another woman but it was me that he really wanted. At this time too I was becoming increasingly mean with money. Now I had far more than ever before in my whole life I found myself not even offering to pay for any drinks and accepting expensive meals and generally being an utterly selfish parasite. I bought no new clothes no perfume no special tit-bits for meals. As I grew mean with money I grew mean in other ways too. The same week I rang Harry Josephs and told him that our weekly date was off because my mother was very ill again. Lying like that was ridiculously easy for me now. Good practice! At home the boiler they said could just about be repaired and so I refused to buy a new one. I regarded the first rewiring estimate as ridiculously high so I got a local odd-job man in to do it for half the price. Not that he made a wonderful success of it. I decided to redecorate the upstairs kitchen myself and I found I thoroughly enjoyed doing it. For years I had put 50p in the collection-plate each Sunday morning. Now I put in 20p. But I still cleaned the church. It was my one pennance and I seemed to take more pride than ever in my self-imposed duties. You will think all of this very strange yet it is exactly how I felt and acted. From the way I have just been talking I am conscious that I have made it sound as if it all took place over a long time. But of course it didn't. It was only just over three weeks until the 26th September.

On that day the five of us met at 7 p.m. at St Frideswide's: Brenda Josephs and Paul Morris and

Lionel Lawson and Philip Lawson and myself. The doors were locked and I received my instructions. The candles were to be lit in the Lady Chapel and prayer books set out as if for thirteen members of a congregation – including the churchwarden's pew! I think that last thing was the worst of all really. Paul was playing something on the organ and he seemed to me to look more strained than any of us. Brenda was standing by the font dressed in a smart two-piece green suit and looking quite expressionless. Lionel was busying himself with what appeared to be the usual preparations for a mass – his face quite normal as far as I could tell. Lionel's brother was just as spruce as when I had last seen him and was sitting in the vestry drinking from a bottle which Lionel had no doubt provided for him. At about 7.15 Lionel asked Brenda and myself to go and stand up at the altar in the Lady Chapel and to stay there until he told us. Almost immediately we heard the key being fitted into the north door and Harry Josephs walked in carrying a fairly large brown-paper parcel under his arm. He looked flushed and excited and it was obvious that he had been drinking quite heavily. He saw the pair of us and nodded – but whether to me or to Brenda I couldn't tell. We sat down on the steps of the altar and I think that both of us were trembling. Then the organ suddenly stopped and Paul came through and pressed his hand lightly on Brenda's shoulder before walking up towards the vestry. For several minutes we could hear the men's mumbled voices and then there was a scuffling of feet followed by a dull low sort of moan. When Lionel fetched us he was dressed in surplice and cope. He was breathing heavily and looked very shaken. He said that when the police came I was to tell them that there had been about a dozen or more in the congregation mostly American visitors and that I had heard Harry cry out for help from the vestry during the playing of the last hymn. Whether Brenda was still with me I can't remember. I just walked slowly down to the vestry in a daze. I could see him clearly. He lay there quite still in his brown suit and the cassock he always wore in church with Lionel Lawson's paper-knife stuck deep in his back.

Of the other deaths in this nightmarish business I know nothing at all. But I am convinced that Lionel himself committed suicide unable to face what he had done. I am only too glad that at least he cannot be accused of the murders of Brenda Josephs and the Morrises. As I now finish this long statement my thoughts are with my mother and I beg of you to look after her for me and to tell her – but I can't think what you can tell her. I suppose it will have to be the truth.

Signed: RUTH RAWLINSON

'Well?'

Morse put down the statement and looked at Lewis with some distaste. He had been away from the station for more than six hours and had left word of his whereabouts to no one. It was now 8 p.m., and he looked tired.

'Whoever typed that isn't very fond of commas, is she?'

'She's a jolly good girl, sir. Wish we had her up at Kidlington.'

'She can't spell "penance".'

'She can take about 130 words a minute, though.'

'Did Miss Rawlinson speak as fast as that?'

'Pretty fast, yes.'

'Strange,' said Morse.

Lewis looked at his chief with an air of weary puzzlement. 'Clears the air a bit, doesn't it, sir?'

'That?' Morse picked up the statement again, separated the last few sheets, tore them across the middle, and deposited them in the wastepaper basket.

'But you can't just tear—'

'What the hell? The factual content of those pages isn't worth a sheet of lavatory paper! If she's decided to persist in her perjury, she'll get twice as long! Surely you can see that, man?'

Lewis saw very little. He'd been pleased with his day's work – still was; but he, too, felt very tired now and shook his head without bitterness. 'I reckon I could do with a bit of rest, sir.'

'Rest? What the hell are you talking about? You save my life for me and all you want to do is indulge in a bit of Egyptian P.T. Rubbish! We're going to celebrate, you and me.'

'I think I'd rather—'

'But don't you want to hear what I've been up to, old friend?' He looked slyly for a minute at Lewis, and then smiled – a smile which but for a slight hint of sadness could have been called wholly triumphant.

The Book of Revelation

CHAPTER FORTY-ONE

THE FRIAR BACON stands a little way back from the A40 Northern Ring Road, its name commemorating the great thirteenth-century scientist and philosopher, and its beer pleasing to the critical palate of Chief Inspector Morse. The sign outside this public house depicts a stout, jolly-looking man in Franciscan habit, pouring out what appears at first glance to be a glass of Guinness, but what on closer scrutiny proves to be a quantity of some chemical liquid being poured from one glass phial to another. Well, that's what Morse said. Inside they ordered beer and sat down. And then Morse spoke as follows.

'There are some extremely odd points in this case, Lewis – or rather there were – each of them in itself suggestive but also puzzling. They puzzled all of us, and perhaps still do to some extent, because by the time we'd finished we'd got no less than five bodies on our hands and we were never in a position to learn what any of the five could have told us. So, if first of all we look for motive, it's likely to be little more than intelligent guesswork, although we've got some little bits of evidence here and there to help us on our way. Let's start with Harry Josephs. He's getting desperately short of money, and what little he manages to get hold of he promptly donates to his bookmaker. Unbeknown to his wife he borrows money from his insurance company against his house – and he's soon through that, too. Then – as I strongly suspect, Lewis – he starts embezzling church funds, of which there are temptingly large sums and to which he has easy access. Then – I'm guessing again – Lionel Lawson must have found out about this; and if he reports the matter we've got the humiliating prospect of a highly respected ex-officer caught pilfering from the till. It would surely be the last straw for a man who's already lost his job and his money, and who's in real danger of losing his wife as well. Then take Lionel Lawson. Rumours are beginning to spread about him – nasty rumours about his relations with the choirboys, and someone soon made him very much aware of them – pretty certainly Paul Morris, whose son Peter was actually in the choir. Again we've got the prospect of public humiliation: a highly respected minister of the C. of E. caught interfering with the choirboys. Then there's Paul Morris himself. He's having what he hopes is a discreet affair with Harry Josephs' wife, but rumours are beginning to spread about that, too, and it's not very long before Harry gets to know what's going on. Next we come to Ruth Rawlinson. She's got her eyes and ears open more than most, and very soon she gets to know a great deal – in fact a great deal more than is good for her. But she's got a good many problems herself, and it's directly because of them that she becomes caught up in the case. Last, there's Lawson's brother, Philip, who as far as I can see only comes permanently on to the Oxford scene last summer. He's been an idle beggar all his life, and he still was then – absolutely on his uppers and looking yet again to his brother for help. Lionel has him to stay at the vicarage, and it isn't long before the old tensions begin to mount again. By the way, Lewis, I'm not making that last bit up, but I'll come back to it later. What have we got then? We've got enough miscellaneous motives here for a multitude of murders. Each of those involved has some cause to fear at least one of the others, and at the same time some hope he might profit from it all. There's enough potential blackmail and hatred to boil up into a very, very ugly situation. The only thing needed to set the whole reaction off is a catalyst, and we know who that catalyst was – the Reverend Lionel Lawson. It's he who's got the one priceless asset in the case – money: about forty thousand pounds of it. What's more, this money means very little to him personally. He's perfectly happy to struggle along on the miserable little stipend he's allowed by the mean-minded Church Commissioners, because whatever weaknesses he may have the love of money is not among 'em. So, he carefully tests the ice, and after a few tentative steps he finds that the ice on the pond is thick enough to hold all of 'em. What does he offer? To his brother Philip – money, and the chance to perpetuate his dissolute life-style for a few more years to come. To Josephs – money, and the chance to clear up his financial affairs and get away to start a new life somewhere else, minus his wife. To Morris – again, doubtless, money, if that's what Morris wanted; but he can also probably ensure that Morris gets Brenda Josephs as well, and the chance for both of 'em to get away and start a new life together, with a healthy bank balance into the bargain. To Ruth Rawlinson – money, and the chance to settle once and for all her chronic anxiety over her domestic problems. So Lionel Lawson sets up his scheme, with the others as his willing accomplices. He fixes up a bogus service to celebrate some non-existent feast – and then the deed is done. The witnesses happily perjure themselves and at the same time vouch for one another's alibis. Lionel is standing at the altar, Paul Morris is playing the organ, Ruth Rawlinson is sitting in the congregation, and Brenda Josephs is across the road at the cinema. If they all stick to their stories, they're all in the clear. All the suspicion, of course, is going to fall on brother Philip; but Lionel has told him – and probably told everyone else – that everything has been most carefully arranged for him: within a few minutes of the murder, he will have caught a train from Oxford station and will be on his way to some pre-arranged hotel booking, with several thousand pounds in his pocket for his troubles. And for all that a little suspicion is a cheap price to pay, wouldn't you say?'

Morse finished his beer and Lewis, who for once had beaten him to it, walked up to the bar. It was quite clear to him, as Morse had said, that there was a whole host of motives in the case interlocking and (if Morse were right) mutually complementary and beneficial. But where did all this *hatred* against Harry Josephs spring from? All right, the lot of them were getting into a terrible mess, but (again, if Morse were right) money seemed to be coping quite adequately with all their problems. And why, oh, why, all this peculiar palaver in the church? It all seemed a ridiculously complicated and quite unnecessary charade. Why not just kill Josephs and dump his body somewhere? Between them that would have been infinitely simpler, surely? And what about the actual murder itself? Morphine poisoning *and* a knife in the back. No. It didn't really add up.

He paid for the beer and walked circumspectly back to their table. He wouldn't be thanked if he slopped as much as a cubic millimetre on to the carpet.

Morse took a mighty swallow from his beer and continued. 'We've now got to ask ourselves the key question: how can we account for enough hatred – on somebody's part – against Harry Josephs? Because unless we can answer that question we're still groping about in the dark. And closely connected with it we've got to ask ourselves why there was all this clumsy kerfuffle at the phoney service, and also why Josephs was killed twice over. Well, let's deal with the last question first. I'm sure you've heard of those firing squads when you get, say, four men with rifles, all quite happy to shoot the poor fellow tied to the post, but three of 'em have blanks up the barrel and only one has a live bullet. The idea is that none of 'em will ever know which one actually fired the fatal shot. Well, I thought that something of the sort may have happened here. There were three of 'em, remember, and let's say none of 'em is too keen on being solely responsible for the killing. Now, if Josephs, as well as being poisoned and stabbed, had also been bashed on the head, I reckon the evidence would have pointed strongly to my being right. But we learned from the post-mortem that there were two causes of death, and not three. Somebody gives Josephs morphine in some red wine; and then somebody, either the same somebody or somebody else, stabs him in the back. Why bother to kill him twice over? Well, it may well be that two of 'em *were* involved in the actual murder; a division of labour could have been agreed for the reason I've just mentioned. But there was a far more important reason than that. Are you ready for a bit of a shock, Lewis?'

'Ready for anything, sir.'

Morse drained his glass. 'By Jove, the beer's good here!'

'It's your turn, sir.'

'Is it?'

The landlord had come through into the lounge-bar, and for a few minutes Lewis could hear him discussing with Morse the crass stupidity of the selectors of the England football team.

'These are on the house,' said Morse, planting the two pints carefully on the Morrells' beer-mats. (For a man proposing to treat his junior officer for services rendered, he seemed to Lewis to be getting away with things extremely lightly.) 'Where was I now? Ah, yes. You didn't ask me where I'd been today, did you? Well, I've been up to Rutland again.'

'Leicestershire, sir.'

Morse appeared not to hear. 'I made one bad blunder in this case, Lewis. Only one. I listened too much to rumour, and rumour's a terrible thing. If I tell everybody that you're having an affair with that comma-less typist of yours, you'd suddenly find yourself trying like hell to prove you weren't – even though there was absolutely no truth in it. Like they say, you throw enough mud and some of it'll stick. Well, I reckon that's what happened with Lionel Lawson. If he was a homo-sexual, he must have been one of the very mildest variety, I think. But once the charge had been sug-gested he found himself in the middle of a good deal of suspicion, and I was one of those prepared to think the worst of him. I even managed to convince myself, without the slightest shred of evidence, that when he was expelled from school it must have been because he was buggering about with some of the younger lads there. But suddenly I began to wonder. What if I'd been quite wrong? What if Lionel Lawson's old headmaster wasn't too unhappy about letting me believe what I did – *because the truth of the matter was far worse?* I thought I knew what this truth was, and I was right. Today I met Meyer again, as well as Lionel's old housemaster. You see, the Lawson brothers were an extremely odd mixture. There was Lionel the elder brother, a hard-working, studious swot, not too gifted academically, struggling along and doing his best, bespectacled even then, lacking in any confidence – in short, Lewis, a bit of a bore all round. And then there was Philip, a clever little beggar, with all the natural gifts any boy could ask for – a fine brain, good at games, popular, good-looking, and yet always idle and selfish. And the parents dote on – guess who? – young, glamour-pants

Philip. It doesn't require much imagination to see the situation from Lionel's point of view, does it? He's jealous of his brother – increasingly and, finally, furiously jealous. From what I've been able to learn there was a young girl mixed up in it all, when Lionel was eighteen and Philip a year or so younger. She wasn't a brilliant looker by all accounts – but she was Lionel's girl. Until, that is, Philip decided to step in; and probably for no other reason than to spite his brother he took her away from him. It was from that point that the whole of the tragedy dates. At home, one weekend, *Lionel Lawson tried to kill his brother.* He tried to use the kitchen-knife, and in fact he wounded him quite seriously – *in the back.* Things were hushed up as far as possible and the police were quite happy to leave the situation in the hands of the school and the parents. Some arrangement was worked out, with both the boys being taken away from the school. No charge was brought, and things, so it seemed, settled down. But the records couldn't be altered, could they, Lewis? The fact was that at the age of eighteen Lionel Lawson had tried unsuccessfully to murder his brother. So if, as I said, we're looking for any festering, insatiable hatred in this case, then we've found it: the hatred that existed between Lionel Lawson and his younger brother.'

It was all very interesting and suggestive, Lewis could see that; but he couldn't really see how it affected many of the problems in the present case. Morse was going on, though, and the shock he'd spoken of was imminent.

'At first I thought that Lionel Lawson had killed

Harry Josephs and had then faked his own suicide by dressing up his brother in clerical get-up and chucking him from the top of the tower. What could be neater? All you'd want was someone who would agree to a wrong identification of the body, and such a person was readily available in Paul Morris, a man who would have profited twofold from the murder of Josephs: first, by pocketing a considerable sum of money; and, second, by having Josephs' wife for himself. But you made the point to me yourself, Lewis, and you were absolutely right: it's one helluva job to dress up a dead man in someone else's clothes. But it's not an *impossible* job, is it? Not if you're all prepared for the difficulties and if you've got plenty of time. But in this particular instance you were right, I'm convinced of that. It was Lionel Lawson, not his brother Philip, who fell from the tower last October. In his own conscience Lionel must have realized that he'd done something so terrible and so unforgivable that he just couldn't live with it any longer. So he took his spectacles off, put them in their case – and jumped. And while we're on this identification business, Lewis, I must confess I had my fair share of doubts about whether the body we found on the tower really was Paul Morris. If it wasn't, the possibilities were staggeringly interesting. But, although we've no satisfactory identification as yet, you can take my word for it that it *was* Paul Morris. Yes, indeed. And so at long last I began to shelve all these fanciful theories, and I just looked at the simple possibility that all of us had completely ignored from the very beginning. Ruth Rawlinson herself came very near to telling the truth and giving the game away in that ridiculous statement of hers when she said that she was prepared to tell one lie – *one lie.* She told us, as you'll remember, that this lie was about the service in St Frideswide's that never took place, and about her silence in the plotting of Harry Josephs' murder. But listen, Lewis! That wasn't the real lie at all. The real lie was about something else: she lied about the identification of the body lying dead in St Frideswide's vestry that night in September! *That* was her one big lie. Because, you see, the body found murdered that night was not the body of Harry Josephs at all! *It was the body of Lionel Lawson's brother – Philip Lawson.*'

CHAPTER FORTY-TWO

Extract from the transcript of proceedings held on 4 July at Oxford Crown Court against Miss Ruth Isabel Rawlinson on the charges of perjury and conspiracy, Mr Gilbert Marshall, Q.C., prosecuting for the Crown, Mr Anthony Johns, Q.C., acting for the defence.

Marshall: Let us turn, if we can, away from these rather nebulous areas of motive, and come to the events of last September, specifically to the evening of Monday the twenty-sixth of that month. The Court will be glad, I know, to hear your own explanation of the events which took place that unholy night.

Morse: It is my view, sir, that a conspiracy had been formed to murder Mr Philip Lawson, and that this conspiracy involved the Reverend Lionel Lawson, Mr Paul Morris and Mr Harry Josephs. I am quite sure in my own mind that the statement made by the defendant about the events of that evening is substantially correct. Correct, that is, as far as it goes, since I am convinced that Miss Rawlinson was not in a position to know the detailed sequence of events, being neither an active party in, nor an actual witness to, the murder itself.

Marshall: Try to confine yourself to the question, Inspector, will you? It is for the Court to determine the degree of the defendant's involvement in this crime — not for you. Please continue.

Morse: If I were to guess the sequence of events that night, sir, it would have to be something like this. Lionel Lawson was able somehow to persuade his brother Philip that it would be greatly to his advantage to be in the church at a certain time that evening. It would have been no great problem to persuade him to drink a glass of red wine whilst they waited there – wine that had already been doctored with morphine. The fact that the man found dead at the church that night could have died, or certainly would have died, of morphine poisoning was clearly established by the post-mortem findings; but the provenance of the morphine itself was never discovered, in spite of extensive police enquiries. However, there was one of the three men who had earlier had direct and daily access to a complete pharmacopoeia, a man who had worked for eighteen months as a chemist's assistant in Oxford. That man, sir, was Harry Josephs. And it was Josephs who, in my view, not only suggested but actually administered the lethal dose of morphine in the wine.

Marshall: Can you tell us why, if the man was already dead, it was necessary to stab him into the bargain?

Morse: I don't think he was already dead, sir, although I agree he would have been unconscious fairly soon after drinking the wine. Whatever happened, though, he had to be dead when the police arrived, because there might always be the outside chance of his recovering and telling the police what he knew. Hence the knife. And so if I may say so, sir, the key question is not why he was stabbed in the back – but why he was given morphine. And in my considered view the reason was this: it was absolutely vital from Lionel Lawson's point of view that his brother's clothes should be changed, and you can't stab a man in the back and then change his clothes without removing the knife and stabbing him again. By arrangement, Josephs had changed from the brown suit which by all accounts he always wore and brought it with him to the church that night. Without any doubt, I should think, the suit was wrapped up in the brown-paper parcel which Miss Rawlinson mentions in her statement. The police would obviously examine the dead man's clothes in the minutest detail, and an actual change of clothes would be the one certain way of making the deception appear absolutely authentic. And so, when Philip Lawson had slumped unconscious in the vestry, his own clothes were removed and Josephs' clothes put on him – a difficult and lengthy job, I should imagine, but there were three of them to do it and time was very much on their side. Then they dressed him in Josephs' cassock and the moment of truth had now arrived for Lionel Lawson. I suspect that he asked the other two to leave him, and then he completed a task which he had attempted once before and in which he had failed so disastrously. He looked down on the brother he had hated for so long, and he stabbed him in the back with his paper-knife. As I say, I don't myself think that Philip Lawson was dead at that point, and the defendant's statement tends to confirm this view, since what she heard must almost certainly have been the dying man's final groans. The police were summoned immediately, the body wrongly identified, both by the defendant and by Paul Morris, and I think you know the rest, sir.

Marshall: Doesn't all this seem to you an extraordinarily complicated business, Inspector? To me, at least, it seems quite ludicrously so. Why didn't the Reverend Lionel Lawson just murder his brother himself?

Judge: It is my duty to remind prosecuting counsel that it is not the Reverend Mr Lawson who is on trial in this court, and it is improper for the witness to answer the question in the form in which it has been phrased.

Marshall: Thank you, m'lord. Will the witness please explain to the Court why, in his view, the Reverend Mr Lawson, supposing him to have been responsible for his brother's death, did not proceed in this matter in a significantly more simple manner?

Morse: In my opinion, sir, two things were absolutely imperative for the Reverend Lawson. First that his brother should die – a matter which, as you suggest, he could perhaps have coped with single-handedly all right if he'd tried. But the second imperative need was far trickier, and one which he could never have coped with by himself, however hard he tried. He had to have someone who was willing to be identified as the dead man and who was also prepared to disappear immediately from the Oxford scene. Let me explain, sir, why I think this was so. Philip Lawson had let it be known to several people, including the defendant, for example, that he was Lionel Lawson's brother. So if he had been murdered and identified as the man who had often been seen at the vicarage, in the church, and so on, it would only have been a matter of time before the police discovered his true identity. And once that was known other facts would have been swift to follow. An attempt had already been made upon the man's life once before – with a knife – by his elder brother. Police enquiries would very quickly have been channelled in the right direction and virtually certain suspicion would have centred on the Reverend Lawson. As I say, sir, it was absolutely vital not only that Philip Lawson should die but also that he should be wrongly identified. As the Court now knows, he was indeed wrongly identified – as Harry Josephs; and Harry Josephs himself disappeared from the scene, although as it happens he didn't disappear very far. That same night he moved into the upstairs flat at 14B Manning Terrace, and he lived there until he died. He'd taken Philip Lawson's clothes from the church and no doubt the idea was that he should destroy them. But for various reasons Josephs grew restless—

Marshall: Before you go on with your evidence, Inspector, I must ask you if it is your view that the defendant's relations with Mr Josephs had ever been in any way more – shall we say? – more intimate than merely providing him with the daily necessities of living?

Morse: No.

Marshall: You are aware, no doubt, of the evidence before the Court from an earlier witness of several visits by Mr Josephs to Manning Terrace during the course of last summer?

Morse: I am, sir.

Marshall: And it is your view that these visits were of a purely – er – purely social nature?

Morse: It is, sir.

Marshall: Please continue, Inspector.

Morse: I think the idea must have been for Josephs to stay where he was until the dust had settled and then to get right away from Oxford somewhere. But that again has to be guesswork. What is certain is that he very soon learned that the Reverend Lionel Lawson had committed suicide and—

Marshall: I'm sorry to interrupt you again, but is it your view that in that death, at least, the late Mr Josephs could have had no hand whatsoever?

Morse: It is, sir. News of Lawson's death, as I say, would have been a big shock to Josephs. He must have wondered what on earth had gone wrong. Specifically he must have wondered many times whether Lawson had left a note and, if so, whether the note in any way incriminated himself and the others. Quite apart from that, though, Josephs had been dependent on Lawson. It was Lawson who had arranged his present hide-out and it was Lawson who was arranging his impending departure from Oxford. But now he was on his own, and he must have felt increasingly isolated. But again that's guesswork. What is clear is that he started going out into Oxford during the early winter months. He wore Philip Lawson's old clothes, with the long dirty great-coat buttoned up to the neck; he wore a pair of dark glasses; he grew a beard; and he found that he could merge quite anonymously into the Oxford background. It was about this time, too, I think, that he must have

310

realized that there was now only one other person who knew exactly what had taken place in the vestry that September evening; and that person was Paul Morris, a man who had robbed him of his wife, a man who was probably going to live with her after the end of the school term, and a man who had done very nicely out of the whole thing, without actually doing very much at all himself. It is my own view, by the way, sir, that Paul Morris may not have been quite so eager to get away with Mrs Josephs as he had been. But Josephs himself could have no inkling of that, and his hatred of Morris grew, as did his sense of power and his rediscovered capacity for the sort of action he had once known as a captain in the Royal Marine Commandos. On some pretext or other Josephs was able to arrange a meeting with Paul Morris at St Frideswide's, where he killed him and hid his body – though probably not, at that point, on the roof of the tower. Remember that no keys had been found in the clothing of the man murdered in the vestry; and it is clear that Josephs kept them for himself, and was therefore able to use the church for the murders of Paul Morris and his son Peter. Not only that, though. He was compelled to use the church. He was disqualified from driving, and without a licence, of course, he couldn't even hire a car. If he'd had a car, he would probably have tried to dispose of the bodies elsewhere; but in this respect, at least, he was a victim of circumstance. Later the same day – at tea-time in fact – he also arranged to meet Peter Morris, and there can be little doubt that the young boy was also murdered in St Frideswide's. I'm pretty sure his first idea was to hide both bodies in the crypt, and as soon as it was dark he put the boy in a sack and opened the door at the south porch. Everything must have seemed safe enough and he got to the grilled entrance to the crypt in the south churchyard all right – it's only about fifteen yards or so from the door. But then something happened. As he was carrying the body down, the ladder snapped and Josephs must have had an awkward fall. He decided that he couldn't or daren't repeat the process with a much bigger and heavier body; so he changed his plans and carried Paul Morris' body up to the tower roof.

Marshall: And then he decided to murder his wife?

Morse: Yes, sir. Whether at this point he knew exactly where she was; whether he had actually been in touch with her; whether he was able to find out anything from Paul Morris – I just don't know. But once the bodies – or just one of them – were found, he was going to make absolutely sure that *she* didn't talk, either; and, in any case, with Paul Morris now out of the way, his jealous hatred was directing itself ever more insanely against his wife. For the moment, however, he had a dangerous job on his hands. He had to get to the Morrises' house in Kidlington and try to make everything there look as if they'd both left in a reasonably normal manner. It was no problem getting into the house. No keys were found on either of the Morrises, although each of them must have had a latch-key. Once inside—

Marshall: Yes, yes. Thank you, Inspector. Could you now tell the Court exactly where the defendant fits into your scheme of things?

Morse: I felt reasonably certain, sir, that Miss Rawlinson would be safe only so long as she herself had no knowledge of the identities of the bodies found in St Frideswide's.

Marshall: But as soon as she did – tell me if I am wrong, Inspector – Josephs decided that he would also murder the defendant?

Morse: That is so, sir. As you know, I was an eyewitness to the attempted murder of Miss Rawlinson, and it was only at that point that I was convinced of the true identity of the murderer – when I recognized the tie he tried to strangle her with: the tie of the Royal Marine Commandos.

Marshall: Yes, very interesting, Inspector. But surely the defendant was always just as much of a threat to the murderer as Brenda Josephs was? Don't you think so? And, if she was, why do you think he treated the two women so differently?

Morse: I believe that Josephs had grown to hate his wife, sir. I made the point earlier in my evidence.

Marshall: But he didn't feel the same hatred towards the defendant – is that it?

Morse: I don't know, sir.

Marshall: You still wish to maintain that there was no special relationship between the defendant and Mr Josephs?

Morse: I have nothing to add to my earlier answer, sir.

Marshall: Very well. Go on, Inspector.

Morse: As I say, sir, I felt convinced that Josephs would attempt to kill Miss Rawlinson almost immediately, since it must have been clear to him that things were beginning to move very fast indeed, and since Miss Rawlinson was the only person left, apart from himself, who knew something of the truth – far too much of it, he must have felt. So my colleague, Sergeant Lewis, and myself decided we would try to bring the murderer out into the open. We allowed a slightly inaccurate report on the case to appear prominently in the *Oxford Mail* with the sole purpose of making him suspect that the net was already beginning to close on him. I thought that wherever he was – and remember that I had no idea whatsoever that he was living in the same house as Miss Rawlinson – he was almost certain to use the church once more. He would know exactly the times when Miss Rawlinson would be cleaning there, and he had his plans all ready. In fact, he got to church very early that morning, and managed to ruin the precautions which we had so carefully taken.

Marshall: But fortunately things worked out all right, Inspector.

Morse: I suppose you could say that. Thanks to Sergeant Lewis.

Marshall: I have no more questions.

Johns: I understand, Inspector, that you heard the conversation between my client and Mr Josephs before the attempt to strangle her was made.

Morse: I did.

Johns: In that conversation, did you hear anything which might be considered by the Court to be mitigating evidence in the case against my client?

Morse: Yes. I heard Miss Rawlinson say that she—

Judge: Will the witness please speak up for the Court?

Morse: I heard Miss Rawlinson say that she had decided to go to the police and make a full statement of all she knew.

Johns: Thank you. No further questions.

Judge: You may stand down, Inspector.

CHAPTER FORTY-THREE

'WHAT BEATS ME,' said Bell, 'is how many crooks there are around – in a church, too! I always thought those sort of people walked straight down the middle of the paths of righteousness.'

'Perhaps most of them do,' said Lewis quietly.

They were sitting in Bell's office just after the verdict and sentence had been passed on Miss Ruth Rawlinson. Guilty; eighteen months' imprisonment.

'It still beats me,' said Bell.

Morse was sitting there, too, silently smoking a cigarette. He either smoked addictively or not at all, and had given up the habit for ever on innumerable occasions. He had listened vaguely to the mumbled conversation, and he knew exactly what Bell had meant, but ... His favourite Gibbon quotation flashed across his mind, the one concerning the fifteenth-century Pope John XXIII, which had so impressed him as a boy and which he had committed to memory those many years ago: 'The most scandalous charges were suppressed; the vicar of Christ was only accused of piracy, murder, rape, sodomy, and incest.' It was no new thing to realize that the Christian church had a great deal to answer for, with so much blood on the hands of its temporal administrators, and so much hatred and bitterness in the hearts of its spiritual lords. But behind it all, as Morse knew – and transcending it all – stood the simple, historical unpalatable figure of its founder – an enigma with which Morse's mind had wrestled so earnestly as a youth, and which even now troubled his pervasive scepticism. He remembered his first visit to a service at St Frideswide's, and the woman singing next to him: 'Wash me, and I shall be whiter than snow.' Wonderful possibility! The Almighty, as it were, wiping the slate clean and not just forgiving, but forgetting, too. And it was forgetting that was the really hard thing. Morse could find it even in his own cynical soul to forgive – but not to forget. How could he forget? For a few blissful moments on that day in St Frideswide's he had felt such a precious affinity with a woman as he had felt only once before; but their orbits, his and hers, had crossed too late in the day, and she, like all other lost souls, like the Lawsons and Josephs and Morris, had erred and strayed from the ways of acceptable human behaviour. But how could his mind not be haunted by the revelations she had made? Should he go to see her now, as she had asked? If he *was* to see her, it would have to be very soon.

Dimly and uninterestedly his mind caught up with the conversation once more: 'Doesn't reflect very well on me, does it, Sergeant? I'm in charge of the case for months, and then Morse here comes along and solves it in a fortnight. Made me look a proper Charley, if you ask me.' He shook his head slowly. 'Clever bugger!'

Lewis tried to say something but he couldn't find the right words. Morse, he knew, had the maddeningly brilliant facility for seeing his way through the dark labyrinths of human motive and human behaviour, and he was proud to be associated with him; proud when Morse had mentioned his name in court that day. But such matters weren't Lewis' forte; he knew that, too. And it was almost a relief – after Morse – to get back to his usual pedestrian and perfunctory duties.

Morse heard his own name mentioned again and realized that Bell was talking to him.

'You know, I still don't understand—'

'Nor do I,' interrupted Morse. Throughout the case he had made so many guesses that he could find no mental reserve to fabricate more. The words of St Paul to the Corinthians were writ large in his brain: 'There is a manifestation and there is a mystery'; and he felt sure that whatever might be puzzling Bell was not likely to be one of the greater mysteries of life. Wasn't one of the real mysteries the source of that poison which had slowly but inexorably dripped and dripped into Lionel Lawson's soul? And that was almost as old as the seed of Adam himself, when Cain and Abel had presented their offerings before the Lord . . .

'Pardon?'

'I said the pubs'll soon be open, sir.'

'Not tonight for me, Lewis. I – er – I don't feel much like it.'

He got up and walked out of the office without a further word, Lewis staring after him in some bewilderment.

'Odd bugger!' said Bell; and for the second time

within a few minutes Lewis felt he had to agree with him.

Obviously Ruth had been crying, but she was now recovered, her voice dull and resigned. 'I just wanted to thank you, Inspector, that's all. You've been – you've been so kind to me, and – and I think if anyone could ever understand me it might have been you.'

'Perhaps so,' said Morse. It was not one of his more memorable utterances.

'And then—' She sighed deeply and a film of tears enveloped her lovely eyes. 'I just wanted to say that when you asked me out that time – do you remember? – and when I said – when I—' Her face betrayed her feelings completely now, and Morse nodded and looked away.

'Don't worry about it. I know what you're going to say. It's all right. I understand.'

She forced herself to speak through her tears. 'But I *want* to say it to you, Inspector. I want you to know that—' Again, she was unable to go on; and Morse touched her shoulder lightly, just as Paul Morris had touched Brenda Josephs lightly on the shoulder on the night of Philip Lawson's murder. Then he got up and made his way quickly out along the corridor. Yes, he understood – and he forgave her, too. But, unlike the Almighty, he was unable to forget.

*

Mrs Emily Walsh-Atkins had been called upon to identi-fy the battered corpse of Harry Josephs. (It was Morse's idea.) She had done so willingly, of course. What an exciting time this last year had been! And the goldfish flashed its tail almost merrily in her mind as she recalled her own part in the tragic events which had centred upon her chosen church. Her name had appeared once more in the *Oxford Mail* – in the *Oxford Times*, too – and she had cut out the paragraphs carefully, just as Ruth Rawlinson before her, and kept them in her handbag with the others. One Sunday morning during the hot summer which followed these events, she prayed earnestly for forgiveness for her sins of pride, and the Reverend Keith Meiklejohn, standing benignly beside the north porch, was kept waiting even longer than usual until she finally emerged into the bright sunshine.

Mrs Alice Rawlinson had been taken to the Old People's Home in Cowley immediately after her daughter's arrest. When Ruth was freed, after serving only eleven of her eighteen months' sentence, the old lady returned to 14A Manning Terrace, still going strong and looking good for several years to come. As she was helped into the ambulance on her way home, one of the young housemen was heard to murmur that anyone who predicted how long a patient had got to live was nothing but a bloody fool.

*

A few books had been found in Harry Josephs' upstairs flat at 14B Manning Terrace; and after the case was over these had been given to Oxfam, and were slowly sold, at ridiculously low prices, at the second-hand charity bookshop in north Oxford. A seventeen-year-old boy (by some curious coincidence, a boy named Peter Morris) bought one of them for five pence in the early summer. He had always been interested in crime, and the large, fat, glossy volume entitled *Murder Ink* had immediately attracted his attention. That same night whilst browsing through the assorted articles, he came to a piece about suicides on page 349, heavily underlined in red biro: *Myopic jumpers invariably remove their eyeglasses and put them in a pocket before jumping.*

CHAPTER FORTY-FOUR

MORSE TOOK HIS holidays later the following year and decided, again, to go to the Greek islands. Yet somehow his passport remained unrenewed in its drawer, and one sunny morning in mid-June the chief inspector caught a bus down from north Oxford into the city. For an hour he wandered contentedly around the Ashmolean where amongst other delights he stood for many minutes in front of the Giorgione and the Tiepolo. Just before midday he walked across to the cocktail-bar at the Randolph and bought a pint of beer, for he would never lend his lips to anything less than that measure. Then another pint. He left at half past twelve, crossed Cornmarket, and walked into St Frideswide's. The north door creaked no longer, but inside the only sign of life was the flickering candles that burned around the statue of the Virgin. The woman he was seeking was not there. As once before, he decided to walk up to north Oxford, although this time he witnessed no accident at the Marston Ferry crossroads. Reaching the Summertown shops, he called into the Dew Drop, drank two further pints of beer, and continued on his way. The carpet-shop, from which Brenda Josephs had once observed her husband, had now been taken over by an insurance firm, but otherwise little seemed to have changed. When he came to Manning Terrace, Morse turned into it, paused at one point for a second or two, and then continued along it. At number 14A he stopped, knocked briskly on the door, and stood there waiting.

'You!'

'I heard you'd come home.'

'Well! Come in! Come in! You're the first visitor I've had.'

'No, I won't do that. I just called by to tell you that I've been thinking a lot about you since you've been – er – away, and you'd blush if I told you what happened in my dreams.'

'Of course I wouldn't!'

'Don't take any notice of me – I've had too much beer.'

'*Please* come in.'

'Your mother's there.'

'Why don't you take me to bed?'

Her large eyes held his, and in that moment a sparkling mutual joy was born.

'Can I use your "gents"?'

'There's one upstairs – it's a "ladies", too.'

'Upstairs?'

'Just a minute!'

She was back almost immediately with a Yale key labelled 14B in her hand.

'Hadn't you better tell your mother—?'

'I don't think so,' she said, and a slow smile spread across her lips as she closed the door of 14A quietly behind her and inserted the key into 14B.

Morse's eyes followed her slim ankles as she climbed the carpeted stairs ahead of him.

'Bedroom or lounge?'

'Let's go into the lounge a few minutes first,' said Morse.

'There's some whisky here. Do you want a drink?'

'I want you.'

'And you can have me. You know that, don't you?'

Morse took her in his arms as they stood there, and kissed her tenderly on her sweet, full lips. Then, as if the moment were too unbearably blissful to be prolonged, he pressed her body tightly to him and laid his cheek against hers.

'I dreamed about you, too,' she whispered in his ear.

'Did I behave myself?'

'I'm afraid so. But you're not going to behave yourself now, are you?'

'Certainly not.'

'What's your Christian name?' she asked.

'I'll tell you afterwards,' said Morse quietly, as his fingers lingered lightly on the zip at the back of her brightly patterned summer dress.